THE PIER FALLS

"Mesmerizing. . . . A top-notch collection." —*Financial Times*

"*The Pier Falls* is pure genius and I'm jealous of every word."
—Douglas Coupland

"Vividly memorable." —*The Wichita Eagle*

"A startlingly good, gripping read." —*The Independent* (London)

"[A] tour de force of memory. . . . Haddon's capacity for literary
variation in this collection is admirable." —*The Buffalo News*

"Superbly gripping." —*The Sunday Times* (London)

"Haddon is a master of haunting detail. . . . [A reminder] of just
how transporting a perfectly constructed short story can be."
—*British GQ*

"If your jaw dropped when you read Haddon's *The Curious Incident
of the Dog in the Night-Time*, it will drop again when you pick up
this exemplary collection. . . . In pristinely detailed prose, Haddon shocks us with the strong sense of our humanity."
—*Library Journal* (starred review)

"Vivid, arresting. . . . When he is good, Haddon is very, very good."   —*The Philadelphia Inquirer*

"Exquisite. . . . [Haddon] writes with the craft of Julian Barnes or, even, Truman Capote."   —Andrew Billen, *The Times* (London)

"Excellent and surprising."   —*The Sunday Telegraph* (London)

"Beautifully written."   —*Publishers Weekly*

"Exceptional. . . . It's really a virtuoso performance from Haddon, whose constantly shifting stylistic choices make every story a capable piece of stand-alone art."   —*The Maine Edge*

"[A] frequently jaw-dropping collection."   —*Toronto Star*

"Every story here has the power to give the reader a jolt, with Haddon's pristine and stately prose only heightening the power of each violent upheaval."   —*The Sydney Morning Herald*

"This collection could easily be the book that [Haddon] is eventually remembered for."   —Alex O'Connell, *The Times* (London)

"Outstanding. . . . Every line makes you believe what [Haddon] writes, his eye misses nothing."   —*The Observer* (London)

"A sustained set of powerfully told stories."
                                    —*London Evening Standard*

Mark Haddon

THE PIER FALLS

Mark Haddon is the author of the bestselling novels *The Red House* and *A Spot of Bother*. His novel *The Curious Incident of the Dog in the Night-Time* won the Whitbread Book of the Year Award and the Los Angeles Times Book Prize for First Fiction and is the basis for the Tony Award–winning play. He is the author of a collection of poetry, *The Talking Horse and the Sad Girl and the Village Under the Sea*, has written and illustrated numerous children's books, and has won awards for both his radio dramas and his television screenplays. He teaches creative writing for the Arvon Foundation and lives in Oxford, England.

ALSO BY MARK HADDON

Fiction

The Curious Incident of the Dog in the Night-Time

A Spot of Bother

The Red House

Poetry

The Talking Horse and the Sad Girl and the Village Under the Sea

THE PIER FALLS

§

THE PIER FALLS

AND OTHER STORIES

§

MARK HADDON

VINTAGE CONTEMPORARIES

Vintage Books

A Division of Penguin Random House LLC

New York

To Fiona

Now, bring it down
in the kind of fire that flows along ceilings,
that knows the spectral blues; that always starts
in donut fryers or boardwalk kindling
in the dead hour before dawn, that leaves pilings
marooned by mindless tides, that sends a plume
of black smoke high enough to stain the halls
of clouds. Now look around your tiny room
And tell me that you haven't got the power.

"The Power," Paul Farley

Sumwhyle wyth wormez he werrez, and with wolues als,
Sumwhyle wyth wodwos, þat woned in þe knarrez,
Boþe wyth bullez and berez, and borez oþerquyle,
And etaynez, þat hym anelede of þe heȝe felle.

Sir Gawain and the Green Knight

CONTENTS

THE PIER FALLS

§

THE PIER FALLS

23 July 1970, the end of the afternoon. A cool breeze off the Channel, a mackerel sky overhead and, far out, a column of sunlight falling onto a trawler as if God had picked it out for some kind of blessing. The upper storeys of the Regency buildings along the front sit above a gaudy rank of coffee houses and fish bars and knick-knack shops with striped awnings selling 99s and dried seahorses in cellophane envelopes. The names of the hotels are writ large in neon and weatherproof paint. The Excelsior, the Camden, the Royal. The word Royal is missing an o.

Gulls wheel and cry. Two thousand people saunter along the prom, some carrying towels and Tizer to the beach, others pausing to put a shilling in the telescope or to lean against a balustrade whose pistachio-green paint has blistered and popped in a hundred years of salt air. A gull picks up a wafer from a dropped ice cream and lifts into the wind.

On the beach a portly woman hammers a windbreak into the sand with the heel of a shoe while a pair of freckled twins build a fort from sand and lolly sticks. The deckchair man is collecting rentals, doling out change from a leather pouch at his hip. "No deeper than your waist," shouts a father. "Susan? No deeper than your waist."

The air on the pier is thick with the smell of engine grease and fried onions spooned onto hot dogs. The boys from the ticket booth ride shotgun on the rubber rims of the bumper cars, the contacts scraping and sparking on the live chicken wire nailed to the roof above their heads. A barrel organ plays Strauss waltzes on repeat.

Nine minutes to five. Ozone and sea-sparkle and carnival licence.

This is how it begins.

A rivet fails, one of eight which should clamp the joint between two weight-bearing girders on the western side of the pier. Five have sheared already in heavy January seas earlier this year. There is a faint tremor underfoot as if a suitcase or a stepladder has been dropped somewhere nearby. No one takes any notice. There are now two rivets holding the tonnage previously supported by eight.

In the aquarium by the marina the dolphins turn in their blue prison.

Twelve and a half minutes later another rivet snaps and a section of the pier drops by half an inch with a soft thump. People turn to look at one another. The same momentary reduction in weight you feel when a lift starts descending. But the pier is always moving in the wind and the tide, so everyone returns to eating their pineapple fritters and rolling coins into the fruit machines.

The noise, when it comes, is like the noise of a redwood being felled, wood and metal bending and splitting under pressure. Everyone looks at their feet, feeling the hum and judder of the struts. The noise stops and there is a moment of silence, as if the sea itself were holding its breath. Then, with a peal of biblical thunder, a wide semicircle of walkway is hauled seaward by the weight of the broken girders underneath. A woman and three children standing at the rail drop instantly. Six more people are poured, scrabbling, down the half-crater of shattered wood into the sea. If you look through the black haystack of planks and beams you can see three figures thrashing in the dark water, a fourth floating face-down and a fifth folded over a weed-covered beam. The rest are trapped underwater somewhere. Up on the pier a man hurls five lifebelts one after the other into the sea. Other holidaymakers drop their possessions as they flee so that the walkway is littered with bottles and sunglasses and cardboard cones of chips. A cocker spaniel runs in circles trailing a blue lead.

Two men are helping an elderly lady to her feet when yet more decking gives way beneath them. The shorter, bearded man grabs the claw foot of an iron bench and hangs onto the woman till a teenage boy is able to lean down and help them both up, but the taller man with the braces and the rolled-up shirtsleeves slides down the buckled planking till he is brought to a halt by a spike of broken rail which enters the small of his back. He wriggles like a fish. No one will go down to help him. The slope is too steep, the structure too untrustworthy. A father turns his daughter's face away.

The men running the big wheel are trying to empty each gondola in turn, but those stuck at the top of the ride are scream-ing and those lower down are unwilling to wait their turn and jump out, some twisting ankles, one breaking a wrist.

On the beach everyone stands and stares at the hole punched

into the familiar view. The coloured lights still flash. Faintly they can hear the "Emperor Waltz." Five men tear off shoes and shirts and trousers and run into the surf.

A line of seven ornamental belvederes runs down the centre of the pier. The western side of this spine is now impassable, so everyone seaward of the fall is squeezing through the bottleneck on the eastern side to reach the turnstiles, the promenade and safety. At the narrowest point people are starting to lose their footing and tumble so that those still upright must either walk on top of them or fall and be trampled in their turn.

Sixty seconds gone, seven people dead, three survivors in the water. The man with the braces and the rolled-up sleeves is still alive but will not be for long. Eight people, three of them children, are being crushed by the crowd pouring over them.

One of the belvederes is listing now, the metal structure being twisted so hard that the twenty-two glass windows explode one after the other.

The pier manager has opened the service gate beside the turnstiles and escapees are fanning onto the pavement, dishevelled, bloody, wide-eyed. A small boy is being carried in the arms of his father. A teenage girl with a shattered femur sticking through the skin of her right leg is suspended between the shoulders of two men.

The traffic along the promenade comes to a halt and a crowd lines the rails. The whole front is so quiet that everyone hears the noise this time.

Two minutes and twenty seconds. The belvedere falls first, dragging the metal framework and the decking after it. Forty-seven people drop into a threshing machine of spars and beams.

Only six of these people will survive, one of them a boy of six whose parents wrap themselves around him as they fall.

The rubberised wires carrying power along the pier spark like fireworks as they are torn apart. All the lights go out on the end of the pier. The barrel organ wheezes to a halt.

The men swimming out to help are lifted on the small tsunami generated by the mass of broken pier entering the water. It passes under them and heads towards the beach where it sends everyone scurrying above the high-water mark as if it were infected by the event which caused it.

The arcade manager sits in his tiny office at the end of the pier, the dead receiver pressed to his ear. He is twenty-five. He has never even been to London. He has no idea what to do.

The pilot of a twin-engined Cessna 76-D looks down. He can't believe what he is seeing. He banks and circles the pier to double-check before radioing Shoreham tower.

The pier is now in two separate sections, the ragged end of one facing the ragged end of the other, forty-five tons of wood and metal knotted in the water between them. Some of those stranded on the seaward section stand at the edge desperate to be seen and heard by anyone who might rescue them. Others hang back, trying to gauge the most dependable part of the structure. Three couples are trapped in the ghost train listening to the noises outside, fearful that if they manage to get out they will find themselves watching the end of the world.

On the landward section two people lie motionless on the decking and three others are too badly injured to move. A woman is shaking the body of her unconscious husband as if he has overslept and is late for work, while a man with tattooed forearms chases the petrified cocker spaniel in a large figure of eight. An elderly lady has had a fatal heart attack and remains seated on a bench, head tilted to one side as if she has dozed off and missed all the excitement.

Faint sirens can be heard from the maze of the town.

Two of the swimming men turn back, frightened that they will be struck by yet more of the pier collapsing, but the other three swim on into the archipelago of bodies and broken wood. The pier looms overhead, so much bigger than it has ever seemed from the beach or up there on the walkway, so much darker, more malign. The men can hear the groan and crunch of girders still settling beneath them in the water.

They find a terrified woman, two girls who turn out to be sisters and a man still wearing his spectacles who floats upright in the swell like a seal, only vaguely aware of his surroundings. The woman is hyperventilating and lashing out so wildly that the men wonder initially if she is caught on something under the surface. Only the sisters seem wholly compos mentis, so one of the rescuers escorts them back to the shore. The man wearing the spectacles asks what has happened then asks for the explanation to be repeated. The panicking woman won't let anyone come near her, so they have to tread water and let her expend all her energy and come perilously close to drowning before she is tractable.

Just beyond the end of the pier five empty lifebelts are making their way out to sea.

A young man on the promenade lifts his Leica and takes three photographs. Only when he reads the paper the following morning will he realise what is happening in these pictures. Immediately he will open the camera and yank the film out of its drum so that the images are burned away by the light.

The air-sea rescue helicopter rises from its painted yellow circle on the runway at Shoreham, tilts into the prevailing wind and swings off the airfield.

Five minutes. Fifty-eight dead.

On the promenade a number of those who ran to safety have failed to find wives or husbands or children or parents. The manager has closed the gate but these people are weeping and shouting, trying to get back onto the pier. There are no police in attendance yet and he can see that keeping them here against their will may be as dangerous as letting them through and he doesn't want this responsibility, so he reopens the gate and twelve of them pour past as if he has opened the doors to a January sale. The last of these is a girl of no more than eight years old. He grabs her collar. She fights and weeps at the end of his arm.

The lifeboat is scrambled.

On the eastern side of the pier a farmer from Bicester is trying to prise the six-year-old boy from between his parents. The boy can surely see that they are dead. Half his father's head is missing. Or perhaps he can't see this. He won't let go of them and his grip is so tight that the man is afraid he will break the boy's arm if he pulls any harder. He asks the boy what his name is but the boy won't answer. The boy is in some private hell which he will never entirely leave. The farmer has no choice but to turn and swim, towing the three of them ashore. Only when he tries to stand will he realise that his ankle is broken.

The tattooed man comes running down the pier clasping the cocker spaniel to his chest and when he runs through the gate onto the promenade the two of them are greeted by cheers and whoops from a crowd eager to celebrate some small good thing.

Eight minutes. Fifty-nine dead.

The helicopter appears in the sun-glare from the west. Every-one on the promenade hears the growing pulse of the rotors and turns to watch.

None of the eleven people running onto the pier find their missing relatives among the injured and unconscious so they stand near the ragged chasm and shout to the people on the other side. Have they seen an old lady in a green windcheater? A little girl with long red hair? But the people on the far side are not interested in the lady in the windcheater and the girl with red hair because they are missing relatives of their own and they are terrified that the rest of the pier will collapse and the only thing they want to know is when they are going to be rescued.

Two ambulances reach the seafront but the traffic is jammed so tight that the crews have to run carrying stretchers and emer-gency bags. Five stay with the injured on the front, three continue onto the pier itself.

Three policemen are trying to push the spectators back, some of whom resent being evicted from ringside seats. Nobody realises how many people have died. Everyone is thinking how they will tell the story to friends and family and workmates.

On the pier a woman is slid sideways onto a spinal board. An elderly man with a broken collarbone is given morphine.

Fourteen minutes. Sixty dead.

On the promenade people are wondering if it was an IRA bomb. No one wants to believe that time and weather can be this dangerous, and it is exciting to think of oneself as a potential target.

As the helicopter hovers over the end of the pier the people below fight to be the first to grab the winchman as he descends, but the downdraught batters them away from its epicentre and he alights in a circle of empty decking. He scoops a little girl from her mother's arms and the sight of her being clipped into a harness shames them. As she is hoisted aloft they start gathering the other children, lining them up in order of age ready for the next lift.

The swimmers come ashore—the sisters, the confused man, the struggling woman, their three rescuers. People rush forward with towels. It looks like a competition to see whose will be chosen. The struggling woman drops to her knees and digs her hands into the sand as if nothing and no one is going to separate her from solid ground ever again.

The body of the old woman who had a heart attack is carried through the service gate under a white sheet into a sudden hush. There are still people on the front who think she is the only person who has died.

The farmer towing the little boy and his dead parents hauls them into the shallows and feels one end of his broken fibula grinding against the other. It should hurt but he can feel no pain. He needs very badly to lie down. He rolls over into the water and looks at the clouds. People rush into the surf, then see his cargo and come to a halt. A young woman steps between them, a nurse from Southampton where she works in the accident and emergency department. She has seen much worse. She is the only black person on the entire beach. She puts her hands flat on the boy's shoulders and some of those watching wonder if she is using voodoo, but it is the steadiness of her voice which enables him to let go of his parents' bodies and turn and be held by someone who is not frightened. The colour of her skin helps too, the fact that she is so different from all these other people among whom he no longer belongs. Her name is Renée. They will stay in touch with one another for the next thirty years.

The fourth child is lifted into the helicopter, then the fifth.

The arcade manager emerges from his tiny office. He realises that if he is the last person winched to safety he will be able to say, "I stayed at my post."

The last couple escape from the ghost train, the husband kicking his way through Frankenstein's Monster painted on the plywood sheeting of the façade.

Twenty-five minutes. Sixty-one dead.

The lifeboat arrives and the crew begin hauling people from the water. Some cannot stop talking. Some slither into the bottom of the boat like netted fish, sodden, glassy-eyed, oblivious. A boy of thirteen floats in a dark recess between two fallen girders. He refuses to come out and will not respond to their calls. A crew member jumps into the water but the boy retreats into the flooded forest of wreckage and they are forced to abandon him.

The winch is stowed and the helicopter swings away with all the children on board. Many of them have left parents on the pier. Several don't know if their parents are alive. For all of them the hammering roar is a comfort, filling their heads so completely that they are unable to entertain the terrifying thoughts that will return only when they are helped down onto the tarmac and run through the wind from the rotors towards the women from the St. John's Ambulance waiting for them outside the little terminal building.

On the promenade a man in a dirty white apron squeezes through the crowd bearing hot dogs and sweet tea from the stand he runs beside the crazy golf. He returns with a second tray.

Other boats are being drawn towards the pier, a Bristol motor cruiser, an aluminium launch with a Mercury outboard, two fibreglass Hornets. They idle just beyond the moraine of bodies and debris, unable either to help or to turn away.

The boy of thirteen will not come out from the flooded forest because he knows that his sister is in there somewhere. He cannot find her. After thirty minutes he is hypothermic and feels desperately cold. Then, quite suddenly, he doesn't feel cold at all. This doesn't seem strange. Nothing seems strange anymore. He wants to take his clothes off but hardly has the energy to stay afloat. Out there, only yards away, the world continues—sunshine, boats, a helicopter. But he feels safe in here. He is not thinking about his sister anymore. He cannot remember having a sister. Only this deep need to be in the dark, to be contained, unseen, some primal circuit still alight on the dimming circuit board of the brainstem. He sinks into the water five times, coughs and forces himself back to the surface, but with less effort each time and with a less distinct sense of what he has just avoided. The sixth time there is so little left of his mind that he lets it go as easily as if it were a book falling from his sleeping hand.

A journalist from the *Argus* stands in a phone box reading the shorthand he has scribbled onto four pages of a ring-bound notebook. "Shortly before five in the afternoon . . ."

One of the men trapped on the far end of the pier is terrified of flying. He is wearing a Leeds United T-shirt. The prospect of being lifted into the helicopter is many times worse than that of the structure collapsing beneath him. He knows that his only other choice is to jump from the pier. He is a strong swimmer but the drop to the water is sixty feet. The two possibilities toggle at increasing speeds in his mind—fly, jump, fly, jump. He feels sick. His wife is airlifted in the second batch and in her absence his thoughts race at increasing speeds until he realises that he will lose his mind and that this possibility is worse than flying or jumping. At which point he sees himself turn away from the crowd and run towards the railing. The sensation of watching himself from a distance is so strong that he wants to cry out to this foolish man to remove his shoes and trousers first. He remembers nothing of the leap itself, only the terrible surprise of waking underwater with no memory of where he is or why. He fights his way to the surface, refills his lungs several times and forces off his double-knotted shoes. He can see now that he is at the seaside and that he is floating in the shadow of some vast object. He turns and the wrecked pier looms over him. He remembers what has happened and turns again and swims hard. After a hundred yards he stops and turns for a third time and finds that the distance has turned the pier into a part of the view. He looks towards the town, the crowds, the blue flashing lights, the Camden, the Royal. He is unaware that people saw him jump and that he is now starring in his own brief episode in the afternoon's greater drama. He feels victorious, unburdened. He swims steadily towards the beach where he is cheered ashore, wrapped in a red blanket and led to an ambulance. His wife will spend three hours thinking he is dead and will not forgive him for a long time.

There is now no one left on the far end of the pier.

The final person dies, deep inside the tangle of planks and girders. He is fifteen years old. He helped his father on the helter-skelter, collecting the mats and going up the ladder at the back when kids got scared or started a fight inside. He has been unconscious since he fell.

The lifeboat returns and the crew retrieve fifteen bodies from the water.

An hour and a half. Sixty-four dead.

A Baptist minister offers the use of his church hall. Survivors are escorted by policemen and firemen over the road, up Hope Street, through a door beside Whelan's Marine Stores and into a large warm room with fluorescent lighting and a parquet floor. The lid of a tea urn is rattling and two ladies are making sandwiches in the kitchenette. People slump onto chairs and onto the floor. They are no longer being observed. They are among people who understand. Some weep openly, some sit and stare. Three children are unaccompanied, two boys and a girl. The parents of the younger boy have been airlifted to Shoreham. The other two children are now orphans. The girl saw her parents die and is inconsolable. The boy has concocted a story in which his parents fell into the sea and were picked up by a fishing boat, a story so detailed and told with such earnestness that the elderly woman to whom he is telling it doesn't realise anything is wrong until he explains that they are now living in France.

A policewoman moves quietly round the room, squatting beside each group in turn. "Are you missing anyone?"

Outside, the lifeboat returns for a third time with a cargo of rope and orange buoys to keep away the curious and the ghoulish.

Three hours and twenty minutes.

Six men from the council works department erect shuttering around the pier entrance, big frames of two-by-four covered with sheets of chipboard.

In the hospital most of the broken bones have been set and the girl with the shattered femur is having it pinned in surgery. A woman has had a splinter the size of a carving knife pulled from her chest.

Evening comes. The front is unnaturally empty. No one wants to look at the pier anymore. They are elsewhere eating scampi and baked Alaska, watching *The Railway Children* at the Coronet, or driving to neighbouring resorts for evening walks against a view that can be comfortably ignored. In spite of which the conversation keeps circling back, because at sometime this week everyone has stood in a spot which is now empty air. Everyone can feel the thrilling shiver of the Reaper passing close, dampened rapidly by the thought of those poor people. But was it a bomb? Was there a man on the front with a radio control and a trip switch? Had they perhaps sat next to him?

Nine people remain buried under wreckage. The authorities know about eight of these. The ninth is a girl of fifteen who ran away from her home in Stockport six months ago. Her parents will never connect her to the event in the newspaper and will spend the rest of their lives waiting for her to come home.

The orphaned boy and girl are driven to the house of a couple who foster for the local social services until their grandparents arrive tomorrow. The boy still believes his parents are living in France.

The reunited families have gone. The hall is almost empty now. The only people who remain are those waiting for family members who will never come.

None of the survivors sleep well. They wake from dreams in which the floor beneath them vanishes. They wake from dreams of being trapped inside a cat's cradle of iron and wood as the tide rises.

2 a.m. Clear skies. The whole town so precise and blue that you could lean down and pick up that moored yacht between your thumb and forefinger. Only the surf moving and a single drunk shouting at the sea. The gaudy lights along the front have been turned off as a mark of respect, leaving a scattering of yellow windows and the hotel names in green and red neon. Excelsior, Camden, Royal.

3 a.m. Mars just visible above the Downs and a choppy stripe of moon across the sea. There is a dull boom as the far end of the pier's landward half drops and twists like a monster shifting in its sleep.

The TV crews arrive at 5 a.m. They set up camp on the prom and outside the police station, smoking and telling jokes and drinking sugary coffee from Thermos flasks.

Dawn comes and for a brief period the wrecked pier is beautiful, but the epicentre of the town is already moving eastwards, down the prom towards the dolphinarium and the saltwater swimming pool. The pier is already becoming something you walk past.

People get their holiday snaps back from the chemist's. Some of the pictures contain the final images of family members who are now dead. They smile, they shade their eyes, they eat chips and hold outsize teddy bears. They have only minutes to live. In one freakish photograph a teenage boy is already falling downwards, his mouth wide open as if he were singing.

Funerals are held and the legal wrangle begins.

Paint peels, metal rusts. Gulls gather on the roundabouts and the belvederes. Bulbs shatter, colours fade. Cormorants nest on the rotten decking. In high winds the gondolas on the big wheel sway and creak. The ghost train becomes a roost for pipistrelles and greater horseshoe bats; the tangled beams and girders underwater become a home for conger eels and octopus.

Three years later a man walking his dog along the beach will find a sea-bleached skull washed up by a winter storm. It will be laid to rest with full funeral rites in a corner of the graveyard of St. Bartholomew's Church under a stone inscribed with the words, "The kingdom of heaven is like unto a net, that was cast into the sea, and gathered of every kind."

Ten years after the disaster the pier is brought down in a series of controlled explosions, and over many months the remnants are lifted laboriously by a floating crane and towed to a marine breakers in Southampton. No other human remains are found.

THE ISLAND

She's dreaming of the pines outside her window in the palace, the way the night wind turns them into a black sea that tumbles and breaks against the stone wall below the sill. She's dreaming of the summer sound of trees being felled farther up the mountain, the hollow tock, tock, tock of the axe, the slow cracking of the trunk and that final thump, all that splintered yellow, still damp with life, the smell of fresh resin in the air and columns of midges rising and falling in the angled sunlight.

She's dreaming of the wood being split and planed and toothed home into a curved keel that will cut an ocean in half. She's dreaming of this morning, standing on the prow with her husband-to-be, the oars churning the waves to foam and the fat sails slapping in the wind, over the horizon his city where they'll marry, behind them the home she'll never see again.

She's dreaming of the wedding, flames dancing in the sconces of a great hall. Flames multiplied in a hundred golden cups, painted plates heavy with roast meats and chickpeas, quinces and saffron and honey cakes.

She's dreaming of the bridal suite, a snowfall of Egyptian cotton on the bed. Hanging above the pillows is a tapestry, the work so fine she could be looking through a window. In the centre of the picture is a woman weeping on a beach, and far out, in the chop and glitter of the woven sea, a single ship sailing steadily towards the border and the world beyond.

She moves a little closer so that she can see the woman's face, and then it hits her like a punch. She's looking at herself.

§

She comes round like a drowning woman breaking the water's surface, thrashing and gasping for air. The light hurts her eyes, her throat is dry and the world is foggy from drink, or drugs, or fever.

She rolls over and finds herself in an empty bed. He must be awake and making preparations for today's journey. She stands with difficulty and realises that she can hear nothing except the cry of gulls and guy ropes humming in the wind. She staggers to the door, uncouples the four leather ties which bind the canvas flaps and steps outside to find herself in a ghost camp, five squares of flattened, yellow grass, fishbones, a single sandal, the torched circle of last night's fire and far out, in the chop and glitter of the sea, a single ship.

She tries to scream but there is a weight on her chest which stops her filling her lungs. Her mind bucks and twists, searching for ways to make this right. He's coming back. The crew have mutinied and kidnapped him or left him somewhere nearby, tied up, beaten, dead. Then she looks down and sees, beside her feet, a jug of water and a loaf of bread, and on the loaf is the ring she gave him as a sign of their eternal love. He has abandoned her.

The sky revolves, she vomits on the wet grass and the world goes dark.

When time begins again she's skidding down the scree on bloody hands and knees towards the beach, then stumbling over the slip and clack of pebbles to the surf. She yells into the wind and her cry echoes round the rocky cove. Her heart thrashes like a netted bird.

The boat shrinks. She has become the woman in the tapestry.

He is the only man she's ever loved, and he has dumped her like ballast. She needs to find an explanation that does not make her a fool and him an animal, but every thought of him is a knife turning in the wound love made. She wants to hurl a stack of figured bowls across a room. She wants to weep till someone comes to comfort her. She wants to find a man who'll track him down and break his neck or make him realise he's wrong and bring him back.

She turns to take it in, this godforsaken place, bracken and sea pink, rye grass jerking in the wind, slabs of basalt rusty with lichen. Lying in a shallow pool, she sees the bloody head of a seal pup hacked off by the men last night then hurled off the cliff before they cooked the body. Its blind eyes have turned white.

She crouches on the hard, wet stones and hugs herself. No one has any idea that she is here except the crew of the departing ship, and no one else would give a damn. She does not know the name of this island. She knows only that this is the place in which she will die. She is off the heart's map and her compass is spinning.

Minutes pass. Water breaks and fizzes on the pebbles. The wind sings and the cold begins to bite. She stands and starts the long climb to the bed they will never share again.

§

She is a princess. In twenty years she has never been alone, never cooked a meal, never cleaned a floor. She has bathed in clean, warm water every morning. Twice a day newly laundered clothes have been laid on her bed. She realises that this will be hard. She does not know the meaning of the word.

She enters the tent and sees his body's imprint on the sheets and has to turn away. She eats the bread and drinks the water, then lies down and waits, as if an easy death is one more luxury some nameless servant will provide.

She cannot believe that anyone is able to bear this kind of pain. She thinks of shepherds sleepless in the blue snow, their furs pulled tight around their shoulders, waiting for the wolves, armed only with a slingshot. She thinks of the soldiers who come back from every summer's campaign with legs and arms missing, the stumps like melted wax. She thinks of women giving birth in stone sheds with leaking roofs and mud floors. She thinks about what it must take to lead such lives, and she starts to understand that wealth has deprived her of the one skill that she needs now.

§

The light begins to die and the dark thickens slowly to a colour she has never seen before. Then the shearwaters come, two hundred thousand birds returning from a day at sea to run the gauntlet of the black-backed gulls, and suddenly the tent is inside a hurricane of screams, the noise that makes young sailors think they have drifted near the mouth of hell. She dares not go outside for fear of what she might find. She covers her ears and curls into a ball in the centre of the single rug and waits for claws and teeth to tear the flimsy canvas walls and shred her body like a deer's. She waits, and waits, and when the silence finally comes it is worse, for she has been stripped of everything that used to shield her from a hard world where every action has a consequence. She has no one else to blame. This is her punishment. She helped him kill her brother. Now it is her turn. When her bones are picked clean the scales will be level once again.

§

She should have listened to her maids and walked around the palace grounds, but she had walked around the palace grounds a thousand times. She knew in tedious detail every carved fountain, every lavender bush with its halo of bees, every shaded bower. She wanted the bustle of the quays, those overflowing baskets of squid and mackerel, the stacked crates and coiled ropes, the shouting and the knock of tarred hulls, that childhood fantasy of walking up a gangplank, casting off and slipping through the cupped hands of the breakwater into the white light of a world outside her family's orbit.

§

They came at every summer's end, a war-price Athens paid to keep the peace, just one more ceremony in a calendar of ceremonies, the Leaping of the Bulls, the Festival of Poppies. Twelve young men and women taken from their ship and housed in the barn above the orchard while this year's pit was dug beside the last, then led out and lined up to have their throats slit and die on top of one another. They were human cattle, and they knew this, shuffling with heads down, already half dead. She gave them no more thought than she gave the enemies her father and her cousins killed in battle.

But her eyes locked briefly with the eyes of the one man who held his head high and she realised that there were many worlds beyond this world and that her own was very small indeed.

Later that night she woke repeatedly, thinking he was standing in the room or lying beside her. She was terrified at first, then disappointed. She felt alive in a way that she had never felt alive before. The cold flags on the floor, the cicadas, the pocked coin of the moon, her own skin . . . She had never seen these things clearly until now.

Shortly after dawn she slipped past the maids in the outer room and walked round the orchard to the stables. She told the guards she wanted to talk to the prisoners and they could think of no adequate reply to this unexpected request. The last of the night was pooling in the big stone rooms, the window slits no wider than a hand. There was sand on the floor and the sound of breathing. She felt the stir her presence caused, warm bodies shifting nervously in the dark. It was a small thing to be brave about but she had never needed to be brave before and mastering her fear was thrilling.

His face materialised behind the bars of the little window. "You came."

She had spent her whole life waiting for this moment and never realised it. She thought stories only happened to men. Now her own was beginning.

"My father is the king," he said. "In time I will become king. If you save us I will make you my queen."

She gave him her ring and he told her what to do. She slid her hands between the bars, let him grip her wrists and cried out for help. When the guard came running and reached through to free her the prince grabbed him. He wrapped one hand around the man's mouth and the other around his neck. He put a foot on the bars and heaved as if he were pulling a rope. The man kicked and thrashed for a long time before he sagged and slid to the floor. She took the keys from his belt and unlocked the door. She had never seen a man being killed. It looked no different from the games her cousins played when they were young.

He took the man's sword and met the second guard running in. He swung it into his belly and lifted him on the point to force it deeper, then let him drop. He put his boot on the man's chest and pulled the blade out with a sucking gurgle. By this time his friends were pouring out of the stables, the men arming themselves with makeshift weapons from the walls—staves, pitchforks, iron bars.

He told them to take her to the harbour and treat her well. For a moment she thought he was going to murder her parents. He laid a hand on her cheek and told her that they would be safe.

He chose two men to accompany him and they ran towards the palace.

§

They said her mother had been raped by a bull and had given birth to a monster who lay chained and snarling in a nest of straw and dung at the centre of a maze beneath the palace, waiting for the young men and women from Athens to be offered to him as fresh meat. Let the peasants keep their stories, her father said. They had precious little else. And it was safer to be feared than to be pitied.

There was some truth in the story for her brother sometimes

seemed like a monster, his bloated head, his rages, the way he lashed out at the men who went into the cellar to sluice him with buckets of water every week, to carry off the foul straw and fill his trough with the same food they gave to the pigs—kitchen scraps, greasy bones, wine gone sour.

They thought he could not speak. They never asked him a question so he never gave them a reply. But she knew. She went down to the cellar most days and sat with him in the light of that single, guttering torch and held his hand. He would lay his head on her lap and tell her about the things the men did to him for their amusement. She gave him fruit and bread which she had hidden under her skirt and while he ate she told him about the world outside, about the ocean that was like the water in the bucket but deeper and broader than he could possibly imagine, about boats that were like floating houses, about music that was sound shaped to make you happy, about the pines outside her window and the woodcutters in the summer.

He wept sometimes but he never asked for help. When he was younger and she was more naïve she suggested that he try to escape, but he did not understand what she was saying for he had never seen anything beyond these damp walls, and thought her stories of oceans and boats and music were simply games to make the darkness bearable. He was right, of course. He could not live outside. The sun would blind him. He would be mocked and taunted and stoned.

Her mother, her father, her cousins, they put him out of their minds, but she could not. She felt his presence constantly, like the distant rumble of thunder, and when she felt the weight of his deformed head in her lap and ran her hand through his patchy hair, the kindness flowed both ways, for he was easing her discomfort as much as she was easing his.

§

They reached the harbour to find that the Athenians had already hoisted six small barrels of pitch out of the hold, set them on fire with flints and torn cloth and slung them onto the decks of the other ships so that the sailors on watch were too preoccupied with trying to extinguish the flames to concern themselves with anything but saving their own vessels.

She was petrified. She could see what it meant to be in the middle of a story, and why the men protected them from this. It was a mistake. She understood that now. A moment's weakness had caused this horror, the way a single spark from those struck flints bloomed into the fires that surrounded her. Metal struck metal, planks split, the air was so full of smoke she was finding it hard to breathe.

Then she saw him running along the quay with his two companions, carrying a sack, pursued by palace guards, and he was a hand reaching down to pull her from the hole into which she had fallen and if only he made it to the boat in time she would be safe and happy. They pushed off and the men jumped the widening gap between the hull and the harbour wall. A guard leapt behind them and was struck in the face with a sword and dropped into the water, his blood spraying the man who killed him. A second leapt and clung briefly to the rail of the boat before his fingers were broken under heels and he fell onto his companion. Then they were too far away for anything but angry yells which were soon drowned in the roar of the fires.

He turned to her and wrapped his arms around her shoulders and pulled her close and she could no longer hear or see the flames, she could only feel the warmth of his body and smell the sour tang of his sweat. Then she looked down at the deck and saw the mouth of the sack fall open to reveal her brother's head.

§

She is woken by the biting cold and the sound of two hundred thousand birds taking flight. Waking to anything solid is a relief after the murky, cycling panic of her dreams. She walks to the door and sees the creatures that petrified her the night before emerging from their burrows and climbing into the air like ashes above a fire, black backs turning into white bellies, the whole flock becoming a cloud of grey flakes drifting out over the ocean.

When they have gone the air is washed and white and she is able to hold the events of the previous day at a distance for a few minutes, as if they happened to someone else, or happened to herself many years ago. Then it all comes back, raw and real, and there is a spasm in her guts. She crouches behind a rock and relieves herself, and the sight of her own excrement sickens her, doubly so when she finds that the earth is too thin to bury it and the handfuls of grass she rips free just blow away in the wind and she is forced to use a stick to push it under the lip of the rock where she will not see it.

She drinks from a muddy pool of rainwater, retches and makes herself drink again. She wraps herself in the rug from the tent floor and walks round the perimeter of the island, a figure of eight with two stony beaches on either side of its narrow waist. It takes her two hours. There are no trees, only clumps of low thorn bushes bent flat by the wind, green cushions of mossy thrift, bracken and sea campions, razorbills and butterflies. The greater part of the coast is sheer cliff, though in places the grass falls away to great slabs of cracked and toppled stone, stained with an orange crust above the waterline and shaggy with weed beneath it. She catches a movement in the corner of her eye and thinks, for a moment, that she is not alone, but it is a group of seals lying beached on a thin promontory, half-fish, half-dog, their wet skins like mottled gemstones. The only signs of human presence are the remains of an ancient stone circle about which there hangs an atmosphere that scares her.

She returns to the tent pitched in the low saddle between the two halves of the island and sheltered from the worst of the wind. She is hungry but has no idea what she can eat. She wonders how long it takes to starve. She knows nothing about such things.

§

He held her till her sobs began to die down then wiped her cheek and looked into her eyes. "I have to command these people. They need to look at me and see someone who has powers they do not possess. They need to know that I can kill monsters." He was not angry. He did not need to be angry. "Your father killed twelve of us every year for ten years. Those people had sisters, they had mothers. Your father was planning to bury us in a ditch. I killed your brother. I could have done a great deal more."

She had no choice. She had to embrace this man and put her brother out of her mind. She had to throw away her old life and become a new person. She wondered if this was what it meant to love someone completely.

§

The second morning, hunger wakes her before dawn. It is like a broken bone. Her body is not going to let her starve.

A cold drizzle is falling. She wants to stay in the tent but the pain in her stomach is worse than the prospect of getting wet, so she makes her way down the scree again to the little beach. She stands at the top of the shingle slope and looks around. She does not know if there is anything edible here. Her food has always been cooked and prepared. She has little idea of what this involves. She is accustomed to eating grapes and pears and quinces but she has seen no fruit on the island. To her left is the seal pup's head but that would need cooking and she has no fire and she cannot look at the object without thinking of her brother.

She tries to chew some seaweed but it is leathery and gritty and covered in a layer of slime. She finds some shells stuck to the sides of a rock pool but they prove impossible to remove. She wades into the shallows. The water is like shackles of ice around her ankles. She bends down, turns the pebbles over and pushes aside the fronds of shaggy weed, nervous of what she might find beneath. She wades a little deeper. Already her sense of danger is being overridden by an animal need which obscures all other thoughts.

She is up to her thighs in the freezing waves now, the stones under her feet are harder to see and searching among them requires her to put her face into the water. Her fingers find a cluster of something sharper and more geometric than the surrounding rocks. She pulls and breaks it free and retrieves a cluster of shells, speckled with stony mortar. She walks out of the water and discovers that the temperature of the ocean makes the air seem warm. She tries to prise open the shells but splits a nail, so she goes up the beach to a flat shelf. She puts the shells down, takes up a large pebble and cracks the shells open. There is a kind of meat inside. She picks away the shards of broken shell and scoops some out. She puts the contents in her mouth. It is like salty phlegm. She waits and swallows. At least she does not need to chew. She eats a second. Then a third.

The air is no longer warm and she is beginning to shiver uncontrollably. She has five more shells. She carries them back up the scree towards the grassy saddle. She goes inside the tent, thinking that she must get warm and dry, but there is water dripping through the roof onto the bed and she has very little energy. She removes her clothing and wraps the deerskin blanket round her and lies down in the dry half of the tent.

She cries and rocks back and forth and manages to descend into a half-sleep that calms her a little. Then the stomach cramps begin. With no warning, she is sick onto the ground in front of her. She rolls over so that she does not have to look at it. The cramps ease a little.

§

He ordered one of the women to bring a cloak from below decks and sat her on a bench to one side of the boat then returned to the other men, commanding them to trim sails and watch for rocks and stow the ropes, sending them to the rowing benches when these tasks were done, to maintain as high a speed as possible. When they were out of sight of land he altered course to throw off any following ships.

She had never been on a boat before. The cleanness and the coldness of the air and the spray coming over the prow took her by surprise. The way the deck yawed and pitched terrified her at first, though everyone else on board seemed oblivious. She tried to pretend it was a child's game, like swinging on a rope, or being thrown into the air and caught by her father.

It was the sheer size of the ocean which unsettled her most. She wondered how deep the water was beneath the hull and felt a nauseous tingle in the back of her legs as if she were standing on a high tower and looking over the edge. She thought of how they were supported by a wooden platform no bigger than a courtyard floating across this sky of water, how none of them could swim and how they were all less than ten steps away from death, and she began to understand how brave sailors were, or how stupid.

The thought of her brother was like a pounding headache. She moved as little as possible and watched and listened hard to what was going on around her and tried to distract herself from the pain.

Finally the rowers broke off and a basket of provisions was brought up from below, olives, salted fish, fresh water and dry biscuits of a kind she had never seen before. He sat beside her but addressed her directly only twice. She liked the way in which she had so rapidly been accepted into the magic circle from which the others were excluded. He had to maintain a public face, she understood that. She was flattered that the private man belonged to her alone.

They anchored in the bay of the island shortly before nightfall. A small boat was lowered on ropes and three men rowed ashore to reconnoitre. They returned with the news that the island was uninhabited and began ferrying boxes and packets and bundles to the beach, taking passengers only when several tents had already been erected on the grassy ridge.

Nightfall frightened her. The firelight at home had always illuminated a stone wall, painted plaster, a woven hanging. She had never seen darkness eat up the world like this. She was losing her bearings a little, and times and places began to overlap. She remembered the stories she had heard as a child, how Chaos gave birth to love and hell, how Kronos castrated his father with a sickle, and these things now seemed no more or less real than her cousin Glaucus nearly drowning in a barrel of honey, or her cousin Catreus trying to ride a goat and breaking his arm.

They ate more of the salted fish and the dried figs which had been compacted into discs like little millwheels. Some of the men found a young seal on the beach and chased its mother away so that they could kill it. They roasted chunks of the flesh over the fire but several of the women found it inedible so she declined, deciding that she could easily wait another two days for proper meat. The sweet wine, in any case, had taken the edges off her hunger.

So novel and so consuming were all these events that she forgot entirely about the one waiting at the evening's end until he drained his final glass and took her hand and led her towards his tent. She knew almost nothing about what he would do to her. She had been told little by her mother and less by her cousins. She had gained more information by overhearing the maids' gossip, and they seemed to find it comical, though the things they described were both repellent and unnerving. She consoled herself that they were talking about men of a kind very different from the one she was marrying.

He closed the door flap and kissed her, for longer this time. She wondered if he would hurt her but he simply slid a hand inside her dress and held one of her breasts. It felt odd and clumsy and wrong. She did not know what she was meant to do in return, if anything. Earlier in the day she trusted him to protect her.

The stakes seemed higher now, the rules less certain. Her life depended on remaining inside the magic circle, and to remain inside the magic circle she had to please him. She had already become a different person this morning. She would have to do it again. She pulled her mouth away from his and said, "What would you like me to do?"

He laughed and lifted her dress and turned her round and bent her over the bed. The maids were right. What he did to her was indeed repellent and unnerving, but oddly comical too. She should have felt adult and sophisticated but it reminded her mostly of being a child again, wrestling, doing handstands, turning cartwheels in the dust. It was demeaning at first, and dirty, then it was good to be a child, to have no responsibilities, to forget everything that had happened today and concentrate only on the present moment.

When he was finished he rolled onto the bed and pulled the deerskin blanket over them. Within minutes he was asleep. She was unable to move without detaching herself from his embrace and she did not want to wake him so she lay listening to the voices outside getting fewer and fainter as everyone made their way to bed and the fidgety orange light of the fire faded. Every so often the wind flicked back a tongue of canvas at the top of the door and she could see a tiny triangle of sky that contained three stars hanging in a darkness that went on forever.

§

Sometime after midday the rain stops, the pain in her stomach disappears and her mind is returned to her. She hangs her sodden clothes on the guy ropes outside the tent so that they will dry in the sun. She does the same thing with the bedclothes and ties back the door of the tent in the hope that the breeze might evaporate some of the water from its muddy floor. She is naked. She cleans up the vomit, scooping it into her hands and carrying it outside, then wiping her fingers clean on the grass. She does this without thinking and, in the middle of doing it, she sees herself from the outside and realises how far she has travelled in such a short time.

She finds a shallow pool of brackish water gathered on the concave top of a mossy rock and drinks, and the coldness of the water makes up for the earthy, vegetable taste.

She begins to think, for the first time, that surviving here might be possible, but that to do so she must become like a fox, hunting constantly and never thinking about tomorrow.

Wrapped only in her blanket and wearing her sandals, she makes her way back to the area of the island where the thorn bushes were thickest and finds that her memory is correct and some of the plants are indeed covered in small red berries. She does not want to repeat the mistake of this morning, so she picks just one and puts it into her mouth. But when she crushes it between her teeth the taste is shockingly sour and she has to spit it out.

She makes her way down the scree to the beach, determined to master her feelings about the seal pup's head. But it has begun to rot and the smell is overpowering, and when she gets close she can see something moving inside.

She has to make a fire. If she can make a fire then she can perhaps cook the shellfish and make them edible. She used to watch her cousins doing it many years ago with tinderboxes stolen from the kitchen before they were caught and beaten. The boxes contained two stones and a wad of lint. She has no lint, but she has an endless supply of rock. She begins searching the drier, top half of the beach, picking up pairs of stones, turning her back to the wind, striking one against the other and watching for that tiny scrap of lightning. She does this for a long time with no success.

She climbs back up to the grass. She is exhausted. Her clothes are dry but she does not have the energy to put them on. Instead she lies in the mouth of the tent watching the shadows of clouds slide across the surface of the water. There is a seductive comfort in doing this and she knows that the longer she spends without eating the harder it will be to find food but she can neither bring herself to stand up nor think of what she might achieve if she did.

§

He was right. Her father had done worse. She thinks of the bodies in the trench. She wonders if any of them were still alive when the earth was shovelled on top of them, and imagines mud in her mouth, that unmovable weight holding her down.

Her father was doubtless privy to events and information of which she knew nothing. Perhaps, from his perspective, these cruelties were simply the price that had to be paid to keep his people safe. She will never know.

She has not talked for three days. She has not heard another human voice. Her thinking is becoming simultaneously clearer and more confused. Those concentric rings of the royal apartments, the public rooms, the gardens, the town beyond the palace walls, seem to her like a beehive or an ants' nest, some beautifully structured object whose working must remain forever mysterious. There is a picture of her father which comes back to her throughout the day. He is standing at one of the big windows looking down towards the harbour. She is sitting at his feet, playing with a set of ivory jacks. His face is lit by the sun coming off the sea. He is not looking at her but he knows that she is there. She must be three, four, five years old. She feels completely safe.

Later she saw him strike her mother. She saw him bring his fist down on an earthenware plate and shatter it, so angry that he did not notice that his hand was bleeding. She saw him send men to be hanged and watched them weep as they were led from the room.

She can see now that her father, too, had a magic circle around him, and that she loved him less on account of who he was than for allowing her inside that circle when so many others were kept out.

§

The following morning she combs the beach again looking for stones that will strike a spark. This time she selects two of every type then ferries them up to the tent where the air is drier and there is no sea spray. She bangs them together in turn and her spirit leaps when she sees that a tiny star is born with a loud crack between two of the stones. She tears a corner from her dress and picks at it with her dirty nails until it is a wren's nest of cream fibres.

Only then does she remember that she has no wood. She feels stupid, and scared by the realisation that she is losing the ability to plan ahead. She thinks of the effort involved in finding that wood and begins to cry. But crying is pointless so after a few minutes she stops. She wraps the deerskin round her once more and walks a circuit of the island.

There are no logs because there are no trees, but she succeeds in gathering an armful of dry branches. She is walking beside the cliffs on the way back to the tent when she sees movement in the waves. She turns and watches two dolphins break the surface, curve through the air and enter the water again, then break the water a second time, as if they are riding the rim of some great, hidden wheel. They are heart-stoppingly beautiful, like long, silver bottles or wingless, grey birds.

But they are mocking her. She cannot swim. She would die out there, whereas they can travel to ten kingdoms and back. For a moment she dreams of having their freedom, then realises how little it would profit her. She would not be wanted in Athens. She would not be wanted at home. Here is as good as anywhere.

The dolphins have gone. She returns to the tent, piles the twigs on the ashes of the last fire and rebuilds the little circle of stones the men built around it. She fetches the two stones and the little nest of cotton lint.

It does not work. The stones spark one time in twenty, and when they do she has no way of directing that spark into the lint. She tries a hundred, two hundred times. Her hands are bloody and bruised. Her arms are exhausted. The lint refuses to catch.

§

She is too tired to remain awake but too uncomfortable to sleep. She drifts halfway between the two states, clipping the edge of nightmares and coming away trailing nameless fears that snap her briefly awake. She thinks she has fallen overboard or is running up an endless slope of shingle, chased by a nameless, seal-faced creature that is and is not her brother.

When dawn comes she lies listening to the shearwaters taking flight. When there is only the muffled sound of the waves left she stands and walks down to the beach, climbing round the rocks at the side of the cove until she is looking down into deeper water. She sits on a rock with her legs dangling. A jellyfish swims below her, a ball of light in a white bag with a charred rim, trailing ragged tentacles. It pulses in the slow wind of the current. She watches, transfixed. She is no longer able to measure time.

The jellyfish is gone. The translucent green water flexes and wobbles like flames dancing in a grate.

There is a rash on the back of her left hand where the skin has reddened and begun to peel away. She runs her fingers over it. There is pain but it does not belong to her.

Clambering back up the scree she hears women's voices and a high metal chime like tiny bells ringing. She climbs faster but by the time she reaches the curved, grass saddle the voices have stopped and there is no one there.

Her bowels clench. She does not bother to find shelter. She squats and relaxes and what comes out is a foul, orange liquid so that she has to clean herself repeatedly with clumps of torn grass.

She walks aimlessly towards the highest point on the island simply to postpone her return to the tent. She does not want to look at the vastness of the sea so she keeps her eyes fixed on the ground. It is peppered with the burrows out of which the shearwaters emerge. She stops and stamps her feet and realises for the first time how hollow the earth sounds and how it must be honeycombed with little tunnels. She gets down on her hands and knees and begins to tear at the mouth of the nearest hole. The earth is woven thick with pale roots and she has to search for a sharp stone to cut through the toughest of them. She digs farther, making a deep furrow. She feels something scratching and flapping at the ends of her fingers and excavates the last two handfuls of earth to find two fat, grey chicks huddled in their subterranean chamber. She had hoped to find eggs but it is too late in the season.

She picks up one of the birds, a puffball of dove-coloured fur. It pecks her with its hooked black beak. She stands up and crushes the head of the chick with the heel of her sandal. She hacks at the chest of the tiny bird with the edge of the stone until it peels back. There is blood all over her hands and tiny feathers stuck to the blood. She bites into the warm innards, chewing at the gristle and swallowing what she can tear off. She is eating feathers along with the meat. She gags but carries on eating. Three mouthfuls. The bird is finished. She gazes down at its brother. It is looking back up at her with its mouth open, waiting to be fed, the black jewels of its eyes glittery in the sunlight.

She walks away, wiping her mouth on the deerskin.

§

She cannot remember her mother's face. She can remember the faces of her brother, her cousins, her father. She can remember the faces of the men who sat around the council table. She can remember the faces of the four male servants who were trusted enough to work in the royal apartments. But she cannot bring her mother's face to mind.

This is the woman who brought her into the world, the woman her father loved. Yet every time she turns her mind's eye in her mother's direction she sees only the men she is talking to, the children she is playing with, the maids to whom she is giving orders. She begins to realise how little her mother did, how rarely she offered an opinion, how the family revolved around her without ever making contact, how small an effect she had on the world.

How alike they are, she and her mother, these blank sheets on which men have written their stories, the white paper under the words, making all their achievements possible and contributing nothing to the meaning.

She realises that she can no longer remember what her own face looks like so she leaves the tent and makes her way to the shallow pool on the rock. She puts her back to the sun and makes a canopy of the deerskin cloak to shield the surface from the glare. She stares down into the water and sees her brother's sister staring up at her, hair matted like his hair, skin filthy like his skin, cheeks sunken, eyes dark, the skull starting to come through.

§

There is a storm at night. The thunder is like buildings coming down, and after every explosion the tent is flooded with a harsh blue light that sings on the back of her eyes for minutes afterwards. She wills the lightning to strike her directly, for everything to be over in an instant, but this does not happen. The canvas bucks and cracks and after several hours she is woken from her half-sleep by the rough cloth smacking her face as the tent collapses around her. The wind fills the canvas like a sail and drags her along the ground. She has lost all sense of direction and is terrified that she will be hauled over a cliff. She does not want to die, not now, not like this. She does not want to lie on rocks with shattered bones or drown like a dog in a sack but she does not possess the strength to wrestle herself free, so she lies flat and prays for the wind to slacken. Eventually a gust hoists her free of the ground, she is swung hard against a boulder, the tent comes to a halt and she can do nothing but block her ears to the roar and the whipping of the canvas so that she can nurse the pain in her side.

Morning comes and the wind dies away. She frees herself and

rolls what remains of the tent into a heap behind the rock that anchored her through half the night. She looks back towards the square of dead grass where it had been pitched. All but two of the pegs have gone. Putting the tent back up is impossible now. She drinks some water then begins the painfully slow process of dragging the torn canvas sheets down to the head of the beach where there is some protection from the wind and she can wrap herself up at night.

There is now a constant throbbing in her head and a churning anger in her guts that she has no way of expending. She lies down and closes her eyes and tries to get some of the rest she should have got last night. As she slips out of consciousness she hears the women's voices again and that distant tinkling, but when she opens her eyes she can hear only the surf. She descends into vivid, fitful dreams. She is in the bridal suite once more, standing by the bed and examining the tapestry of the weeping woman and the receding ship. This time, however, she sees a part of the picture she had not noticed before. In the lower left-hand corner of the great, woven square, on the green of the island, she can see a band of figures. They are walking towards the weeping woman. She does not know whether they are coming to help the woman or whether they are hunting her down. She steps forward to examine them more closely and the dream evaporates.

§

The sun is overhead and the air is warm again. She decides that she must make use of what little energy she has left to find some food. Picking up the sharpened stone she climbs to the grassy plateau where the shrubs grow. Half of her is in her body, half hovers in the air above. She moves fluidly and for once walking is easy. She can smell the perfume of the small blue flowers and see two gulls hanging on the breeze.

She finds the largest plant, breaks off the straightest, toughest branch then uses the sharpened stone to whittle a point at one end. She walks to the place where she first saw the seals. She has no idea how many days ago that was. She simply assumes that they will still be there and indeed they are, three adults and a pup. She sits on the grassy ledge and looks down. There is a drop, perhaps twice the height of a man, to a slab of rock that slopes smoothly down to the little channel beside which they are lying. Holding the makeshift weapon in her teeth she turns, lowers herself as far as she can then lets go.

She feels, briefly, as if she is flying, then she lands badly. The pain is so bright and sharp that she cannot breathe, only cradle herself and moan till it dies away, before rolling onto her back. She examines her left hand. The little finger is bent backwards and will not respond to any commands. She cannot bear to touch it. She is sweating profusely.

She looks up to the grassy ledge. She can see no way of getting back. She looks down. The seals are still there. They seem unbothered by her presence. She tells herself that this is good. They are tame. She can do what she came to do.

Her stick has slid down the rocks. She stands up, intending to walk over and retrieve it, but as she does so a flock of tiny, white insects swarms across her field of vision. She sits and waits then shuffles sideways, using her one good hand until she has the stick in her possession again.

She begins moving towards the seals. Two of the adults are watching her. She is fifteen paces away now. They are bigger than she had thought, their bodies as bulky as the bodies of oxen. One of the adults nudges the pup into the water then slips through the surface after it. She is ten paces away now, and she can see, for all their ungainliness, how strong these animals are and how much they weigh. She realises that what she is about to do is dangerous. She cannot remember precisely why she is doing it but changing her mind and doing something different seems like the hardest thing of all. She is five paces away. One of the seals lumbers towards her, rears up, opens its mouth and barks. It sounds like the bottom of a great jar being scraped. It is talking to her and no one has talked to her in a long time. She almost says something back. These animals are going to save her. She wonders why she did not come here sooner. It would have made everything so much easier.

Putting her right hand flat on the ground she gets slowly to her feet. She is a little giddy but there are no stars this time. The seal rears and barks again. She grips the stick tightly, steps forward and shoves the point into the flesh of the seal's head. It moves with surprising speed, flicking the stick away and swinging immediately back to sink its teeth into her ankle, then swinging its head a third time so that her leg is yanked out from underneath her. The seal lets go and she is tumbling towards the channel. She puts out her hands but the stone is slimy with weed and she cannot get sufficient grip. She crashes into the water, her arms flailing. She's hunting desperately for handholds but there are none to be found. Her head goes under, she breathes a mouthful of salty water and coughs it out. She grabs two hanks of weed and pulls her head above the surface. She looks round, thinking the seal is going to attack again, but they are all gone. She wonders if they are circling beneath her, biding their time. She looks down but she cannot even see her own feet. What she can see is the pink froth and clouds of blood in the water.

She holds the weed tight and breathes as slowly and as calmly as she can then hauls herself sideways along the channel to the point where the bottom rises and she is standing in waist-deep water. Everything hurts. She is cold to her bones and unable to stop herself shivering but getting out of the water means lifting herself onto a seaweed-covered shelf. It is all of a hand's breadth above the surface of the water but even that effort is beyond her imagination.

The world slips out of focus then comes back. She sees her stick a little farther up the rock, the stripped wood of its point still red with the seal's blood. She remembers eating a baby bird. Was that yesterday or the day before? It is hard to be clear about these things. Why did she not dig another bird out of its nest instead of coming down here to kill an animal ten times her size? She has no answers to these questions.

With no warning, the water rises around her and a seal breaks the surface only a few feet away and lunges at her. She has no idea how she does it but she is suddenly out of the water and crawling up the rocky slope. She collapses and looks back, panting. The seal is no longer there. She examines her leg. There is a deep gash on her ankle. Inside it she can see something white which might or might not be bone. She looks away.

§

She went down to the cellar one time and found her brother's head covered in blood. She asked him what had happened, but he would say nothing at first. She fetched some water from the bucket and washed the wound, then tore a strip of cloth from her skirt and bandaged it. She put her arms around him and asked if one of the men had done this to him. He shook his head. She pulled back and looked into his eyes.

"Tell me."

"I did it."

"You did it?"

"I did it."

"You hurt yourself? How?"

"Wall." He nodded to one of the arches of the brick vault and she saw the bloodstains.

"Why?"

"I want it to stop."

"What do you want to stop?"

"Everything. I want everything to stop."

She pretended not to understand. She can see now that she was a coward. She can see now that if she had been braver, if she had really loved her brother, she would have taken a knife down those dark stairs and slipped it between his ribs and let him die in her arms.

§

Night comes and in the darkness, after the shearwaters have flown ashore, she hears animals that are neither seals nor birds. She hears lions and leopards and wolves. She hears the clanking of chains. She hears drunken shouting and the crackle of a fire and something large breathing close to her ear. She hears the air going in and out of its nostrils and smells the rot of its yellow teeth. She feels the heat of its breath.

§

Grey light. Intense cold. A fine rain is falling. She cannot move her leg. She cannot move her hand. The world is a tiny, bright thing, so small she can hold it in her hand.

She looks up to the fringe of green grass high above her head. That was the place she had come from. There was a bed somewhere up there. But if there is a way back she is unable to see it from here. She can move her other leg a little. She thinks about trying to stand so that she can find a route but this rock is a kind of bed, too, and she has a memory of the other bed blowing away. She can smell the ammonia on her breath. She looks down at her damaged hand. One of the fingers is the wrong shape. It looks like a badly drawn picture of a hand.

§

She is in a garden. There are fountains and lavender bushes covered in bees that rise in angry, humming clouds when her cousins hit them with sticks before the nurse drags them away. She trod on a bee once and her foot swelled to twice its size. There are bowers, too, where she can sit out of the heat of the sun. From her favourite she can look down over the wall to the quays and to the ships entering or leaving the harbour. She likes to imagine the countries from which they have come, the countries the old men talk about, countries made entirely of sand, countries where the people have skin as black and glossy as plums, countries where there are water lizards as long as a rowing boat.

She is playing with a hoop made of stripped willow branches, the ends tapered and bound together with little spirals of fibre. If no one gets in the way she can run alongside it, batting it with a stick to keep it rolling, and do a circuit of the entire garden.

It is the most beautiful garden in the world. She never wants to leave. If only she could remember where it is.

§

There is a high wind and the sea explodes on the rocks below. The moon is full and the waves come in like black hills with a crest of blue snow, swelling and flexing and dropping onto the rocky shelf where they turn to freezing spray which falls on her like rain. She thinks how calm it must be out there, under those waves, in that dark that goes down and down, where the dolphins swim and the jellyfish drift on the current and the forests of seaweed swing back and forth, so much better than up here where everything hurts.

§

Dawn comes. Her throat and mouth are dry and she cannot generate enough saliva to swallow. Her lips are cracked and bleeding. She can see nothing but fog through her right eye.

There is a flock of gulls standing farther down the rock, all looking out to sea, preening their grey wings with their orange beaks and shaking out their feathers. Their eyes are little yellow stones with black holes drilled through them. The ocean is beaten silver. The seals have come back.

She can hear the cymbals again, a distant, high ringing that comes and goes on the breeze, now louder, now quieter. She wonders if there is something wrong with her ears. Then she hears the faint but unmistakable sound of a big animal growling, that lazy rumble like a barrel on cobbles. The gulls scatter and the seals slip into the waves, leaving only circles of wash behind them.

Everything is briefly still and silent. Then she sees him. He is a big man, naked except for a ragged cloak of red cloth, taller than she remembers from the boat, and more muscular. His head is too large and there is blood on his face. A leopard pads at his side. Behind him are six naked men and six naked women. Some have made themselves crowns and belts of creepers and green branches, some are carrying freshly killed animals—rabbits, foxes, pheasants.

He stands in front of her, breathing heavily. His chest and shoulders are covered with wiry black hair and she can see now that he has horns. There is dung on his legs and his penis is thick and erect. He bends down and picks her up. She can smell wine on his breath and the rot of his teeth. He licks her. She recognises him from somewhere. She does not feel frightened. No one can hurt her anymore. There is no longer enough of her to be hurt.

He turns her over and lays her down and pushes himself into her. The movement back and forth inside her is the movement of the waves back and forth against the rock, the coming and going of the birds, the pulse of day and night, summer turning into autumn, to winter, to spring to summer again, the heart squeezing and releasing, the pulse of the blood.

Then they are on top of her, the men and women, biting, tearing, ripping her skin, pulling out her hair, breaking her fingers, gouging her eyes, hacking out the fat and muscle, pulling free the greasy tubes and bags of her innards till she is finally free of her body. Rising now, she looks down at the skeleton lying on the rocks, gulls picking at the remaining shreds of meat and gristle.

She sees the grass blowing in the wind, the fringe of restless surf, the island shrinking till it is no more than a lump in the fastness of the sea, the sea an azure tear on the surface of the globe itself which shrinks rapidly in the haze of the sun as she floats into the great, black vault, becoming a buckled ring of seven stars, Corona Borealis, the northern crown.

She is immortal.

BUNNY

He loved Mars bars and KitKats. He loved Double Deckers and
Galaxy Caramels and Yorkies. He loved Reese's Pieces and Cadbury's Creme Eggs. He could eat a whole box of Quality Street
in one sitting and had done so on several occasions, perhaps more
than several. He loved white chocolate. He was not particularly
keen on Maltesers, Wispas and Crunchies which were airy and
insubstantial, though he wouldn't turn his nose up at any of them
if they were on offer. He disliked boiled and gummy sweets. He
loved chocolate digestives. He loved Oreos and chocolate Bour-
bons. He loved coconut macaroons and Scottish shortbread. He
would never buy a cereal bar but a moist, chunky flapjack was one
of the most irresistible foods on the planet.

He loved thick, sweet custard. He loved Frosties and Weeta-
bix with several dessertspoons of sugar. He loved chunks of cheese
broken from a block in the fridge, Red Leicester preferably or
cheap, rubbery mozzarella. He loved Yazoo banana milk, the stuff
you got from garages and service stations in squat plastic bottles
with foil seals under chunky screw-tops. He could eat a litre tub
of yogurt if he added brown sugar or maple syrup.

He loved hot dogs and burgers, especially with tomato ketchup in a soft white bun thickly spread with butter. He loved battered cod and chips with salt and no vinegar. He loved roast chicken, he loved bacon, he loved steak. He loved every flavour of ice cream he had ever sampled—rum and raisin, Dime bar crunch, peanut butter, tiramisu . . .

At least he used to love these things. His eating was now largely mechanical and joyless. It was the sugar and the fat he needed, though it gave him little pleasure. More often than not it made the cravings worse. He hated people using the phrase "comfort eating." He had not been comfortable for a very long time, except sometimes in dreams where he ran and swam, and from which he occasionally woke up weeping.

He was twenty-eight years old and weighed thirty-seven stone.

There was a creased and sun-bleached photograph of him at nine, standing in the corridor outside the Burnside flat wearing his new uniform for the first day at St. Jude's. His mother had run back inside at the last minute to get the camera, as if she'd feared he might not be coming home again and had wanted a memento, or a picture to give to the police. He'd been wearing grey flannel shorts and a sky-blue Aertex shirt. He could still smell the damp, fungal carpet and hear the coo and clatter of the pigeons on the window ledge. He remembered how overweight he felt, even then. Whenever he looked at the photo, however, his first thought was what a beautiful boy he had been. So he stopped looking at the photo. He dared not tear it up for fear of invoking some terrible voodoo. Instead he asked one of his care assistants to put it on top of a cupboard where he couldn't reach it.

Three weeks before his tenth birthday his father disappeared overnight to live in Wrexham with a woman whose name Bunny was never allowed to know. At supper he was there, by breakfast he had gone. His mother was a different person afterwards, more brittle, less kind. Bunny believed that she blamed him for his father's departure. It seemed entirely possible. His father played cricket. As a young man he'd had a trial for Gloucestershire. He was very much not the parent of an overweight, unathletic child.

To Bunny's surprise he wasn't bullied at St. Jude's. Mostly the other children ignored him, understanding perhaps that isolation was both the cruellest and the easiest punishment they could inflict. His friend Karl said, "I'm sorry. I can only talk to you outside school." Karl was a wedding photographer now and lived in Derby.

Bunny had kissed three girls. The first was drunk, the second, he learnt later, had lost a bet. The third, Emma Cullen, let him put his hand inside her knickers. He didn't wash it for a week. But she was chubby and he was aroused and disgusted and utterly aware of his own hypocrisy, and the tangle in his head when he was with her was more painful than the longing when he wasn't so he cold-shouldered her until she walked away.

He scraped through a business diploma from the CFE then worked for five years as an assistant housing officer for the county council until he was no longer able to drive. His GP said, "You are slowly killing yourself," as if this had not occurred to Bunny before. He took a job in university admin, digitising paper records, but he was getting larger and increasingly unwell. He had a series of gallstones and two bouts of acute pancreatitis. He had his gall bladder removed but his weight made the operation more traumatic and the recovery harder than it should have been. Sitting was uncomfortable and standing made him feel faint so he lay down at home and after four weeks of statutory sick pay he got a letter telling him not to return to work. His sister, Kate, said it was illegal and maybe she was right but he was tired and in pain and he felt increasingly vulnerable outside the house so he applied for Disability Living Allowance.

His sister said a lot of things that were meant to be helpful, over the phone from Jesmond mostly and very occasionally in person. She had married a man with a red Audi RS3 who owned three wine bars. They had two children and a spotless house which Bunny had seen only in pictures.

Bunny's few friends began to drift away. For a brief period his most frequent visitor was a bear of a man from the local Baptist church who was charming and funny until it became clear that Bunny was not going to see the light, at which point he too was gone.

Bunny had visited his mother every fortnight since he left home, though she had always given the impression that it was she who was doing him the favour, stepping off the merry-go-round of her busy life to make tea, feed him biscuits and chat. She worked in the Marie Curie shop and had an allotment. At fifty-seven she had started internet dating using a public terminal at the library and lightly dropped so many different names into the conversation that he didn't know whether she was promiscuous or picky or whether no one stuck around after the second date. Despite the two miles between them she had come to his house over the past few years only when he was bedbound after his three visits to hospital. Now he couldn't keep her away. She collected his benefit and spent most of it on his weekly shop. She made him eat wholemeal bread and green beans and sardines. She said, "I'm going to save your life."

Once a week, using a walking frame, he made an expedition

to the Londis at the end of the street where he bought a bag of sugar and a slab of butter. He left the butter out till it softened then mixed the two into a paste and ate it over three or four sittings. He would have done it every day if he had more money and cared less about what Mrs. Khan and her son thought of him.

§

Bunny's paternal grandfather had been a policeman before the Second World War. He joined the 6th Armoured Division and was burnt to death in his Matilda II tank during the run for Tunis in December 1942. Bunny had a library of books and DVDs about the North Africa Campaign. He read biographies of Alexander and Auchinleck, Rommel and von Arnim. He made ferociously accurate military dioramas, sharing photos and tips and techniques with other enthusiasts around the world on military modelling forums: filters, pre-washing, pin-shading, Tamiya buff dust spray . . .

He watched porn sometimes. He didn't like images of lean men with big cocks which served only to make him acutely aware of his own body's shortcomings. He preferred pictures and videos of solitary women masturbating. He liked to imagine that he had found a hole in the wall of a shower cubicle or a dormitory.

§

He had thrush in the folds between his gut and his thighs. His joints were sore, which might or might not have been the beginnings of arthritis. His ankles were swollen by lymphoedema. He had diabetes for which he took Metformin every morning. God alone knew what his blood pressure was. He ate Rennies steadily throughout the day to counteract his stomach reflux.

Moving from room to room made him breathless. He had fallen badly climbing the stairs a while back, dislocating his knee and giving himself a black eye on the newel post so he slept now on a fold-out sofa in what had previously been the dining room, and used the toilet beside the kitchen. Carers came in to give him a bed bath twice a week.

Sometimes the kids on the estate threw stones at his windows or put dog shit through the letter box. For a period of several weeks one of them with some kind of developmental problem stood with his face pressed to the glass. Bunny would shut the curtains and open them half an hour later only to find that the boy was still standing there.

He played *Rome Total War* and *Halo*. He watched daytime television—*The Real Housewives of Orange County*, *Kojak*, *Homes Under the Hammer* . . . He spent a great deal of time simply looking out of the window. He couldn't see much—the backs of the houses on Erskine Close, mainly, and the top corner of next door's Carioca motorhome. But in between, on clear days, there was a triangle of moorland. If the weather was good he watched the shadows of cloud moving across the grass and gorse and heather and imagined that he was one of the buzzards who sometimes came off the hills and drifted over the edge of town.

On the mantelpiece there were photos of Kate's children, his niece and nephew, Debbie and Raylan, blonde, washed-out, borderline albino, in generic grey-blue cardboard frames with thin gold borders and fold-out stands at the back. He hadn't seen them in seven years and did not expect to see them again for a long time. Next to the photos was a small wooden donkey with two baskets of tiny oranges slung across its back, a memento of his only foreign holiday, in Puerto de Sóller, when he was nineteen.

Mostly he was tired. Hunger and disappointment were, in their own way, as painful as pancreatitis and he would have willingly swapped the former for the latter. And while his mother thought she could save his life, there were days when he wondered whether it was worth saving.

Then Leah came.

§

It was meant to be a temporary arrangement. She would live with her father until she got back on her feet and had sufficient money in the bank to feel safe. Gavin had pushed her out of the front door with nothing, not even her wallet. In Barclays she discovered that the joint account was overdrawn. Too ashamed to put in a reverse-charge call home she spent the first night walking around the centre of Manchester, sitting at bus stops when she grew too tired to stand, kept awake by the fear that she would be preyed upon in some way. She rang her father the following morning but he took too long to arrange the money transfer. It was a further twenty-four hours before she could pick up her train fare from the building society, so she spent the second night in the women's hostel to which the police had directed her. It was not an experience she wanted to repeat.

Leaving the estate had been the first part of the grand plan. But you never did leave the estate, not really. You carried a little bit of it inside you wherever you went, something grubby and broken and windswept. You never trusted anyone who was kind. You married a man who made you feel ugly and weak and scared just like your mother once did, because deep down there was a comfort in being hurt in the old, familiar ways. So in the end the two miscarriages seemed almost a blessing, because they would have been Gavin's children, just like it had been Gavin's house and Gavin's car and Gavin's money. He would have let her do all the hard work then rolled up one day, lifted them out of the playpen and taken them away like he'd done with everything else.

So here she was, working as a dental receptionist and returning each evening to the front room where she'd spent her childhood, sitting on the dove-grey leatherette sofa which stuck to the back of her legs in hot weather, filling the dishwasher in precisely the way her father said it had to be filled, having tea at six forty-five every day and never, ever moving the speakers off the masking tape rectangles on the carpet despite the fact that her father only played R&B and soul from the sixties and seventies which was music about dancing and sex and not giving a fuck about whether the mugs were on the top or the bottom rack of the dishwasher, because her father was coping with retirement and loneliness and ageing in the same way he had coped with her mother, in the same way he had coped with being a parent, by looking the other way and concentrating very hard on something of no importance whatsoever.

She met Bunny while scouring the neighbourhood for a strimmer. Her father's was broken and chores which took her out of the house were becoming increasingly attractive. She rang the doorbell twice because she could hear the television and after forty strimmerless houses it was becoming a challenge. She'd given up and was walking back down the path when the door opened behind her. "Leah Curtis." She was too shocked by the size and shape of him to hear what he was saying. The liquid waddle, the waist which touched both sides of the doorway. "You were at St. Jude's. You won't remember me."

He was right. She had no memory whatsoever. "You haven't got a strimmer, have you?"

"Come in." He rotated then rocked from side to side as he made his way back towards the front room.

There was a yeasty, unwashed smell in the hallway so she left the front door open.

He bent his knees and rolled backwards onto a large, mustard-yellow sofa bed. *Storage Hunters* was on the TV. The wallpaper must have gone up circa 1975, psychedelic bamboo shoots in red and orange, peeling a little at the edges. On the table beside the sofa was a tiny model battlefield—soldiers, sand dunes, an armoured car—and beside the battlefield, a neatly organised collection of paint tubs, aerosols, brushes, folded rags and scalpels, the tips of their blades pushed into corks.

"I get out of breath," he said. "Have a look in the utility room. Kitchen. Turn right. Bunny Wallis. I was in the year above."

There was a garden chair, a bin liner of unwanted clothing and a broken bedside lamp. Maybe she did remember. "Chubby Checker" they called him. She hadn't talked to him once in five years. She wondered if this was all their fault in some obscure way. She grabbed the orange cord snaking out from under the ironing board and pulled. She said she'd bring it back as soon as she'd finished.

"Whenever you want. I'm not leaving the country."

§

She bought him four bottles of Black Sheep Ale as a thank-you. Only when she was standing on the doorstep did she realise that it might not be medically appropriate but he just smiled and said, "Don't tell my mother."

"Does she live here?"

"It sometimes feels like that. Do you want a cup of tea?"

She said yes and was sent to make it. He remembered enough about her to be flattering—that she and Abby had run away to Sheffield, that she had a signed photograph of Shane McGowan— but not so much as to seem creepy. The milk was slightly off but he was good company. He gave her a Panzer captain from the Afrika Korps together with a magnifying glass so that she could see the details in the face.

She was going to say how much her father would like it, the neatness, the precision, but she didn't want to think of the two men as having anything in common, because in half an hour Bunny had asked more questions than her father had asked in two months.

He said his mother had put him on a penitential diet about which he could do nothing, so she came back a few days later with a box of chocolates. His doctor would probably not be happy but it would make a change from the broccoli and the Brussels sprouts.

§

When she was five years old Leah's mother had taken her to the gravel pit to watch her drown Beauty's new kittens. It was a long walk and Leah cried the whole way, hearing them mewl and struggle inside the duffel bag. Her mother said it would toughen her up. She laughed as she held the bag underwater, not out loud but quietly to herself as if she were remembering a funny story. She wanted Leah to know what she was capable of. It was so much more efficient than hitting her. After that she could make Leah feel sick inside just by narrowing her eyes.

When they had guests her mother called her "darling." So how could Leah tell anyone? It was fathers who abused their children. Cruel mothers were the stuff of fairy tales.

§

Bunny didn't find her attractive at first. She was oddly shapeless, a skinny girl carrying too much weight. Her hair was flat and there was something sour about the expression into which her face fell when she didn't think she was being watched. But she woke something which had been going slowly to sleep inside him over the past couple of years. He pictured her naked, moving through the house, perched on the armchair, wiping herself on the toilet, standing at the sink. He could no longer get an erection let alone masturbate so there was no relief from these images and every fantasy left a small bruise on his heart. She was kind and bought him sweet, sticky things. They never talked about his weight and she understood the tyranny of mothers. Five minutes into their second meeting he realised how badly he needed her to keep coming.

§

The first carer Leah met was a pinched Polish woman who didn't offer her name and acted as if Leah were not in the room. She treated Bunny like a recalcitrant child with whom she'd been saddled for half an hour. Leah could see him flinching as she dried his hair. The second, Deolinda, was a big woman from Zimbabwe who kept up a steady stream of stories about the latest episode of *MasterChef*, about her uncle who had been tortured by the police back home, about the proposed landfill site in Totton . . . Then they were replaced by two different carers who were quickly replaced in their turn, and Leah could see that Bunny would prefer someone dour and ill-tempered if only they stuck around and knew where the shampoo was kept, took care of the models and made him a mug of sugary tea without being asked.

§

Her father went to the Wainwright and drank a half of Guinness three nights a week. Her father played the Blackbyrds and the Contours. Her father wore a green V-neck sweater or a red V-neck sweater. Her father smoked thirty cigarettes a day standing under the little awning outside the back door. Her father put the big plates on the right and the smaller side plates on the left and insisted that all knives pointed downwards in the cutlery basket. Her father recorded TV travel programmes and watched them at convenient times—the Great Wall of China, the Atacama Desert, the Everglades.

She hadn't hated him when she was little. If anything she had thought of him as an elder sibling who was keeping a low profile for the same reasons she was. But now, looking back? How could you turn away from your own child? She said, "You never stuck up for me."

Her father said, "Your mother was a difficult and troubled woman."

She said, "That's not the point."

Her father said, "I think something went wrong after you were born."

She said, "That's not the point, either."

He never understood that she was asking for an apology. Or perhaps he understood but didn't feel an apology was appropriate. Either way, if you had to ask then it counted for nothing.

§

One morning Bunny's mother crouched on the far side of his bed and retrieved a crackly, transparent punnet which had once contained twenty Tesco mini flapjack bites and which Leah must have forgotten to remove the night before. "What in God's name is this?"

He said, "I've got a friend."

She said, "Do you know how hard I try to keep you healthy?"

After washing up and hoovering she returned to the living room and said, "Who?"

He said nothing. He had leverage for once and wanted to savour it briefly.

"Well?"

"I used to go to school with her."

"What's her name?"

He was surprised by how upset his mother was, and worried that she might go to Leah's house and confront her.

"How often does she come round?"

"Now and then."

"Every week?"

"I have a friend. She brought me some biscuits. There's no reason to be upset."

She punished him by not coming round for five days but found, on her return, that Leah had done the housework in her absence, and marked her territory by leaving four crumpled Cadbury's Fruit and Nut wrappers on the draining board.

§

She should have gone to London with Abby and Nisha and Sam straight after college. She'd be living in a flat in Haringey now, taking the Piccadilly Line to an office in Farringdon or Bank, winding down on a Friday evening with Jägerbombs and chicken tikka skewers in the Crypt. She might be married to someone halfway human. She might have children.

There was jubilation on Facebook when she confessed that her marriage was over, perhaps a little more jubilation than she wanted. She didn't go into detail. Nisha said, "Get your arse down here. You are going to die in that place."

Why didn't she pack her bags? Was she dead already? Did the memory of that close-knit foursome at school seem less rosy now that there was a real possibility of her joining them? Or was it Bunny? He was funny, he was kind, he was grateful. For the first time in her life she had someone who needed her, and she couldn't imagine sitting by the boating lake in Ally Pally or walking down Shaftesbury Avenue knowing she'd abandoned him to a life that was shrinking rapidly to a single room four hundred miles away.

§

Bunny liked her to read the paper out loud. He liked to beat her at chess and lose to her at Monopoly. They watched DVDs she picked up from the bargain box in Blockbuster. Often she would bring a cake, take a small piece for herself and make no comment as he worked his way through the rest. Sometimes she would go into the back garden to smoke and come back ten minutes later smelling of cigarettes. He yearned for her to lean over one day and push her dirty tongue into his mouth. Could you ask someone to do that kind of thing? Just as a favour? Because the thought of never being kissed again tore open a hole in his chest.

§

One evening when they were watching a documentary about Bletchley Park Bunny's mother let herself in. She called out a casual hello, hung up her coat, came into the living room and said, "So we meet at last," as if this were a surprise. "I don't think Bunny has ever told me your name."

"Leah." She didn't hold out her hand.

The two women swapped pleasantries for a couple of scratchy minutes then his mother said, "You bring him biscuits."

"Sometimes," said Leah.

"You know you're killing him."

"They're just biscuits."

"I've looked after my son for nearly thirty years."

"You don't like me coming here, do you?" said Leah. "You want him all to yourself."

His mother straightened her back. "I just don't want him spending his time with someone like you."

Bunny knew he should intervene but he was not in the habit of telling either of them what they should or should not do, and in truth he was flattered to find himself being fought over.

"Someone like me?" said Leah. "What does that mean, precisely?"

Bunny had imagined this argument many times. He had always wanted Leah to win, but now that it was happening he wondered if his mother might be right after all. Leah was not his wife, not his girlfriend, not a part of his family. She could abandon him tomorrow.

His mother stepped close to Leah and said, quietly, "You little bitch. I've got your number."

On the table beside the sofa there was a diorama of five British soldiers surrounding a crashed Messerschmitt, the dead pilot slumped forward in the smashed cockpit. Bunny had spent five weeks making it. His mother swept it off the table and walked out of the house, slamming the door behind her.

§

It was the end of summer, but instead of cool winds and rainy days a thick grey cloud settled over the town so that the air felt tepid and second-hand. Two children at the end of the street were killed by a police car chasing a stolen van. Nasir Iqbal and Javed Burrows. The rear wheels lost traction on the bend and the vehicle mounted the pavement knocking over a brick wall behind which the boys were playing cricket. He knew their names because they were painted on the street in big white letters. The driver of the car and his colleague were spirited away before the family and neighbours fully understood what had happened. The next police officers at the scene were greeted by a volley of stones and glass bottles and one of their cars was rolled onto its roof.

There was a small riot every evening for a fortnight. Through the curtains Bunny saw the blue lights of police vans and heard whoops and explosions which sounded to him more like people celebrating a victory than mourning a loss.

He decided that for the time being he wouldn't leave the house. He did not want to find himself surrounded by an angry crowd in search of an easy target. But when the streets finally became calm once more he found he was still afraid. He told himself that he would go out when he felt stronger, but even as he was telling himself this he knew it wasn't true.

§

She got back from work one Wednesday evening to find her father sitting at the dining table with his palms flat on the place-mat in front of him as if he were engaged in a one-man séance. He was wearing his red V-neck jumper. He looked directly at her and said, "My trouble."

"Your what?" said Leah.

"My trouble leg," he said, slurring his words.

She assumed he was drunk but when she came closer she could see that the left-hand side of his face was sagging. She tried helping him to the sofa so that he could lie down but he couldn't hold his own weight and she had to hoist him back onto the chair. He was unable to say how long he had been in this state.

The ambulance took twenty-five minutes to arrive. Her father seemed completely unbothered by the gravity of the situation. The paramedic slipped a line into the crook of his arm and held it down with a fat crucifix of white tape. The siren was on the whole way, a dreamy mismatch between the antiseptic calm and the speed with which they sliced through the world.

When they arrived at the hospital her father was partially blind and there were many words he could no longer say, Leah's name being one of them. It was the length of time he had spent sitting at the table, so the doctor said. However long that was. After the golden hour the odds went through the floor. Leah wondered if he had realised that he was being offered a neat, uncomplicated exit and had decided to take it, because God forbid that he should ever find himself bedbound or incontinent or needing to be fed by someone else.

He had the second stroke just after midnight.

She sat in the hard glare of the relatives' room looking at a shitty painting of a fishing boat and a lighthouse. It was the lack of justice which hurt most, the way his cowardice turned out to have been such a good game plan, the possibility that he had never really suffered.

She took a taxi back to the house but couldn't sleep, repeatedly dropping off then crashing back into wakefulness convinced that her mother was in the room.

She rang in sick the following morning and went round to Bunny's house. She wasn't sure he understood but he held her while she cried and that was enough. She told him about the kittens. She told him how her mother had called her "a mistake" and "a disappointment." She told him how her mother had made balls of lard and peanuts and hung them from strings outside the dining-room window in the winter for chaffinches and coal tits and robins. She told him how quickly the MS had progressed, how she wasn't allowed into her mother's bedroom during the final months, how her mother died and how Leah kept forgetting this because nothing in the house had changed.

Bunny said, "I hate my father. I haven't seen him for twenty years. I have no idea what he looks like. But every time there's a crowd on TV I find myself scanning the faces, looking for him."

She told him that she had trouble sleeping. He said she could move in upstairs if she wanted, and tried very hard not to show how pleased he was when she accepted the offer.

§

She took Bunny's old bedroom. He hadn't been upstairs for a long time. The rusted hot tap in the sink no longer turned and there was velvety green fungus in the corners of the bathroom window. On the dusty sill sat a pair of rusty nail clippers, a dog-eared box of sticking plasters and a little brown tub of diazepam tablets with a water-blurred label.

The first night she drank whisky in warm milk to get herself to sleep but was woken a couple of hours later by Bunny's snoring. She lay motionless in the half-dark. The gaps between his snores were growing longer and she could tell that something was not right. She went downstairs and pushed the living-room door open. Bunny now slept on an adjustable bed which had replaced the yellow sofa bed. The smell was rank and cloistered. She drew the curtain back and opened the smaller window.

He was lying on his back, his skin unnaturally white, his arms swimming as if he were underwater and struggling to reach the surface. His breathing stopped for three, four, five seconds then restarted like an old motor. She wondered if she should do something. His breathing stopped again. And started. And stopped. Suddenly he was awake, wide-eyed and fighting for breath.

"Bunny?" She took his hand. "It's Leah. I'm here."

It was the fat around his throat, the doctor said, the sheer weight of his chest, the weakness of his muscles. If he carried on sleeping on his back he would suffocate. He had to remain propped up twenty-four hours a day.

§

Towards the end of the second week she returned from work to find that he had soiled himself. That morning's carer had not turned up and he could hold on no longer. She smelt it as soon as she came in. She considered quietly reclosing the door and going back to her father's empty house. Then Bunny called out, "Leah?"

She stepped into the living room.

He said, "I'm so sorry."

She filled a plastic bowl with hot water. Soap, flannels, toilet rolls, a towel from upstairs. She helped Bunny roll onto his side. His flesh was raw and spotty and covered in large port-wine blotches. Some of the shit was on the sheet, some of it was wedged into the crack between his buttocks. She used wads of toilet paper to scrape most of it off, dumping the shit and the used paper in a plastic bag. She unhooked the corners of the cotton sheet and the plastic mattress protector beneath it and bunched them up, using the material to wipe him clean as she did so. She put the sheet in the washing machine and the protector into a second plastic bag.

It wasn't as bad as she had expected. This was what she would have done for her children if life had turned out differently.

She dipped the flannels in the soapy water and wiped him, lifting the flesh to get into the folds. She towelled him dry and left him to lie on his side exposed to the air for a while. She put the flannels and the towel into the washing machine with the sheet. She bleached the plastic bowl. She remade the bed with a clean sheet and a new mattress protector from the cupboard in the kitchen. She dusted him with anti-fungal powder then let him roll back into his usual position.

He said, "You are the kindest person I have ever met."

§

She found a letter from the council lying on her father's doormat saying that the tenancy had come to an end with her father's death and unless representations were made the house would have to be vacated by the end of the month.

She took the records to the Oxfam shop in town. "Higher

and Higher" by Jackie Wilson, "Up, Up and Away" by the Fifth Dimension, "Nothing Can Stop Me" by Gene Chandler . . . She brought a small cardboard box home from the Co-op and filled it with the only possessions that seemed worth keeping, objects she remembered from her childhood, mostly—an owl made of yellow glass, a box of tarnished apostle spoons on faded purple plush, a decorative wall plate with a view of Robin Hood's Bay. She locked the door and posted the keys through the letter box. She stowed the cardboard box under the bed at Bunny's house.

§

It was a Friday after work. She'd just come out of Boots and was passing Kenyons en route to the bus station. The two women were sitting at a table in the window. She could see immediately that they were from out of town by the way they held themselves, the way they owned the space around them. The woman facing her had sunglasses pushed up into an auburn crop, tanned shoulders and a canary-yellow dress to show them off. Leah felt a little stab of something between envy and affront. The woman caught her eye. Leah walked away in embarrassment and five steps farther down the street realised that she had been looking at Abby and Nisha. She was about to break into a run when Nisha emerged from the doors of the restaurant. She blocked Leah's path, looked her up and down theatrically and said, "What the fuck happened to you, girl?"

Leah had forgotten how it worked, the spiky repartee that bound them together and kept outsiders away. She looked down at her grey tights and elderly trainers. "I've just come from work."

"Inside," said Nisha, nodding towards the door of the restaurant as if it were a cell Leah was being returned to.

The two of them were back for Abby's brother's wedding. "Number Four. I can't even remember her name. Albanian? Slovenian? She looks like those pictures in the papers of women who've killed their kids." Abby and Vince were now living in Muswell Hill. "The Great White Highlands." And Sam was pregnant for a second time. "Ten months. He practically fucked her in the delivery suite."

The waiter materialised with his little flip pad. Leah tried to make her excuses but Abby held her eye. "I don't know what you've got planned for this evening but I know for a fact that it will be shit compared to this."

She ate grilled tuna with a salad of cannellini beans, roasted red peppers, olives, anchovies and rocket followed by lemon tart and crème frâiche. They drank two bottles of Montepulciano d'Abruzzo between them. A bill for a hundred and ten pounds and a fifteen-pound tip. They smoked in the little garden at the back, next to one of the patio heaters.

"How's your dad?" asked Nisha.

"He died," said Leah.

Nisha looked at her long and hard. No condolence, no consolation. "We've got a sofa bed. If you haven't found a job and a room in a shared house by the end of the month I'll stick you on the bus back up here."

"I'm sorry," said Leah. "I can't do it."

Nisha shrugged. "It's your funeral."

§

Two of the toes on Bunny's left foot went black. They kept the window open all day because of the smell. There was nothing to be done, the doctor said. Leah should keep them tightly bandaged

until they fell off, then wash the wounds in salt water twice a
day until they healed. Ten days later she found them in the bed
while Bunny was sleeping. She flicked them onto a newspaper as
if they were dead bees, carried them outside and dropped them
into the bin.

A fine, spitty rain was coming in off the hills. There was no
one around. A wing mirror hung off a battered brown Honda.
The names of the dead boys were still readable on the tarmac. At
her feet grass was forcing its way up through cracks in the concrete. If everyone abandoned these streets she wondered how long
it would take for the forest to take them back, roots and creepers
bringing the walls down piece by piece, wolves moving through
the ruins.

She was crying but she didn't know whether it was for herself
or for Bunny.

§

He knew that something was wrong. She was making an
effort to be cheerful, to be attentive, to be patient. He had known
all along that it would come to this. If he were braver he would let
her go. She'd given him more happiness than he'd expected to get
from anyone. But he had never been brave. And he couldn't bring
himself to have one day less of her company.

He couldn't take his eyes off her. Now that she was about to
be taken from him she had become unutterably beautiful. He
finally understood the songs: the sweetness, the hurt, the cost
of it all. He would be wiser next time. It was just a shame there
wouldn't be a next time.

§

She went to Sainsbury's and bought a chicken jalfrezi and pilau rice, a king prawn masala and some oven chips. She bought two tins of treacle pudding, two tubs of Taste the Difference vanilla custard and a bottle of Jacob's Creek Cool Harvest Shiraz Rosé.

He saw her negotiating the hallway with three bags. "You bought the shop."

"I'm cooking you a posh supper."

"Why?" asked Bunny. "Not that I'm complaining."

"Big occasion," said Leah.

"What big occasion?"

She could hear the anxiety in his voice. She put the bags down and stuck her head round the door of the living room. "Trust me." She turned the oven on and poured him a glass of the rosé. "I would never do anything to hurt you." She kissed his forehead.

While everything was cooking she lit two candles and turned the lights down. She carefully moved Bunny's models off the table and put them out of harm's way. Then she fetched a chair from the dining room so that she could sit and eat beside him. She laid the cutlery out and gave Bunny the chequered green tea towel to use as a serviette. She brought the dishes in one by one, the prawn masala, the chicken, the chips, the rice. She sat down and held up her glass. "Cheers."

He said, "I know you're leaving, and I know you're trying to be kind about it."

"I'm not leaving."

"Really?" He spoke very quietly, as if her decision were a house of cards which might collapse at any minute.

"Really." She took a sip of the rosé. It was slightly warm. She should have put it in the freezer for ten minutes.

"Wow." He lay back against his pillows and exhaled. He was trying not to cry. "I was so scared."

"The food's going cold," she said.

He was still unsure. "So what are we celebrating?"

"Eat first. Then I'll tell you."

He gingerly put a forkful of chicken into his mouth and chewed. She could see the tension slowly leaving his body. He swallowed, took another deep breath and fanned his face with a comedy flap of his hands. "I got a bit worked up back there."

"There's no need to apologise." She refilled his glass.

They ate in silence for a while. He finished the chicken and the rice and the side plate of chips. "That was fantastic. Thank you."

"Treacle pudding to come."

"No expense spared."

She put her glass down. "But first . . ."

"Go on." His face tensed again.

"Bunny Wallis . . ." She paused for effect. "Will you marry me?"

He stared at her.

"Do I need to repeat the question?"

"Yes," said Bunny. "You do need to repeat the question."

"Will you marry me?" She waited. "If I have to say it a third time then I'm going to withdraw the offer."

"Why?" asked Bunny. "Why would you want to marry me?"

"Because I love you."

"This is the most extraordinary day of my life."

"Does that mean 'yes'?"

He took a deep breath. "Of course it does."

"Good." She leaned over and kissed him on the lips then sat down and poured him a third glass. "To us."

"To us." He clinked his glass against hers and drank. She could see tears forming in the corners of his eyes. He said, "I have never been this happy. Never."

She stood up. "I think that calls for treacle pudding."

When she came back into the room his eyes were closed. She set the bowls down and stroked his forearm. "Bunny?"

"I just . . ." He shook his head like a dog coming out of a pond. "I'm so sorry. You ask me to marry you and I fall asleep."

"You're tired, that's all." She handed him the treacle pudding.

He was squeezing his eyes shut and opening them again, trying to focus. He filled his spoon with pudding and custard and lifted it halfway to his mouth but had to put it down again. "Can you . . . ?" He gave her the bowl. Taking his hand away he knocked the spoon onto the bedcovers. "Shit. Sorry."

"It's no problem."

He leaned back and closed his eyes once more. She licked the spoon and scraped the dropped food back into the bowl. She dipped the corner of the tea towel in her glass of water and rubbed gently at the stain. She squeezed his hand. "How are you doing in there?" He squeezed back then slowly loosened his grip. She took the bowls into the kitchen, dumped the remaining treacle pudding into the bin and set the bowls in the sink. She went back into the living room and watched him for a while.

"Let's make you more comfortable." She put her hand behind his neck, pulled him forward and slipped the top pillow out from behind his head. He roused himself a little then became still. She waited for thirty seconds then pulled him forward once more to remove the next pillow. The third and last was harder to remove. Gently, she eased it free by pulling it from side to side, taking care not to wake him, until it slipped out.

He was now lying flat on his back. His breathing stopped for a few seconds then restarted. His arms circled, reaching for some invisible thing just above the bed, then they were still again. A couple of minutes later he went through the same cycle without waking. "Bunny?" she said quietly, but there was no response.

Quarter past eight. She waited till half past. The periods when he was not breathing grew longer but some automatic response kicked in every time. Had she miscalculated? Eight forty. She put her hand on his arm. "Come on, Bunny. Help me out here."

Eight forty-five. He was no longer lifting his arms off the bed, just the ghost of a movement. He looked shattered, as if he were reaching the end of a long fight against a much stronger opponent.

"It's OK, Bunny. You can let go."

She could no longer see his chest rising and falling. She could no longer hear him breathing, only a tiny, broken hiss that stopped and started and stopped and started and finally, just before nine o'clock, stopped altogether.

She waited another five minutes to be sure, then she leaned over and kissed him. It was nothing, really, when you thought about it, like turning off a light. You were here, then you were gone.

She took the little brown tub from her pocket, unscrewed the lid and gently dropped both of them onto the carpet on the far side of the bed. She poured the remains of his wine onto the table and laid the glass on its side. She carried her own glass into the kitchen where she washed the crockery, cutlery and glassware and left it to dry. She double-bagged the packaging and the uneaten food and dropped everything in the bin outside the front door. She washed and dried her hands and went into the garden for a cigarette.

She would discover him when she came down in the morning. She would notice the glass but she would fail to see the diazepam. She would check his pulse and his breathing but she would know from the look of him that he had been dead for some time. She would call an ambulance and wait outside for it to arrive. She would call Bunny's mother. She would call Bunny's sister. She would say, "He seemed so happy." She would wrap the owl and the apostle spoons and the wall plate in newspaper and put them at the bottom of her suitcase, but she wouldn't leave town till after the funeral. The idea of him being rolled through those curtains without a friend in the room was almost unbearable.

WODWO

It is late afternoon on Christmas Eve and the predicted snow has begun, a long front of white teeth sweeping down the weather map of the Baltic and fastening itself into the curved rump of England. Kelmarsh, Clipston, Sibbertoft: red sandstone and rolling green hills, thatched roofs, cattle farms and boxy Saxon churches. Scattered flakes at first, whiter than the darkening sky behind them, that magical childhood silence settling on everything, only the peal of church bells and the chatter of distant trains being carried in the cold, clean air.

Madeleine Cooper is cooking a smoked salmon quiche with honey-glazed carrots and broccoli, getting everything ready for the final bake and steam when the three children and their respective families have safely arrived. There is a chocolate and raspberry pavlova in the fridge.

Her husband, Martin, has completed his allotted, minimal task of setting the table and is now sitting in his study listening to the *St. Matthew Passion* (the 2001 Nikolaus Harnoncourt recording) and reading Roger Crowley's *Empires of the Sea: The Final Battle for the Mediterranean, 1521–1580*. He has set the table wrong, laying nine places instead of ten. It is a drama they play out so often they hardly notice anymore: his feigned incompetence followed by her feigned exasperation ("Can you honestly not count the members of your own family?") which makes her feel more important and him more justified in not providing any further help. He retired two years ago after thirty-six years of neurosurgery, at St. George's, Tooting, then Frenchay in Bristol, then out into the sticks for a final few laps at Leicester Royal Infirmary. She worried about him falling to pieces in the time-honoured manner of returning Vietnam vets now that no lives were on the line but he applies to books, music, golf and grade 5 piano the same unsentimental rigour he previously applied to leucotomies, aneurysms and pituitary adenomas.

Madeleine worries about most things. She has been anxious for the greater part of her adult life. She rarely talks about this to anyone, though it is obvious to those around her, Martin included. He believes that she suffers from a basic flaw in her psychological make-up which has been exacerbated by a life in which she has taken very few risks and spent too much time in her own company. It being something he is powerless to change he sees little point in discussing the subject.

§

Just after four o'clock their eldest daughter, Sarah, and her husband, Robert, arrive. Sarah is the service manager for business development at Hampshire County Council, a job which used to involve building children's homes, rolling out broadband and getting social workers into GP surgeries but which now mostly involves sacking employees, closing down projects and saving money. Robert is the fund manager for Appalachian, a small wealth management company he set up three years ago with two escapees from Deutsche Bank, which they run from an office in Reading to which he commutes from Winchester three days a week.

They have one child, a teenage daughter, Ellie, who is spending Christmas with her boyfriend's family in Winchester because she and Daniel are still in the honeymoon period and his parents are "so, so, so much more relaxed than you," meaning, presumably, that she has not yet had a meltdown in their presence.

Sarah is bloody hard work. That's her father's blunt diagnosis. Sarah puts it down to her being a woman and, unlike her mother, having a job and opinions, some of which are not the same as her father's.

Robert likes the fact that Sarah is argumentative and opinionated, though this is made easier by the fact that he agrees with most of those opinions and most of the arguments are therefore had with other people, but he dislikes visiting his parents-in-law in whose presence Sarah can sometimes regress to the teenage girl he guesses she once was, a teenage girl not unlike their own teenage daughter in her less charming moods. It is a subject he has tried to broach with Sarah. It is not a subject he is going to broach again. There is a constant and generous supply of alcohol at the Rookery, however, which he treats as a medical necessity, like a morphine drip on a low setting.

"Hello, darling." Madeleine hugs her daughter.

Robert gives Madeleine their traditional uneasy embrace. There is a surge of choral music (". . . *Ich will dir mein Herze schenken* . . .") and Martin appears from the opened study door for the golf-club handshake which always strikes Robert as too muscular for a man who previously worked inside the brains of living human beings. He waves the cordless in his free hand. "That was Leo and Sofie. They'll be here in twenty minutes."

"And Gavin?" asks Sarah.

"No news yet," says Martin.

"So," says Sarah, "if the weather keeps up . . ."

"Now now," says Madeleine, "don't start before he's even got here."

"He was an arse last year," says Sarah, "and I'm sure he'll be an arse this year."

Martin looks at Robert and rubs his hands together. "Drink?"

§

The sky is blacker now. Snow deepens in sheltered corners and on the windward side of walls. It lies in Advent calendar curves on windowsills. It blots and softens the top of every object like icing on a plum pudding. Hedges, telegraph wires, cars, post-boxes, recycling bins. The world is losing its edges. Look upwards and it seems as if the stars themselves are being poured from the sky and turn out not to be vast and fiery globes after all but tiny, frozen things which melt in the palm of your hand.

Martin tells Madeleine to stop fretting and insists that Gavin and Emmy will be fine, because it is one of his guiding principles that everything is always fine until occasionally it isn't and you should therefore save your energy for coping with that rare eventuality. In the back of his mind he ponders the satisfying conundrum of what he would do if he were stuck in a car overnight in weather like this. How long would the engine run in neutral to power the heating system, for example? The snow would act as an insulator of course, but you would have to be wary of carbon monoxide poisoning.

§

A green VW Touran turns off the main road, two cones of halogen light swinging through the slowly falling flakes. The car slides briefly sideways then finds traction again, compacted snow squeaking as the tyre treads bite. Leo, Martin and Madeleine's younger son, is driving. His wife, Sofie, is in the passenger seat and David (eleven) and Anya (ten) are in the back. Leo decides against attempting the potentially ruinous bottleneck of the stone gateposts and leaves the car at a jaunty angle halfway over the hidden kerb. He rests his head on the steering wheel. "Jesus. I am knackered."

He teaches history at Durham. When he was a small boy he wondered regularly whether he had been adopted and the suspicion has never entirely gone away. Family gatherings of all kinds are purgatorial, leaving him longing for a solitary walking holiday in some remote corner of the earth. In truth he is like his mother, or like the person his mother might have been if she were not warped by the deforming gravity of the husband around whom she has orbited for nearly all her life. He listens more than he talks. In most rooms he has a good sense of what other people are feeling, and if any of them are uneasy he cannot help but share that unease. A family Christmas is a guaranteed generator of unease.

Sofie translates from Icelandic and her native Danish, mostly business, a bit of crime writing over the last couple of years. She feels no closer to Leo's family than he does but she keeps her distance by pretending to be more foreign and less intelligent than she is, misusing words and faking bafflement at quirky native customs, and is both insulted and relieved that none of them see through the blatant subterfuge.

Anya is going through a period of ferocious conformity that both Leo and Sofie find deeply dispiriting (Sims, *Frozen*, One Direction) though not as dispiriting as David's rank oddity which Leo, in particular, fears may be an expression of the same car-crash genes which have yo-yoed Sofie's uncle in and out of a psychiatric hospital in Augustenborg for his whole adult life. All the books Leo has read on the subject suggest that psychosis only rears its ugly head in the late teens for boys, which is some reassurance. Still, it's hard not to be disturbed by the collection of dead animals (crow, mouse, stag beetle, toad) that he keeps wrapped in tissue paper in a line of cardboard boxes on his bedroom bookshelf like so many little coffins, and by the incomprehensible language in which he talks to himself sometimes, which he claims to be Tagalog but isn't because Leo has checked.

They take their luggage from the boot. Anya has a yellow, black and white rucksack in the shape of one of the Minions from *Despicable Me*. David has an antique leather satchel given to him by his Danish grandfather which he dubbins regularly and which gives him the air of a tiny Renaissance clerk.

Leo stops and looks around at all this crystal, blue-black darkness and listens to . . . absolutely nothing. Apart from his son and daughter arguing about who knocked the bagged-up duvet into the snow the silence is fathomless. He forgets it every year until some detail brings it back (the eggshell glass of a broken bauble, a Salvation Army brass band playing "I Saw Three Ships," thick snowfall . . .), how extraordinary Christmas once was, how extraordinary everything once was all year round, each individual moment a thing to be swallowed or solved or suffered. But now . . . ? So much coasting, so many blanks, as if there was an infinite supply of time and those same seconds could be brushed from the table like spilt salt.

"I know you'd like to spend all night standing out here." Sofie touches his arm. "But it really is very cold."

They trudge up the drive into the sudden glare of the intruder light. By the time they reach the porch Sarah is opening the door with its two stained-glass panels (a shepherd on the left, three sheep on the right). "Hey, little brother." It is a thing she does in one way or another every time they meet, gently but firmly asserting her superior place in the pecking order, but with enough warmth to make a complaint seem churlish.

Deep breath. Ten seconds down, thirty-six hours to go. "No Gavin yet?" says Leo. "I didn't see the car."

"With any luck they'll be spending Christmas in a Travelodge on the M1."

Sofie stamps the snow off her boots while Sarah gives the children mock-regal handshakes. "Anya . . . David . . ."

"I greet you in the name of the seven kingdoms," says David. "I feared that we would not make it through the mountains."

But Sofie is looking over the top of his head. "You spoke too soon."

They turn as one to see Gavin and Emmy walking up the drive and even in the dark it is possible to tell from her weary, Scott/Shackleton gait that they have been forced to leave the car some distance away.

"Ahoy there," shouts Gavin. "I hope you have a blazing log fire and large whiskies waiting."

§

Gavin is an extravagantly gifted man whose critical short-coming, aside from his monstrous ego, is that he has never been struck by a passionate interest which will direct his manifold talents and offer him the prospect of achieving something which matters more than achievement itself.

Leo's theory is that since his preternatural growth spurt at twelve a natural magnetism has made him, always, the centre of a group of people who want to be in his presence and he has never been sufficiently free of their noise to hear what is going on inside his own mind, nor bored enough to discover what genuinely pleases him.

Deep down Gavin believes that he should now be head of the family—Sarah's gender disqualifies her so completely that he never thinks of her as his older sister—and he resents the fact that his father has not ceded his position by dying or slackening his mental grip on the world. The simple fact of driving to his parents' house at Christmas is an act of obeisance which he finds demeaning and which the inclement weather has only made more irksome.

Eighteen years ago he got a rugby Blue at Cambridge, played briefly for the Harlequins, had his jaw shattered in his seventh game and experienced a rare moment of revelation lying in St. Thomas' Hospital, to the effect that he would never get an international cap and should therefore take the job Ove Arup had offered him four months previously. He got back in touch and, being a man into whose lap so many things simply fell, it seemed only natural that the woman who had taken the job he spurned had been killed in a light-plane crash on Namibia's Skeleton Coast only the week before and that his prospective departmental boss was a rugby fan who bore no grudge for Gavin's initial rejection.

The company, which had worked on the Chinese National Aquatics Centre for the Olympics and the new Terminal 5 at JFK, however, assigned him to the A8 Belfast to Larne dual carriageway and he was soon champing at the bit. Thankfully the benign fates arranged a meeting with an old friend from Peterhouse which led to him doing a few slots of commentary and interviewing for Sky. He was articulate, quick-witted and wholly at ease looking into a camera through which three million people might be looking back at him. He expanded sideways from rugby into athletics and cycling but soon became bored, again, with what he saw as the unchallenging nature of the job, and hungry for more prestige, at which point those same benign fates came to his aid for a third time and placed him and the head of factual programming for BBC4 at adjacent urinals after the Royal Television Society Awards, which led, by a somewhat drunken and circuitous route, to a heated argument about the respective merits of the wealthy, self-promoting Brunel and the lower-class, self-effacing Stephenson and from there, by a less drunken but equally circuitous route, to Gavin presenting a TV series about ten outstanding feats of British engineering (the Thrust SSC racing car, the East Hill funicular in Hastings, Pitstone Windmill . . .). He wrote the accompanying book without the help of a ghost and began a regular technology column for *The Times*, the guiding principle of which was that he would write about nothing that had either a keyboard or a screen. He took lucrative speaking engagements and, while filming a further series about great bridges of the world, met and married Kirstin Gomez. She was not, it's fair to say, the sharpest knife in the box. If she were she might not have married Gavin. But she was cartoon-sexy and one of very few people who were genuinely rude to him. They bought a house in Richmond and had a son, Thom, now eleven years old. He was a surprisingly good husband and father, certainly better than many of those who knew him predicted he would be, until yet again he became bored with what he saw as the unchallenging nature of the job which, in truth, he had only ever done part-time, and Thom now lived with his mother ten thousand miles away within sight of the bridge whose 503-metre arch span had been the cause of their parents' meeting.

He took legal advice about what the overexcitable young man at Dagmar-Prestell unhelpfully referred to as "the kidnap" but decided, ultimately, that he did not want to run the risk of a settlement which saw him having his son actually living with him for significant chunks of the year. The separation did not cause him the pain and distress it might have caused someone without his geological self-confidence, but there was a part of his memory which he simply did not visit, and of whose existence other people could only guess, like a locked cellar in a large house from which inexplicable noises might occasionally be heard during the quieter parts of the night, the precise nature of which were irrelevant because the door was bolted fast and only a fool would go down that narrow, mildewed staircase.

His new wife, Emmy, is an actress, and a very good one (the National, the Donmar, some TV, a little film, but still mainly, and passionately, stage), who possesses precisely what he lacks, a commitment to a project larger than herself, and who lacks precisely what he possesses, that solid sense of self whose absence leaves her feeling lost between the job of being one imaginary person and the job of being another imaginary person. He likes her arresting good looks—"Bond Villain's Assistant" is Sarah's less than generous description—and the reflected glory therefrom, but in truth it is the mutual absences which have kept their two hearts fond over these last three years. Indeed, thanks to Henrik Ibsen and Gavin's work schedule this is only the fourth evening they have spent together since early November.

They are sitting now in his parents' kitchen drinking mugs of tea and wearing makeshift skirts of clean towels while their sodden jeans tumble like acrobats in the dryer. Gavin is feeling jovial. He enjoys a bit of adventure (he is in the process of trying to sell the BBC a documentary series in which he walks the Silk Road) and would happily have trudged five times the distance through snow twice as deep. And if Emmy is not feeling jovial she is warm at last and greatly relieved to have survived Gavin's overconfident driving.

§

The good mood continues into and throughout the meal, helped partly by the exceptional quality of the quiche and the pavlova, partly by Gavin's good humour and partly by the fact that Emmy recently had a very small role in *The Second Best Exotic Marigold Hotel* and is therefore possessed of scandalous gossip about a group of famous actors, some of whom are refusing to age gracefully, and everyone, including Martin who professes to float at some Olympian height above such vulgar tittle-tattle, is agog.

§

At the end of the meal Sarah insists that her mother stays seated while she clears the table with help from Emmy and Sofie. It is an unspoken tradition that they comply with old-fashioned gender stereotypes while they are here, making a little panto-mime of it to show that this is, of course, not how they act at home. They put the kettle on, scrape the leftovers from plates into the green bin below the sink, fill the dishwasher, set it going and return to the dining room with a pot of coffee and two peppermint teas, a small box of which Sofie has brought with her from Durham. They leave the cheese plate in the centre of the table in case the men want to continue grazing.

They take the second set of smaller wineglasses from the cabinet and hand them round. There is brandy, there is Sauternes, a ninety-pound bottle of Château Suduiraut courtesy of Gavin who gets a perverse pleasure from the knowing that no one apart from his father appreciates the extent of his largesse. There is also a three-quid box of After Eights brought by Sarah so as to deliberately undercut the grander gesture she knows her brother was guaranteed to make.

Martin would like some entertainment. It has become a regular thing, a regular thing in which everyone takes part under various levels of duress, a ceremony which dramatises Martin's dominion over this little court. Reading from a book is acceptable but generally considered a poor effort. Reciting from memory is better. Performing something of one's own creation beats both if one's own creation passes muster. Only Sofie is exempted on condition that she does pencil sketches of other family members performing, some of which have been framed and now hang in the hallway beside the downstairs toilet. Emmy never acts because she is too good an actor and no one is allowed to steal Martin's show. Instead she does low-rent magic tricks, a skill she picked up while performing in an experimental production of *The Tempest* at the Edinburgh Fringe many years ago (David and Anya still talk about the twenty-pound note which vanished and reappeared

inside a mince pie Grandpa was eating). At a low point in diplo-
matic relations some years back Sarah recited a poem by Sharon
Olds which contained the word "cunt," but her father caught the
ball and belted it straight down the pitch into the back of her net
by saying he thought it was fantastic and whose turn was it next?

This year marks a period of détente in that department and
tonight's event promises to pass off smoothly. Anya has brought
her violin and is planning to play an unaccompanied piece by
Leclair which she is learning for her grade 4 exam while her
grandfather is planning to play the allegretto con moto from
Frank Bridge's first set of "Miniature Pastorals." There will be
some Tennyson and some Carol Ann Duffy. Emmy will do some
mind-reading.

"So," says Martin, "who is going to get the evening rolling?"

And Sarah says, "Christing shit!" which are very much not
words anyone is allowed to say in this room.

In unison they follow her eyes to the French windows, outside
which the intruder light has snapped on to reveal a tall black man
in a black woolly hat, sporting a big salt-and-pepper beard and
wearing a long black coat over camouflage trousers and big black
boots. He is looking in at them all as if they are exhibits in a zoo.
Or perhaps it is the other way round.

"Who in God's name is that?" says Gavin.

"I have absolutely no idea," says Martin, sounding more
intrigued than startled.

"Is he a neighbour?" asks Sofie.

"Of course he's not a bloody neighbour," says Gavin.

"Why is that a stupid question?" asks Sofie.

Leo puts a consoling hand on Sofie's back. He has tried to

stand up for his wife in the face of his brother's rudeness before and it has never turned out well. "Is someone planning to let him in?" he asks.

Madeleine says, "He does not look like the kind of man I want inside the house."

The stranger knocks twice on the glass, slowly and deliberately.

"Nor," says Martin, "does he look like someone you'd want to leave standing in your garden." He does not recognise the man. He has dealt with a good number of eccentric, difficult and unpredictable people in his time, some of them patients, some of them family members of patients. He has on a small number of occasions been threatened. Brain surgery is a risky business and desperate people do not handle statistics well.

"I'm actually quite scared?" says Anya. The question thing is something she has been doing for the last few months, not wanting to be assertive or seem needy.

"It's all right." Sofie strokes her hair. "He's probably just cold and hungry."

"Grandad is going to kill him," says David, as if this is obvious and unremarkable. It is precisely this kind of comment that makes his father worry that his son will spend a significant part of his adult life in mental institutions.

"Let's see what he wants." Martin gets to his feet.

Madeleine says, "Do not let him in."

Her husband pauses. "I'm not sure sitting here watching him is a long-term option."

"Perhaps we should call the police," says Madeleine.

"And say what?" asks Gavin. "'There's a black chap knocking on the French windows'?"

"In the absence of any better ideas . . ." Martin unlocks the door and swings it open. A great belch of snow and freezing air enter the room. A couple of cards fall from the mantelpiece, clattering softly onto the log basket and from there to the floor.

"What can we do for you, sir?"

"Are you not going to ask me in?" The man has a breathy tenor voice. They'd expected Trinidad or Hackney but the accent is from some less obvious third place.

"I wasn't planning on it, no."

"It's bitter weather out here, and I've come a good distance."

"I'm less interested in where you've come from," says Martin, "and more interested in what you're doing in my garden."

"That is a poor welcome on a cold night."

"I think it's a pretty decent welcome in the circumstances," says Martin.

"This is freaking me out quite a bit," says Sarah.

"Better than listening to Leo reading Seamus bloody Heaney again," says Gavin, just loud enough for Leo to hear.

"Do you want money?" asks Martin.

"I was hoping for hospitality."

"Let the chap in," says Gavin.

"Gavin, for God's sake," whispers Madeleine.

"Give him a glass of brandy and a mince pie so he can warm up and tootle off on his merry way," says Gavin. "Spirit of the season and so forth."

Leo says, "Gavin, I am really not sure that's a good idea."

Anya shifts her chair next to her mother's chair and squirrels under her protecting arm.

"Five minutes," says Martin.

The stranger steps inside. He wipes his feet in the same slow, deliberate way in which he knocked on the glass, like someone demonstrating the wiping of feet to people who have not seen it before. Martin closes the door behind him. The stranger takes off his woolly hat and dunks it into a pocket.

They can smell him now, more agricultural than homeless. Leather, dung and smoke, something very old about it, Mongol horses on the high steppe. Yurts and eagles. His greatcoat is Napoleonic, scuffed black serge with actual brass buttons and a ragged hem. Snow melts on his shoulders.

"Compliments of the season." Gavin hands him the promised victuals. "Made by my mother's own fair hand. Five stars. Lots of fruit in the mincemeat."

"Please, Gavin," says Leo quietly, "don't be a twat."

The stranger sips the brandy, savours it and swallows. He takes a bite of the mince pie. He closes his eyes. To an outside observer it might look as if the family were waiting for a score out of ten.

Martin is turning over old memories. If the man had shorter hair and no beard . . .

The stranger nods. The mince pie is good. The room relaxes. He takes a second sip of the brandy and steps forward to put the glass and the mince pie down on the table. Emmy and Sofie scooch their chairs back a little to avoid being touched. The damp hem of the stranger's coat brushes Emmy's knee. He steps back into the centre of the room. There are pastry crumbs in his beard. "Who wants to play a game?"

"None of us want to play a game," says Martin firmly. "We want to get on with the pleasant evening we were having before you arrived."

The stranger ignores, or perhaps fails to hear, the edge in Martin's reply. "Surely someone wants to play a game."

"You've had something to drink," says Martin. "You've had something to eat. I think that now it might be a good idea if you were to continue with your travels."

"I was on my way here," says the stranger.

There is a short silence while everyone digests this, then Gavin says, "Stop dicking us around, all right?"

"Gavin," hisses Sarah. "Jesus Christ."

The stranger opens his greatcoat. There is a deep poacher's pocket on the left-hand side which sags open with the weight of a sawn-off shotgun. Anya's intake of breath sounds like a hiccup. David says, "Wow." The stranger lifts the gun out of the pocket, pushes the After Eights and the cheese plate to one side, slides the spare wicker mat into the cleared area and lays the gun gently on top of it so that it doesn't scratch the polished walnut veneer.

"Oh my God," says Madeleine.

Leo's mouth hangs open.

Anya begins to cry.

"Is that a real gun?" asks David.

"Let's assume it is, shall we?" says Martin.

But David's question is apposite, because there is something odd about the gun, a hint of steampunk about it, the faintest possibility that it could be a theatrical prop, despite the weight everyone could sense when it touched the surface of the table.

"Oh my God," says Madeleine again. She is hyperventilating. "Oh my God."

"Someone really, really needs to call the police," says Sofie.

"Have we met before?" Martin asks the stranger. He has

decided that this is, ultimately, a medical problem and this has allowed him to step back into a role he hasn't filled for a long time and which feels very comfortable indeed.

"Surely one of you wants to play a game," says the stranger.

Emmy gets to her feet.

"Stay with us," says the stranger.

Emmy sits down again. Gavin pats her hand reassuringly.

"I'm afraid you need to leave," says Martin, "and you need to leave now."

"Are we in a hostage situation here?" asks Gavin. "Just out of interest."

"Are none of you brave enough to play my game?" asks the stranger.

"Fucking hell," says Gavin. "This is not about being brave. This is about you interrupting our hitherto very enjoyable festive family meal and assuming that we want to take part in some deranged pantomime of your own creation."

"Gavin?" says his father calmly, meaning, I'll take it from here. He turns to the stranger. "Time's up, I'm afraid."

The stranger smiles. He looks slowly around the room, as if assessing each of them in turn.

Sofie squeezes Anya's hand and says, "It's going to be OK, darling."

"That's it," says Gavin, getting to his feet, irked not just by the stranger's intrusion but by the way his father's relaxed competence has placed him in a subordinate position.

"Gavin," Sarah half growls under her breath.

Gavin picks up the gun.

"No," says Emmy. "Gavin, please."

Gavin steps away from the table and pushes his chair back under.

"Holy fuck," says Leo, putting his face in his hands.

Gavin himself has not thought about what he will do with the gun, only that it is the source of power in the room, the sceptre, the conch. Now that it is in his hands, however, he is less sure about this. Should he hand the gun back to the stranger and order him to take it away? Should he confiscate it? Should he use it to threaten the man? "Time to go, I'm afraid."

Martin has been wrong-footed. The most dangerous person in the room is now his older son. He was not expecting this and is not immediately sure what to do about it. Family has always been so much more complex than work.

The stranger smiles. "So you *are* willing to play my game?"

"What, precisely, is this game you want us to play?" Gavin does not want to be asking questions, he wants to be giving orders, but he is being outplayed.

"Shoot me," says the stranger.

Madeleine yelps, the kind of noise you might make if you fell down a flight of stairs.

Gavin laughs. "Oh, I don't think that's going to happen." How odd it is to be holding a weapon yet to have no control over the situation.

"Gavin," says his father, "I think it might be a good idea for you to put the gun down."

He agrees with his father and he would very much like to put the gun down but he does not want the stranger to see him doing something his father has asked him to do.

The stranger walks very slowly towards Gavin. He seems

utterly unbothered by the gun. It is the most menacing thing he has done since his arrival.

"Whoa," says Gavin. "Whoa, whoa. Stop right there." His voice is not as low or as calm as he would like it to be.

The stranger comes to a halt a couple of metres away from Gavin. They are two magnets of identical polarity pressed into close proximity. You can almost see curved lines of force penned on the air.

"No closer," says Gavin.

"Gavin," says his father, "you need to be very careful."

"No shit, Sherlock," says Gavin.

The exchange makes both men seem smaller.

The stranger makes the tiniest of moves, perhaps no more than shifting his weight from one foot to another. Gavin responds immediately by raising the gun. He is not aware of having taken this decision, only that it has happened and that he cannot now undo it.

"Oh fuck," says Sarah. "Fucking fuck."

Gavin is now pointing a gun at another human being. He has occasionally imagined doing such a thing but he has never imagined it coupled with this level of anxiety and unease.

Anya gets up and runs from the room. No one follows her for fear of doing even more to upset the precarious balance upon which everything seems now to depend. David has no thought of leaving. He is gripped. He senses no danger. He wonders if it is all part of Grandpa's Christmas extravaganza. Perhaps the stranger is a friend of Emmy's. Later on, when he gets up to his room and digs out his phone he is going to have the most amazing story to text to Ryan and Yah ya.

"You're going now," says Gavin to the stranger.

It is quite obvious to everyone that the stranger is not going.

Leo softly pushes his chair back, half stands and reaches out towards Gavin, intending to nudge the barrel of the gun towards the carpet. But Gavin swings the gun towards Leo. He does not think about how the gesture might be read. It seems obvious to pretty much everyone in the room that it means *I could shoot you, too.* Leo sits back down.

Martin can think of nothing more that he can contribute. He would rather David, Sofie, Sarah, Emmy and Madeleine were not in the room but otherwise he finds the situation perversely fascinating.

"Pull the trigger," says the stranger.

"This man is not well, Gavin," says Leo. "Gavin? Listen to me."

"I don't think it's a real gun," says Gavin. "That's why our friend is so relaxed." He doesn't quite believe this. The gun feels real. He simply needs something to say. If he keeps talking then maybe he can find a way to get a grip on the situation.

The stranger says nothing and does not move.

"Put the fucking gun down, Gavin," says Sarah, "and stop playing this stupid, bloody childish game, all right?"

"I don't think shouting is helpful," says Emmy.

"Well, gentle persuasion is not working out terribly well," says Sarah.

Gavin steps forward and pokes the stranger in the chest with the barrel of the gun.

"Brilliant," says Sarah.

Madeleine's face is white. Sofie's hand is over her mouth.

"No, no, no, no, no," says Martin quietly, holding his index finger up, like a schoolteacher wanting a pupil to pause so he can redirect them towards the correct answer. "That's a very bad idea, Gavin."

Emmy says, "Gavin, this is really scaring me. This is really scaring all of us."

Martin reaches towards his son. And this is when it happens. Everyone's attention is momentarily distracted by Martin's movement. Everyone, that is, except David who has no interest in his grandfather and eyes only for the gun. So it is only he and Gavin who are looking directly at the stranger when he is hit in the chest at point-blank range by two barrels of shot. He has no memory of the noise because the sight is so extraordinary. It is like a huge, invisible airbag going off between the two men, lifting them and hurling them away from each other, the stranger's torso propelled by the shot, Gavin's torso propelled by the butt of the gun which punches him hard in the ribs. He has seen this kind of image in films. What he has never seen in a film is the way the spray of shot passes instantly through the stranger's chest, shredding and liquidising its contents and splashing them all over the curtains and the grandmother clock and the hand-coloured map of Bedfordshire while the stranger himself is still airborne.

Then the stranger is no longer airborne. He is lying on the floor on his back, his head hard against the base of the clock which is still rocking from the impact, his greatcoat spread to either side like a great pair of bat wings. Mirroring him on the opposite side of the central rug Gavin, too, lies on his back, arms thrown to the side, unconscious but with his eyes and mouth open as if he has just noticed the amazing pattern of blood on the ceiling. A fat S of sulphurous grey smoke disperses slowly in the air between the two men.

Madeleine screams, stops to catch her breath then screams again as if she is in a screaming competition.

"Gavin . . . ?" says Emmy, but she is wary of getting too close. "Gavin . . . ?"

There is blood on the sofa. There is blood on the standard lamp. There is a growing pool of blood beneath the stranger's body. It is viscous with a plump, rounded outline, the colour of good port. There is blood on three of the dining chairs. There is a thin lasso of blood across the dining table, bisecting the cheese plate exactly. There is a little marble of blood sinking very slowly in a glass of Sauternes. Sofie has blood in her hair. She is wiping it robotically with a napkin, keeping her eyes fixed on the light switch on the far wall.

Anya appears at the doorway. Granny is screaming. She sees two men lying on the floor. She sees oceanic amounts of blood. Her assumption is that the stranger is killing everyone in the house. She turns and runs, as quietly as she can, upstairs and into the guest bathroom on the second floor. She has imagined this happening many times. She thinks, often, about the car crashing, about bombs on the train, about tsunamis, about volcanoes, about ISIS, about Boko Haram. Whenever she finds herself in a new building she works out escape routes and hiding places. She finds it comforting, imagining the jackboots on the floorboards over-head and the sad cries of the foolish children who have failed to plan for this eventuality. It's not comforting now that it is happening in real life but at least she is prepared. There is a panel beside the bath. She slides her fingernails under the rim, pulls it away and squeezes through the hole into the little loft above Granny and Grandpa's bedroom, pulling the panel back into place behind her. The cramped, triangular space between the water tank and the roof is thick with cobwebs. It is also shockingly cold. She has only been in here once before, at the height of summer two years ago when she read an entire *Tracy Beaker* by torchlight. She had assumed it would be the same temperature all year round but she is sitting on the insulation which keeps the rest of the house warm. She should have grabbed a coat or a jumper. It is too late now. She hugs herself and starts to shiver.

Downstairs, Martin puts his hand on his wife's shoulder. "You need to stop that now. Go into the kitchen and take some diazepam."

She does not hear her husband. She hears a doctor talking. She stops screaming, gets automatically to her feet, walks into the kitchen and takes the foil pack from the shortbread tin behind the chutney. She pops out three 2mg tablets and swallows them with a glass of milk. She wonders if she has woken from a particularly vivid nightmare. She will sit and wait for someone to come and find her and tell her what is going on.

In the living room Gavin groans, rolls onto his side and contracts slowly into a foetal curl, nursing what will turn out to be two broken ribs. Emmy kneels beside him and rubs his shoulder, alternating between relief that her husband is still alive and horror at his having shot someone.

"Dad?" Leo pushes the abandoned gun to the skirting board with the tip of his right shoe. "You're a doctor. You need to do something."

Martin is looking down at his older son. His older son has killed someone.

"Not for Gavin," says Leo. "For him." He points at the stranger but can't look at the body directly.

Martin walks over to the stranger. He stands beside what remains of the man, hands in the pockets of his racing-green cardigan. The man's chest cavity has been hollowed out and is now a rough bowl of red mush, torn membranes and the jagged ends of shattered bone. Martin hasn't seen anything like this since he was a junior doctor, perhaps not even then. He remembers a motorcyclist who'd gone under a lorry but that was just a crushed pelvis and a missing leg. What was the point of showing anyone in this state to a doctor?

"Can't you do CPR?" asks Leo.

"No C, no P," says Martin. "Which makes the R impossible."

"I have no idea what you're talking about," says Leo.

"No heart, no lungs," says Martin. "Cardiopulmonary. CP."

Emmy vomits into her cupped hands. Leo hands her a napkin and she runs to the toilet in the hallway.

Gavin puts the flat of his hand on the floor and pushes himself slowly up into a sitting position. He rubs his eyes with the thumb and forefinger of his free hand. He has the fuzzy, pained look of someone waking to a heavy-duty hangover. He looks over at the stranger's body. He says, "It just went off."

"You killed him," says Sarah. "You've fucking killed him."

"That's not going to help anyone," says Martin.

"I'm not thinking about helping anyone," says Sarah. "The only person who needs help is fucking dead. I'm just getting it off my chest that my fucking brother acted like an arrogant fuckwit, as per usual, except this time he actually ended up murdering someone."

Robert touches her arm. "Hey, hey, come on."

"Get the fuck off me," says Sarah. "I'm right. He knows I'm right. Everyone knows I'm right. So don't you dare try and shut me up."

Robert makes the universal gesture of surrender and sits back in his chair.

Sofie is trying to hustle David out of the room but he is refusing to go, shaking her hand off his shoulder. He is pretty sure now that the man was not one of Emmy's friends. He feels sick and frightened but he wants to be able to say, "My sister ran away, but I didn't."

"He was an intruder," says Gavin slowly. "He had a gun. We got into a fight. The gun went off."

"Shut the fuck up, Gavin," says Sarah. "You picked up the gun. You were told to put it down. You refused to put it down. You shoved it into his chest. You shot him."

"It was a mistake," says Gavin.

"Oh well, that's fine then," says Sarah.

Martin sits down and rubs his face. He would so much rather be buried in a car overnight.

Emmy appears in the doorway, drying her ashen face with the little purple towel from the handrail by the sink, remaining just beyond the threshold like a member of the public behind the crime-scene tape.

Upstairs, in the little loft above her grandparents' bedroom, Anya cannot stop herself shaking from the cold. She is not afraid. The possibility that her entire family may now be dead has induced a terrible calm. Slowly but steadily her core temperature falls.

Her mother is not worried about where her daughter is. Her daughter has not crossed her mind. At the moment, for Sofie, the world beyond this room simply does not exist.

"I'm calling the police," says Sarah. She walks towards the door. Emmy steps back to let her through.

"Wait," says her father.

She stops in her tracks. It's one of the things which angers her most about her father, the hotline he has to some primitive part of her brain, the way she has to override her knee-jerk subservience.

"I think you're very probably right," says her father carefully, because he, in turn, has had to learn how to override his own automatic response to his daughter's periodic outbursts, "but perhaps we should consider the consequences of irreversible actions."

"Are you seriously suggesting that we don't call the police?" says Sarah. She does the words-fail-me face where she blows up her cheeks and shakes her head. "His insides are all over the fucking ceiling."

The last time he told his daughter to calm down she threw a dinner plate at him. He says, "Give me two minutes."

"One," says Sarah.

"Your brother could go to prison for a very long time."

Gavin shakes his head. "That is not going to happen."

His sister says, "I don't want to fucking hear from you right now."

He clenches his teeth and presses his hand to his pained ribs to excuse his failure to think of a decent reply.

She turns to her father. "Fifty seconds."

"He was an intruder—"

"He was a guest."

"With a gun."

"Which he wasn't even holding."

If Martin were a lawyer he might be able to see a way out of this particularly impenetrable thicket but God alone knows what form it might take.

David wonders if he can take his phone out and get a photo of the corpse. He does not know if it would be considered more than usually insensitive because of it being a dead person or whether the extraordinariness of the situation would give him some moral wiggle room.

"You're asking nine people to lie," says Sarah. "And you're asking them to tell exactly the same lie, down to the last detail, for the rest of their lives. How is that going to work exactly?"

His daughter should have been a lawyer, thinks Martin. And his son is going to prison. What a bizarre and wholly unexpected turn of events. His job will be to minimise the effect this has on Madeleine. It will be a difficult job and not one he relishes. He will start by sealing off this room and getting it cleaned and redecorated.

"Any other objections?" Sarah revolves slowly, making eye contact with all the adults in turn. They know she is right. They are also mightily relieved that she is the one who is planning to set the inevitable process in motion. But Sarah does not call the police, because the silence is broken by a loud, sucking gurgle coming from the stranger's body. Emmy screams and does a little dance, running on the spot and flapping her hands in front of her face, which would be very funny in almost any other context.

"Emmy . . . ?" says Martin. "Emmy?" He waits for her to calm down a little. "It's trapped gases being released." Also, very possibly, the man's bowels emptying beneath him, though it seems unnecessary to add this clarification. He wonders how Madeleine is doing in the kitchen. Perhaps he ought to go and check on her.

The stranger sits up and opens his eyes.

Emmy sits down, slumps forward, headbutts her coffee cup then rolls sideways off her chair, too swiftly for Robert to catch her. Gavin makes a noise that can only be described as a dog-whimper. David is bedazzled. It is, by a country mile, the most amazing thing he has ever seen. Perhaps it was a magic trick after all.

Apart from the fact that he is missing most of his internal organs, the stranger seems in better condition than Gavin. He strokes his bloody beard back into shape and gets to his feet as if he had merely stumbled in the street. He walks across the room and as he does so everyone can hear the soles of his boots alternately sticking to and becoming unstuck from the bloody floor. He retrieves his sawn-off shotgun. He walks over to Gavin and stands looking down at him. Gavin's whimper becomes a low keening. The stranger smiles. He has the contented look of a man who has downed a good meal in fine company.

Gavin is certain that these are the last few seconds of his life and he wishes he were able to act in a more manly fashion but the pain of his broken ribs and the emotional roller coaster of the last twenty minutes have left him too drained to do anything but close his eyes and wait for the lights to go out.

The lights do not go out. The stranger says, "I will see you next Christmas." He slips the gun into his poacher's pocket and buttons his greatcoat over the carnage of his chest. "Then it will be my turn." He straightens his back and turns so that he can address his last words to everyone in the room. "I bid you all good night and a merry Christmas."

He strides to the French windows, swings them open and walks through the resulting gust of flakes into the dark.

§

Gavin sits with his head in his hands, staring into the wood-grain of the kitchen tabletop, waiting for his mother's codeine to take effect. Sarah has made a pot of tea and put out a plate of biscuits and most of them seem comforted in some small degree by a custard cream and a hot mug they can wrap their hands around. Emmy has a livid bruise on her temple.

David is finally beginning to understand the enormity of the situation. For a while he rang with excitement like a beaten gong, having sailed through a test of manhood the like of which his friends would never undertake. Disappointed that he had failed to get a photograph of the dead man, however, he sneaked into the off-limits dining room with his phone. The bloodstains themselves did not affect him, but his photograph of the bloodstains looked undeniably like the photograph of a murder scene, sad and sordid and profoundly unglamorous, and he realised for the first time that he had just watched his uncle kill someone. This fact was made no more acceptable by having watched the dead man get up afterwards and announce that he would kill his uncle next year.

Upstairs, Sofie moves from room to room in a rising panic. "Anya . . . ?" Is it possible that her daughter was so frightened that she left the house and ran into the night? In the little loft her daughter is unconscious and unable to hear her mother calling. Eventually Sofie returns to the kitchen. "I can't find Anya."

"She can't have gone far," says Leo.

"No," says Sofie. "Listen to me. Anya is not here."

It takes a long moment for the penny to drop. "She ran out of the room."

"She ran out of the house," says Sofie.

"Oh fuck." Leo is on his feet. "Dad. Find me a torch."

§

Leo and Robert scour the garden. They check inside the shed and behind the climbing roses which cover the long wooden trellis. They look in the compost bin. They take bamboo canes from the pot beside the kitchen door and push them into drifts. Leo tries not to think that if he finds his daughter using this method then she will almost certainly be dead.

Ten minutes later, sitting in the kitchen, David says, casually, "There's a place you can hide. In the top bathroom. There's a kind of hatch in the wall."

Sofie runs upstairs. At her lowest point, in a couple of years' time, she will slap her son viciously across the face and call him an "evil little shit" for not revealing this information earlier. And when her marriage to Leo falls apart she will know, deep down, that it was her son's fault for sitting eating biscuits, untroubled by the fact that his sister was dying upstairs.

She kicks open the bathroom door, tears the panel from the wall and pulls her daughter out through the hatch. Anya's limbs are limp, her face grey, her flesh cold and damp. Sofie carries her daughter along the corridor to the bedroom. Martin takes charge. They undress Anya and put her into her dry rabbit onesie and lie her under the duvet. Sarah is made to sit with the hairdryer feeding hot air into the space around her shaking body. Emmy fetches her a bobble hat.

Sofie says, "She needs to be in a hospital."

"And how would she get there?" says Martin. "This is what they would do for her in a hospital."

Sofie says, "Will she be all right?"

Martin says, "I honestly don't know," and this is what Sofie will remember, not that her father-in-law helped saved her daughter's life but his cool acceptance of the fact that he might not be able to.

Madeleine arrives with a mug of hot sweet tea in one of the spouted beakers she has saved from when the grandchildren were small. Sofie works it between Anya's lips and says, "Come on, darling, drink."

They call Leo and Robert. Leo returns, relieved that his daughter is alive then terrified all over again when he sees how unresponsive she is, the distance in her eyes. He leans down and kisses her. "Hey, little one."

It is a small bedroom and filling it with useless people is no help to anyone, so Sarah and Emmy retreat downstairs and wash up while Robert does what can be done in the dining room. He wipes down the clock. He rolls and bags the blood-soaked rug and puts it in the garden. He removes the map of Bedfordshire from its soiled frame and lays it in a drawer so that the frame and the glass can be soaped clean. He sponges bodily matter from pitted wallpaper. He takes down the curtains and leaves them to soak in a bucket of water. He turns off the light, closes the door and puts a symbolic chair in front of it.

Throughout all of this Gavin sits at the kitchen table saying very little. He is not greatly troubled by the pain. There is a rough-and-tumble, tree-climbing, small-boy part of him which enjoys physical discomfort. Nor is he troubled by what has happened and what might be happening to Anya. He has always possessed the ability to ignore things to which he is not immediately connected. What troubles him is that he cannot see a way in which these events might be turned to his advantage, and this is a situation he has not been in before.

Emmy hovers nearby, drying pans and casserole dishes. She

longs to be back in London, stepping out of her mundane self every night and into that pretend sitting room with its view of the rainy fjord to greet Pastor Manders—"How good of you to come so early. We can get our business done before supper . . ." Because it was Gavin's invulnerability, above everything else, which drew her to him and counterbalanced the arrogance and insensitivity. She knows now that he can be broken and she cannot shake the suspicion that she has climbed into the wrong lifeboat.

§

Only Madeleine sleeps, and she does so only until 4 a.m. when the bloody images begin to sharpen in the clearing diazepam fog. Leo tells Sofie to take a rest but she can't until she sees Anya up and walking and, in truth, he feels the same way. Sarah is too angry to sleep and Robert's job is clearly to remain awake in order to absorb, defuse and deflect some of his wife's anger so that she doesn't complicate an already difficult situation.

As for Martin it is the stranger's resurrection which keeps him awake. The man was dead, then the man was not dead. They have been the victims of an extraordinarily sophisticated trick. But how was it done? By whom? And for what reason?

David cannot sleep because when he went upstairs to see how his sister was doing his mother hissed at him to stay away, a note of unmistakable hatred in her voice. His father came out into the corridor and said that Mummy was feeling very tense, but an apology on someone else's behalf wasn't a real apology. Everyone knew that.

He forgot about Anya's hiding place. Then he remembered. Why is he not being congratulated? The answer is the same as it has always been. Because Anya was premature, the fairy child, the blessed one, who only just made it into the world. And sometimes he does wish she were dead, because everyone tells you to be good and look after yourself and not make a fuss and remember how lucky you are because Mummy and Daddy have a lot on their plate right now, so you are good and you look after yourself and don't make a fuss and your reward is to be ignored.

He dreams sometimes of having a terrible disease. He dreams of being crippled in a car accident. Sometimes he leans a little too far out of windows. Sometimes he pushes the tip of a penknife into his wrist till blood comes out. Sometime he googles fatal doses.

And here he is again, standing in the wings of "The Anya Show."

§

Gavin lies under the duvet for the latter half of the night, so as to rest if not to sleep. The daylight, when it comes, restores some of his self-belief and lends the events of the previous day an otherworldly cast which allows him to frame and neuter them. He asks Emmy to fetch him more codeine, strong coffee and toast, and when the analgesia kicks in he showers slowly and carefully, comes downstairs and suggests a preprandial family walk.

Sarah is speechless. How is it possible for him to ignore what happened in the next room? And why is everyone else colluding in this act of communal amnesia? She wants it talked about. She wants justice done. At the very least she wants her brother to admit that he did a dreadful, dreadful thing.

It is one of the reasons many people are attracted to Gavin and many people find Sarah difficult, one of the reasons why the universe so often bends unfairly to his will and throws obstacles in her way. He is all momentum and confidence. He is entertained by the new and the interesting and bored by the old and the difficult. And he makes this choice seem noble and right.

Madeleine's hip is not good so Sofie stays behind to help with lunch. Anya, up and mobile now, is scared of what lies outside the house but decides to throw in her lot with the larger crowd for safety's sake and they don Wellingtons and gloves and set off towards the church. Other villagers halloo them like fellow Eskimos across the snowy waste. A golden retriever bounces in and out of the deepest drifts, appearing and disappearing like a furred yellow dolphin.

Robert sees David trailing at the rear and senses something off-kilter, an echo from his own childhood perhaps, when he was shunted between international schools. Worthless superficial glamour and loneliness in fourteen languages.

"How's it going, buddy?"

David stares at him with the utter contempt of the young, and the image that comes to Robert is that of a child who has fallen down a well, so that any conversation they muster is pointless because the shaft is deep and there is no ladder. It is a moment that will haunt Robert over the coming years when he hears, periodically, about the successive downward steps of David's long descent. And deep snow will always come overlaid with this faint image of his nephew's sour little face and the parents who didn't realise which of their children was in danger.

§

Exercised and de-booted, everyone arranges themselves around the kitchen table for a stripped-down Christmas lunch to suit the less-than-festive mood, the younger and more limber perching on stools or sitting on the washing machine and eating on their laps. The turkey is good, and only Martin complains about the absence of swede and Brussels. The mincemeat tart and custard are even better and everyone is quietly pleased to finish the meal without feeling bloated for once, and while no one wishes to tempt fate by referring, even indirectly, to the reason why they are eating in this unorthodox manner it is tacitly admitted by the majority of the family that it is a very nice Christmas lunch.

Gavin raises his glass of Malbec. "God bless you one and all."

§

After lunch gifts are handed out and what is sometimes a rather tense affair goes off without a hitch (last year Gavin's present to his father of two walking poles was considered insulting and unsubtle). David gets the latest edition of *FIFA*. Martin gets a box set of the complete Beethoven sonatas for piano and violin by Isabelle Faust and Alexander Melnikov. Sarah attempts yet again to broaden her mother's cultural horizons by buying her a contemporary novel by a woman which will be shelved, unread, along with the others in what Gavin refers to as "the Black Lesbian Fiction Section" behind the gramophone. Leo and Sofie, in contrast, have brought many jars of blackberry jam from their allotment, ornately hand-labelled by Anya, which seem parsimonious at the time but are consumed more completely and with more enjoyment than any of the other gifts (Martin never reaches disc four of the Beethoven).

The wrapping paper is cleared away and cake served. In other circumstances they might watch *Skyfall* but the television is anchored to the aerial socket in the dining room. Consequently the events of the previous evening begin to rise up in the absence of commensurable distraction. While the others play Monopoly Leo and Robert escape the house to retrieve Emmy and Gavin's suitcase and discover that their car is parked on a road which has, miraculously, been snow-ploughed and gritted. Within the hour, Monopoly has been abandoned and Gavin and Emmy are heading south on the M1, Emmy at the wheel, Gavin reclined and semi-conscious in the passenger seat.

Her brother gone, Sarah expresses her feelings about him loudly and at length. Her father asks why she has saved her anger precisely for the people who do not deserve it. This does not go down well and she exits in high dudgeon shortly thereafter taking Robert with her so that, come eight in the evening, Leo, Sofie and the children are the only remaining guests, and when Anya says that she won't be able to sleep in the house Leo and Sofie seize the opportunity with poorly disguised relief, and set off on a night drive to Durham.

By ten o'clock Martin and Madeleine are alone and about to experience a night of such profound ill-ease that they will spend the next seven days in a damp little holiday cottage in Shropshire, Martin arranging from afar for Andrezj, the Polish builder who did the conservatory after the alder fell on it, to return the dining room to the condition it was in before "a very troubled ex-patient forced his way into the house and tried to take his own life."

§

Gavin and Emmy spend the evening of Christmas Day on hard plastic chairs in the A&E department of the West Middlesex Hospital, waiting for an X-ray. "Last Christmas" by Wham! comes round seven times on the PA before Gavin gives up counting.

On Boxing Day Gavin asks a friend at the BBC to dig up any

information about a rumoured shooting in his parents' village. A blank is drawn and he puts the matter from his mind.

Emmy suffers occasional post-traumatic flashbacks over the next few weeks (the glutinous line of blood across the cheese plate, the gurgling noise . . .) but Gavin seems untroubled and this calms her. She wonders, sometimes, if it really happened and is reassured by her uncertainty, a sign that the event is rolling into the long grass at the edges of her memory.

One night in late January, however, Gavin is woken by a gunshot. He opens his eyes and sees a ragged splash of fresh gore on the ceiling above the bed, little stalactites of blood turning, one by one, into drops which fall in slow motion towards the bed. He puts his hand to his chest and feels . . . absolutely nothing, lungs, heart, stomach, all gone. Something moves in the corner of his eye. The stranger is standing in the doorway, same camouflage trousers, same brass buttons, same insolent smile, preposterous steampunk weapon smoking. An eagle turns on the wind coming off the mountains. Smoke and dung.

"Gavin?" Emmy is shaking him. "You're safe. Please. Stop shouting."

This is how the unravelling begins.

He remains awake for the rest of the night. He reads more of *The Silk Road: A New History* by Valerie Hansen. He googles locations in and around Kashgar. He sacks the graphic designer who has failed to come up with a decent identity for the production company he and Tony Weisz are setting up. The following morning he drives to the Standedge Tunnel near Huddersfield where they are filming the second season of *Isambard's Kingdom*. He manages not to think about his nocturnal hallucination until the middle of the afternoon when Annie, the director, sits beside him and says, casually, "You look exhausted. On camera. Which is not good." She affects a swagger he would accept in a man but finds grating in a woman. She is very possibly a lesbian though they are unlikely to have the kind of tête-à-tête in which such intimacies are shared. She is certainly immune to his charm in a way that puzzles and irritates him. He counts to three in his head, the way Tony has advised him to do. "I broke two ribs at Christmas. I'm still in some pain. I didn't sleep well last night."

Nor does he sleep the following night at the hotel, despite *Hellboy* on the Mac, two Paracodol and three whiskies from the minibar. He stares into the grainy, monochrome dark, listening to the low, irregular timpani of the heating pipes, unable to let go of the world. He knows that if he falls asleep the stranger will enter the room and slaughter him. It is more than simple fear, however. He has never really thought of himself as possessing an unconscious. He has seldom looked inwards and has seen little on those rare occasions. He loves busyness, company, tasks, exercise. Belatedly he is realising that there is a vital part of the mind which can go badly wrong but which cannot be easily accessed. He is forty-one years old and only now becoming aware of a problem his less confident contemporaries were grappling with on the windswept edge of the playground at St. Aloysius Primary School.

The following afternoon Veronique, the executive producer from Palomar, pitches up and makes polite enquiries into Gavin's health. He forgets to count to three and uses the phrase "the fucking matriarchy." He is told to take four days off while the crew shoot background footage in Manchester and Edinburgh. "Yoga, sex, pills, whatever. Get some rest. You look like the walking dead."

§

Tony's advice was intended to apply only to work situations, but when Emmy tells him to go to the doctor Gavin yet again fails to count to three, the upside being that Emmy moves into Pastor Manders's guest room in Chiswick for a week "to make sure two careers don't go down the tube," and he is able to jam chairs under the handle of the bedroom door, sleep with the light on and leave Radio 4 chattering through the small hours.

After four days he returns to Huddersfield and maybe he isn't as sharp or as energetic as he was before but Annie says nothing and he makes it through the rest of the filming without medical assistance, which seems to him to be the most important thing of all, to have been his own saviour.

But the week Emmy intends to spend sleeping elsewhere so that she arrives fresh onstage every night becomes two, then four. In week number six the much-delayed *Fog* finally opens. It is a low-budget Mike Singer film, shot the previous spring on the north Norfolk coast, in which Emmy plays the mother of a pro-foundly handicapped boy who might or might not be possessed by the Devil. Technically horror, it is hugely affecting and very beautiful and the reviews for Emmy's performance in particular are ecstatic. In week number ten she is offered one of the female co-leads in *Lockdown*, a new crime seven-parter for ITV alongside Gemma Arterton and Matt Smith.

When she meets Gavin for lunch at Honey & Co. on War-ren Street the following day he seems unimpressed by her news which, in other circumstances, might offend her except that it is clearly part of some deeper problem with which he is wrestling. If only he were to ask for help, in however coded a fashion, she would find it impossible to refuse. But he doesn't reach out, and if she has learnt one thing in their three years not-quite-together it is to say nothing which presupposes weakness on his part. So she leaves the last few forkfuls of her chestnut and rum cake, kisses him on the cheek and walks out knowing, even as she does so, that this is the unexpected minor cadence of their marriage ending.

§

He gets an email from Sarah. She writes, "I would have preferred not to be in contact at all," and it is this phrase which strikes Gavin with more force than the news that their father has slipped on an icy kerb en route to the newsagent and broken the top of his right femur. He should drive up to Leicester but he cannot bring himself to obey a summons, least of all from his sister. So he rings his mother, says that he's filming, and asks her to send his father good wishes for a speedy recovery.

§

Tony is having trouble finding a broadcaster for the Silk Road series. There are rumours about Gavin's temperament but that shouldn't matter. Viewing figures for *Isambard's Kingdom* were consistently high and commissioners rarely care about interpersonal friction on set if it stays out of the papers. Two of the commissioners are new, however, and eager to personalise their fiefdoms and consequently disinclined to favour projects with which their predecessors had been toying.

"It's the wrong part of the cycle," says Tony. "We hunker down, stay busy, give it twelve months, repackage . . ."

"And that's it?" says Gavin. "That's your answer?"

Tony pauses and says, "Gavin. You can fuck other people off, up to a point, but you do it to me and it's curtains."

§

At which point the process of decline might still be reversible so long as Gavin tightens his belt, accepts all the public speaking engagements he's offered, writes the text for *The World's Most Amazing Buildings*, a children's book Walker have commissioned, and does a few of the less-than-appealing adverts his agent is putting his way. Instead he does something so stupid that he will never be able fully to explain it either to himself or to anyone else.

He is in the Hospital Club in Covent Garden, the membership of which is one of the expenses he might be wise to forgo until he has a steady income again. He is sitting in the bar writing the book for Walker because he dislikes being alone for long periods, which is one of the reasons he is unwilling to forgo the membership. He is drinking, just enough to take the edge off. It is shortly before three in the afternoon.

"Gavin?"

He looks up to find Edward Cole smiling down at him. Pastor Manders, the owner of the house to which his wife fled when she left him. The man makes him uneasy. Gay men in general make him uneasy. It's the physical aspect, of course, but it's also a sense that he is being mocked in a language that sounds superficially like English but which he doesn't quite understand.

"How are you doing?"

"Yeh. I'm doing fine, Edward. Cheers."

"Emmy says she's worried about you."

The following day Tony will say, "You're a public figure, for Christ's sake," though the more pertinent fact is that Emmy is a public figure and Gavin is particularly galled to see that every article describing the incident describes him as "the estranged husband of . . ."

He says, "Fuck you, Edward."

"Goodness." Edward raises an eyebrow. "I see what she means."

"You have no fucking idea what she means."

"If you want my advice," says Edward, because if someone snaps your olive branch then you are surely allowed to poke them with the broken end, "I'd stick to Earl Grey before the sun's over the yardarm."

In the photo you can't see the punch landing, which is one of the reasons why Gavin doesn't end up being prosecuted for GBH, though there will be times, later in the year, when he thinks prison might have been the preferable option.

He spends the night in the cells at the West End Central police station and is granted bail the following afternoon. He calls Tony but doesn't realise the depth and nature of the shit he is in till Tony throws a copy of the *Daily Mail* into his lap. Their relationship, personal and business, ends before they reach Richmond. Walking the last two miles home Gavin is stopped by a boy of nine or ten who wants a joint selfie. Gavin tells him to go fuck himself and the boy starts to cry. He realises that the boy knows nothing of what happened the day before. The boy's father says to Gavin, "What is *wrong* with you?"

§

His financial adviser is "tied up with other clients" so he sits in one of the smaller meeting rooms at Crace & Lawner being talked at by a pustular underling who advises him to draw up a budget, liquidate some of his investments, rent out the house and move into a flat, and whose tone says, unmistakably, "We are no longer flattered by your custom."

§

Martin comes out of hospital with his femur pinned. He walks slowly and will use a frame for the first few weeks. Madeleine assumes that it is the pain and the drugs he is taking to dull it which are making him blurred and unmotivated, but when the dosage comes down and he begins walking unaided she can see that the fall has shattered something which is not physical, and that his redoubtable grip, on himself, on his family and on the world, had been a prolonged act of will he no longer has the energy to repeat.

§

In Durham David puts a plastic bag over his head, pulling it tight by holding the loose material at the base of his skull like a ponytail. If he rides out the automatic reflex to uncover his mouth and nose he enters a place of great calm. He begins to feel woozy, his fist uncurls, the bag comes loose and he starts to breathe again. He does this often. He imagines his parents finding his body on the bedroom floor. He imagines a dog walker finding his body on nearby waste ground, decayed and bloated after a week's search. He imagines being in a persistent vegetative state. All these things comfort him in different ways.

§

Gavin remains drunk for most of the next three months, never blind, never stumbling, but starting with a whisky at breakfast and maintaining a modest but steady intake during the day so as to keep the world at two or three removes.

When the Hospital Club withdraws his membership he transfers his custom to a string of less salubrious establishments in Covent Garden and Soho, moving on each time friendly advice is offered concerning his health and welfare.

He does not open his post. He does not answer the phone. He does, however, open an email from Kirstin in Sydney. It says, "You forgot Thom's birthday. I reminded you and you still forgot. If I write any more I will just get angry and I'm tired of being angry. Please don't contact us again. Thom has a new father now. He is kind and generous and reliable. There is nothing good you can add to his life."

Every night for the next week when the stranger appears he is holding Thom by the scruff of the neck, pressing the barrel of the shotgun to the side of the boy's head. Gavin tries to reach them but the intervening air is viscous and obstructive, the way it is in dreams, and the stranger pulls the trigger before he is halfway across the room so that Thom's head becomes a spray of wet, red vapour.

§

He is sitting in the Mem-Saab on Stukeley Street pretending to eat chicken tikka shashlik. It is the price of spending several hours in the warm human buzz, drinking his way through four bottles of Cobra. He has a ring-bound notebook with him and a big Phaidon volume on the architecture of Alvar Aalto so as to look and feel purposeful.

Amber, whose name is very possibly not Amber, would have

rung alarm bells three months ago: the confidence which doesn't quite hide the damage, the blowsy, dog-eared glamour, a blurry tattoo swallow just below her left ear. What catches him off guard, however, is the way she sits herself down across the table and says, "I'm more of a Mies van der Rohe fan myself. Clean lines, white space. You want to be modern? Be modern. Don't go off half-cocked."

She doesn't pry or criticise. She says, "Life's a bitch," and while she's referring explicitly to her father, who died when she was five years old, her eyes hold his long enough to let him know that she understands that he has been through a hard time himself recently. It should worry him, the speed and ease of this seeming rapport, but he is lonelier than he dares admit.

She's been an art student and an architecture student, though she finished neither course. She's lived in Barcelona, Dublin, Norwich and Copenhagen. She has a pilot's licence and knows how to build a drystone wall and the Swedish poem she recites sounds convincing to his untutored ear. The swift hop from story to story suggests that she wants none of them examined too closely but she has genuine charm, and when she disappears to the toilet and returns wiping her nose and talking too fast he is not dismissive and superior as he might previously have been.

They take a taxi to Richmond where she slips off her shoes and socks and unbuttons her jeans and says, "I suppose you'll want to fuck me now." She seems ten years younger suddenly, her earlier confidence gone entirely. He doesn't know if it is a piece of play-acting, or whether she is wearily bowing to the inevitable, offering him the use of her body in return for something she hasn't yet spelled out. He's several drinks beyond all but the most rudimentary moral judgement and she's naked now, scrawny with big breasts, not a million miles from Emmy, or indeed Kirstin, if the clock were wound back and they'd led rougher lives. There is a big bruise on her left thigh.

He takes the path of least resistance and they fuck on the sofa. He is inside her for a minute at most, no condom, no thought for her pleasure. Afterwards she wraps herself in the baby-blue cashmere rug he bought for Emmy's birthday and smokes a cigarette. No one has ever smoked in the house but he says nothing and of all the day's events it is this which most clearly marks the point past which he gives in to the momentum of the fall.

He opens a bottle of Château Puy-Blanquet. They watch *Shutter Island* and say very little to one another, though whether this is because of a shared shame or a wordless bond he doesn't know. They are conspirators now and don't need to ask or answer such questions.

In the middle of the night she takes hold of his hand, puts it between her legs and rubs herself with his fingers until she comes. She is crying as she does this. He pretends to be only half awake so that he does not have to ask what's wrong. He falls back to sleep and dreams vividly about his son: playing chicken-in-the-waves in Half Moon Bay, the velociraptor cake Kirstin baked for his seventh birthday, reading *Zagazoo* together, reading *Bear Hunt* together. He hasn't thought about his son this much in years. He dreams about the shouting competition the two of them had in the Malvern Hills and how neither of them could speak for two days afterwards. He knows, somehow, that he is asleep, and that when he wakes he will enter a day of harrowing loneliness. But how does one remain inside a dream?

Then suddenly his eyes are open and he can smell cigarette smoke and hear loud music coming from downstairs.

§

When Leo reads about his brother in the paper what he feels is schadenfreude mostly. He still blames Gavin for the problems which have plagued Anya and interrupted her schooling since Christmas—the headaches, the fatigue, the stomach pains—and for the arguments he and Sofie have about how to deal with them. Nevertheless he tries to contact Gavin in order to put his mother's mind at rest, and it is only when he gets no response to his emails and phone calls that he becomes genuinely worried.

He contacts Kirstin and Emmy and Tony but the last reliable sighting is seven weeks old and he is haunted by the image of his brother twisting on a makeshift noose while the rest of them feel smug about his comeuppance. He should ask Sarah to go to London—she is nearer and richer—but he is not immune to the sibling rivalry he usually pretends to rise above, so he pays a king's ransom and takes a five-hour train journey to London at the crack of dawn one Saturday in early May.

There is no answer to his knock at the door so he reads four chapters of *God's Traitors* by Jessie Childs over a panini in Costa. An hour later there still is no answer and he is angry with himself for having conceived such a simplistic plan when his brother could be in Bali for all they know. He walks to Kew Gardens and back brooding on the string of insults, spoken and unspoken, which peppered his childhood in the shadow of the golden boy—the second-hand duffel coat, the afternoon he was pushed out of the tree house, the shelves his father hand-built for Gavin's bedroom whose true purpose had nothing to do with the books and toys they were too weak to support. He receives no answer to his third and final knocking but leans over the thorny anti-burglar hedge before leaving so that he can look through the side window, half hoping now to discover, if not a body, then some demeaning squalor at the very least. What he sees instead is a woman staring back at him, wearing a Clash T-shirt which is too big for her, drinking from a racing-green mug and smoking a cigarette. She must be in her late twenties, greasy blonde hair, a sleazy, car-crash aura, the kind of person he has only ever encountered in films or TV documentaries. She does not react and he realises that she is looking at her own reflection. He backs away slowly, telling himself as he walks to the station that his brother's life is falling apart but unable to suppress the thought that he is living out a sexual fantasy of a kind that was never available, and will never be available, to his younger, less adventurous brother.

§

Gavin gets out of bed and heads down to the living room intending to tell Amber that she must leave, but he can't bring himself to do it. In spite of the music and the smoking and the knowledge that she is accelerating his descent towards some as yet undefined crash, there is sufficient consolation in Amber's presence to make it preferable to the empty house with the menacing pile of unopened mail and the phone that rings and stops and rings and stops and the framed photographs which he has hidden in drawers.

The two of them come and go and after a couple of days Gavin realises that she has got her own key cut. He can't remember her asking if she could do this but his memory of the recent past is increasingly fogged by alcohol and the hangovers he keeps failing to alleviate with painkillers and willpower despite the repeated promises he makes to himself.

Amber has been in residence for nearly a week when he returns from Tesco one lunchtime to find her arguing with a tracksuited man in the kitchen. He has a sinewy, underfed air and Gavin can smell both his deodorant and the sweat it is failing to disguise.

"What are you doing in my house?"

"Amber and I are talking." The man doesn't even turn his head.

"Amber . . . ?"

She says, "I'm so sorry, Gavin."

The man laughs. "She's not fucking sorry. You're never fucking sorry, are you, babe?"

Gavin tells himself he is protecting Amber's honour but his anger is overwhelming and undirected and his main intention is to wipe out his shame at having allowed this whole sorry situation to happen.

He is a big man and still strong despite having done little exercise for the past three months but his smaller opponent has clearly been in fights before. They grapple briefly, falling together onto a chair which shatters beneath them. Then the man breaks Gavin's nose with a headbutt. The shock loosens Gavin's grip, the man gets to his feet, kicks Gavin hard in the small of the back and drags Amber from the house. Gavin does not care what might happen to her. He is not even greatly concerned with the damage to his face. Mostly he is frightened by the fact that he is now alone.

He walks to A&E where he is both relieved and distressed that no one recognises him. He returns five hours later with a bandage over his nose to find that the iPhone and wallet he left on the hall table have been stolen along with the TV, the hi-fi, his MacBook Air and his passport. He rings the bank to cancel the card but the current account has already been emptied of three thousand pounds. He rings a locksmith then has to ring back and cancel the visit when he remembers that he has no way of paying the man. He drinks half a bottle of whisky, lies down on the sofa, loses consciousness and wakes up an hour later, face down in his own vomit.

§

The following day he goes to the bank to get hold of some cash. He has a vicious hangover, a bandage over his face, no proof of identification and a very short fuse. He leaves before the police are called but returns to find another locksmith has come, employed by the bailiffs who have now repossessed the house. There is an envelope Sellotaped to the door explaining how he can retrieve his possessions. He tries to smash the blue recycling bin through the front window but the individual panes are too small. The glass shatters, the top of the box comes free and bottles fall around his feet, some shattering, some emptying dregs of wine and beer onto his trousers.

He has five and a half thousand pounds in a deposit account he cannot access and six pounds forty-three in his pocket. He wants a strong drink, he is hungry and he needs painkillers. He can afford only one of these things. He buys a packet of Paracodol from Boots then has to return and ask for a glass of water so that he can swallow them because his throat is too dry. He sits in the library for three hours, reading the newspaper and staring into space.

He does not consider contacting any of the people he has called friends over the past few years. It is not what the word "friend" means to him and, indeed, if they had treated him in a similar way he would have seen it as an imposition. His main concern is that other people do not find out about his present state.

When the library closes he heads up to the Star and Garter Gate and into the park. He needs to walk long and hard to burn off a churning anger. He is not homeless, he is simply without a home for the present. He has made mistakes. They can be undone. He walks for five hours and spends the night in the Isabella Plantation, sleeping in short bursts from which he is rapidly woken either by the imaginary stranger or by real animals moving through undergrowth nearby.

The following morning he returns to the bank in a more conciliatory state of mind. The woman at the counter says, "It's Mr. Cooper, isn't it?" She is excited for a second or so then goes very quiet. He is ushered into a private room. He explains to a man in a cheap suit that he was burgled. He recites his mother's maiden name, his pin number and his last three addresses and walks out with an envelope containing two thousand pounds. He takes the bandage off his face and throws it away.

He calls the bailiffs who explain that it will cost seventy pounds to retrieve his possessions. He counts silently to three and puts the phone down.

If he spends the next week in a hotel he will rapidly run out of money and find himself back at square one. He needs to ration his resources and ride out this period of turbulence.

He buys a sleeping bag, a cheap one-person tent and a waterproof coat from Millets in Epsom. He buys two packs of sandwiches from the reduced section in Sainsbury's and two plastic litre bottles of water which he can refill. People stare at him, either because of his broken nose or because they recognise him. It is impossible to tell which. If they stare for too long he stares

back. If they do not look away he tells them to fuck off. He buys
more Paracodol. He does not think about going to the Citizens
Advice Bureau. He does not think about finding a hostel. He does
not think about foodbanks or day centres. He wants nothing to
do with homeless people or those who make it their business to
care for them.

He sleeps in the park for a second night, camping in the trees
at the end of Pen Ponds. He is woken by the police in the small
hours. They are very polite. He packs his tent and makes a show
of walking towards Robin Hood Gate but veers into a stand of
trees when they can no longer see him. They're less polite when
they wake him the following night.

He walks upriver. Eel Pie Island, Ham Lands, Kingston,
Hampton Court. He climbs a fence and pitches his tent behind
the waterworks on Desborough Island. The following day he
stands under Chertsey Bridge and watches heavy summer rain
stipple the Thames for two solid hours. Laleham, Staines. He
passes under the M25. He has now left London. Above him, one
by one, planes rise from Heathrow and are swallowed by the sky.
Wraysbury, Windsor.

The days are warm and long, but the path is busy so he must
pitch his tent after dark and take it down soon after dawn. He
camps in a little copse near the A332. He camps in a wood near
Cliveden.

It is August. He does not know the precise date. A year ago he
was diving in the Maldives with Emmy, accompanied by manta
rays and blacktail barracuda, living a life that seems fictional now,
its inhabitants as glossy and shallow as actors in TV adverts.

He is embarrassed by his filthy clothing and his unwashed
smell but the dirtier and more ragged he becomes the less he

attracts people's attention and this is some relief. He does very little. He spends most of his day by the river, walking, sitting. He has never taken much notice of the non-human world. He rowed for two terms at Cambridge but the river was little more than background. He sees mink, he sees water voles, he watches iridescent-blue dragonflies hover among the reeds. He sees a shiny, black terrapin with red eyeballs sitting on a wet stone. He likes it best in the early mornings when the water is a mirror and flotillas of geese and ducks sleep in the last of the mist.

August becomes September. The weather turns. The Paracodol which previously kept him asleep till four o'clock are becoming less effective. He is wary of damaging his liver and kidneys by taking more.

He falls into conversation with a man who has already pitched his ramshackle tent in the little wood where Gavin himself was planning to spend the night. Terry has worked as a librarian and a cook and a gardener. He is reading a battered copy of Primo Levi's *The Periodic Table*.

They talk about the crayfish Terry has caught in the river and will be cooking for his supper. They talk about Cornelius Drebbel who piloted a submarine ten miles from Westminster to Greenwich in 1621 under the eyes of James I. Gavin asks him why he is camping rough and Terry explains that he knows the identity of Prince Harry's real father and for this reason he is being hunted down by the security services. He weeps a little and apologises for this. "I've been running for a long time. It's hard to keep my spirits up." Gavin wishes him well and continues walking in order to pitch his tent elsewhere.

There are tiny insects of some kind in his hair. He has a rash up his right arm and over his shoulder which might or might not be scabies. He has what feels like a constant, low-level chest infection.

He discovers that staff at the Co-op in Pangbourne throw food past its sell-by date into a skip at the rear of the shop at the end of the working day.

One morning he sees a boy walking over a bridge. He is certain that it is Thom. He fights his way up a steep bank and through a hedge but when he reaches the road he can see no one. He sees the boy several more times, never his face, only ever the back of his head. He vanishes when Gavin gives chase.

September becomes October. Goring, Moulsford, North Stoke. He sees a dead dog float past, its legs in the air like a cartoon of a dead dog. He gives up buying food. He saves his remaining money for Paracodol. He doubles his dose then triples it. A security guard finds him going through the bins behind Tesco in Wallingford and attacks him with a fury out of all proportion to the offence, pushing him to the ground, kicking him repeatedly and calling him "you thieving, fucking scum."

He understands now that taking your own life might not be a weakness. He has travelled a long way. It is a different country out here and everything looks different. To carry on living or to end one's life in a manner of one's own choosing? The answer is not obvious. To fill one's pockets with stones could be a decent bet against poor odds.

October becomes November. If the sun is out he finds that he can lie on his back for hours watching the clouds move and change above him, but the sun is rarely out. Most often the sky is low and grey. For a period of two weeks there is heavy rain every day. He is caught off guard on several occasions and unable to find shelter in time. His clothing is now permanently damp.

Oxford, Eynsham, Bablock Hythe, Newbridge. There are very few people around now. He wishes he were an animal so that he could simply hunt and eat and sleep in a burrow and not have to dwell on the past and worry about the future.

He has no money left. He runs out of Paracodol. He feels constantly frightened. It is impossible to tell how much of this is due to codeine withdrawal and how much is due to his rapidly declining health. It is too cold to sleep at night. He sleeps instead for brief periods during the day. When the dark comes down he finds a wall against which he can sit, hoping that he will not be attacked from behind.

He has a low fever. His head pulses and his joints ache. He no longer has the energy or the wit to find a source of clean water. He drinks from the river. In the middle of the night he has stomach cramps followed by diarrhoea.

He has lost the tent. He has no memory of how this happened. It is possible that it was stolen, though by whom he has no idea. He is now blind in his left eye.

He cannot drown himself. He knows that the creature to which his mind is inextricably bound will fight to stay alive and he will simply come out of the water a couple of hundred metres downstream colder and sicker. So he turns and makes his way back to Oxford where he saw a train passing north on the far side of a flooding meadow some days ago.

He comes off the river at Godstow Nunnery and walks through the village before turning back onto the meadow itself. There are cows and ragged horses. The train track has been separated from the grazing land by a high metal fence he no longer has the energy to climb, so he follows it south until it disappears into an area of high scrub. He wades through the brambles and the long grass until he finds an elderly wooden fence he can climb with ease.

He sits between the small trees on the earthen bank that runs beside the rails. A train passes. Ten minutes later another train passes in the opposite direction. He thinks about his father. He thinks about Thom. He thinks about Emmy. They seem a very long way away. A third train passes.

Walking down the meadow he regretted not having some alcohol or Paracodol to provide him with Dutch courage but it doesn't seem necessary now. Indeed with each train that passes he feels less and less comfortable sitting here and more strongly drawn to that invisible doorway only ten metres away through which he can pass into a place where there is no pain and there are no problems to solve.

He waits for another three trains to pass. When he sees a seventh some two hundred metres away he gets to his feet and walks down the little slope onto the gravel and steps over the nearest rail. He sets his feet firmly on a single black sleeper and leans forward with his hands on his knees so that the front of the train will strike his head and there will be no chance of his being thrown clear and finding himself alive and badly injured beside the track.

A hundred and fifty metres. The train horn sounds, followed by the grating skreek of metal on metal. A hundred metres. It will be over in seconds.

He sees movement from the corner of his eye, a figure moving among the trees where he was sitting earlier. Is it Thom again? He must not turn his head. He stares hard into the dirty pebbles between his toes. The horn. The skreek. Twenty metres. Ten.

A hand grabs his upper arm and roughly hauls him sideways. He thinks at first that it is the impact of the train. His head is filled with thunder. Metal hammers and flashes. He wonders why he is still thinking. He can feel his hands. He can feel his legs. He cannot be dead. The thunder stops. He opens his eyes and sees the sky. A black retriever licks his face.

"Give me your hand." A man is staring down at him. "The police will be on their way. We need to leave quickly."

Gavin is too perturbed to do anything but obey. The man is surprisingly strong. He hoists Gavin to his feet and lets go. He feels dizzy. He steadies himself and starts to walk. After three tentative steps, however, his knees buckle. He pitches forward and cannot even summon the energy to raise his hands to protect himself. He hits the gravel face first and passes out.

§

The room is warm and clean and uncluttered, a cube of three white walls, a white ceiling and a window which constitutes most of the fourth wall, through which he can see a line of trees and a featureless, off-white sky beyond. He wonders briefly if this is the laboratory to which you are returned after the experiment of your life has been allowed to run its full course. He can smell lavender fabric conditioner and an antiseptic he remembers from his childhood.

He is able to see out of his left eye. It is still foggy but he can discern colours and rough outlines. His hands look like the hands of a much older man. They have been cleaned but there is still dirt under the nails and in the deeper cracks of his skin. A rash of dry red scabs leads up his wrist under the sleeve of green cotton pyjamas. He remembers that he was homeless. He remembers that he tried to take his own life. He feels tearful but cannot tell whether this is relief or disappointment.

He rolls over and swings his feet carefully onto the bare waxed wood of the floor. His body is stiff. He has no clear sense of how long he has been unconscious. It feels like days. He stands slowly and walks to the window. He expects to see the treetops give way to roofs and chimneys and aerials but he finds himself looking instead onto rolling English farmland of the kind he remembers from his childhood, a dense wood of oak and beech to his left, a ploughed field falling away on the far side of a stone wall then rising again like a wave in a Japanese woodcut, a fringe of trees on the brow of the hill, a spire in the distance. The old comfort, the old claustrophobia. A beauty that sings to something deep inside him.

He turns. There is a white door set into the opposite wall. He has no idea what might lie beyond it. He does not want any more complications. He is already exhausted by his journey to the window. He returns to the bed, lies down, closes his eyes and slips back out of the world.

§

A woman is sitting in a simple chair of blond wood that wasn't there when he last woke. It is later the same day. Or perhaps it is the following day. She has a chestnut bob. She wear jeans and a cream woollen poncho. Her feet are bare. He recognises her but is equally convinced that they have never met. Panic flutters in his chest. He wonders if he has been in this place for years and this encounter has happened hundreds of times before, only to be forgotten repeatedly.

The woman sits in silence for a long time and seems entirely comfortable with this. He says nothing, wary of popping the fragile bubble and finding himself beside the river once again. Eventually she says, "You should come and have something to eat," and only then does he recognise the ache in his abdomen as hunger. She stands up. "I'm sure you can find your way." She leaves the door ajar.

Through the gap he can see more wood, more light, more white paint, a narrow sliver of another big window and, beyond it, more trees. He can smell an open fire. If he leaves this room he will have to deal with things he does not have the strength to deal with. But he is wary, too, of offending his hosts, whoever they might be. He gets to his feet and makes his way to the door, pausing briefly with his hand on the frame in order to get his breath back.

The bedroom is one of seven rooms off a first-floor balcony which runs around three sides of a boxy, light-filled atrium. Below him, over the rail, is the focal point of the house, three low sofas and an open hearth where several logs are burning. In front of him is another wall of glass, two storeys high, divided into big squares so that the view of the long lawn and the small lake and the surrounding trees seems like a video projection. It is, by some distance, the most beautiful house he has ever seen, the kind of house he dreamed of living in as a teenager, the polar opposite of the Rookery, with its low ceilings and thick walls and dark corners, every surface patterned and every cranny occupied by some antique thing.

He descends very slowly to the ground floor on a staircase of open risers and wooden treads which are warm beneath his unslippered feet. The atrium, he can see now, leads to open-plan dining and kitchen areas of smaller proportions but equally filled with light. The woman is standing at the stove. She spoons porridge from a small black pan into an earthenware bowl. "Have a seat."

The same familiarity, the same unnerving possibility that this is a ritual they have gone through before, because while he would never previously think of eating porridge, as soon as she says the word he knows that it is what he wants. He sits at the table and she places the bowl in front of him. "Coffee?"

He nods. He does not want to speak out loud. There is a game being played, the rules of which he does not understand and whose stakes, he thinks, could be very high indeed.

The kettle whistles as it comes to the boil. She turns the hot plate down and pours the bustling water into a cafetière. A column of steam rises above her head as she fits the plunger into the glass jug and places it on the table. Before taking her own seat across the table she gently folds back the sleeve of his pyjamas with two fingers to examine the rash on his wrist. She nods to herself then dips her hand into her pocket and retrieves a little blue-and-white tube of permethrin cream and hands it to him. "I've already put some on. You'll need to use it a couple more times."

"Thank you." His voice is croaky and he has to clear his throat and repeat himself. "Thank you."

"Eat."

The porridge is good, more milk than water. The coffee is good, too. He works his way slowly through both. There is a long painting on the wall to his right, a semi-abstract landscape from the forties or fifties, a patchwork of green, blue and grey planes, rough black lines in the foreground which could be trees or people. Just as he was with the woman he is convinced that he has seen the picture somewhere before but he cannot say precisely where. The woman is reading a book. The cover is not visible and the text seems to be in a foreign language, though having only one good eye he cannot see it clearly.

He finishes the porridge and the coffee. The tabletop is a single piece of oak. He runs his hand across its surface and feels the soft burr of the sanded grain under his fingers. He looks around. He has never lived in a house where it is a pleasure simply to sit and enjoy the geometry of the internal space. If he stayed here would it fade? Would he become blind to this room just as one becomes blind to any room one sees every day?

The woman is looking at him. He has the sense that something is about to happen and, indeed, at that very moment the light changes, a spooky dimming. Eclipse light. He turns and sees, through the window, that it has begun to snow. It is so warm in the house and he has been so comfortable in his pyjamas that he has forgotten what time of year it is.

The woman seems to know what he is thinking. Or perhaps she's simply remarking upon the serendipity. "Christmas Eve."

And this is when the stranger enters.

Gavin does not recognise him at first. He no longer has a beard and his head is shaved. He is wearing a tailored charcoal suit with tan brogues, an open white shirt and no tie. Padding quietly by his side is the black retriever Gavin remembers only now from their last meeting on the railway line. Gavin is struck at first only by how out of place he looks, in this building, in this landscape. At school there was one Indian boy, Rajneesh. Everyone else was white. Everyone in his parents' village is white.

The stranger sits and pours himself a cup of coffee. "You are a very lucky man."

It is only when he speaks that Gavin remembers the accent he could not place first time round. Lucky is the very last thing he feels. Not once in the last twelve months has he thought about the stranger's parting promise, and only now does he begin to wonder if the detail which seemed least important has in fact been the crux upon which the whole year has turned. "Are you going to shoot me?" He hears his own voice. It sounds like the voice of a child.

The stranger considers this, or perhaps just pretends to consider it, before smiling and saying, "I think you've probably suffered enough." The snow is thickening now, big white flakes against the deep green of the trees, the flakes falling nearest the house catching the peach-pink glow of the fire and the house lights. "But it is easy to forget the lessons we have learnt unless we have some permanent reminder." His hand idly scratches behind the ears of the dog sitting at his side.

Gavin shot this man in the chest. He wants to say sorry but it seems an insultingly small word. Perhaps this is what the stranger means.

"Let's not waste what you have gone through." The stranger leans across the table and takes hold of Gavin's wrists. He does not grip tightly but Gavin can feel how strong he is. His expression is calm and kind, the expression of a father holding a child who must undergo some painful medical procedure for their own good.

The woman gets to her feet, walks round the breakfast bar and opens a drawer which is too small to contain the sawn-off shotgun. Gavin thinks she is going to take out a knife but when she returns to the table he sees that she is carrying a bolt cutter in one hand and a white hand towel and a first-aid kit in the other. Gavin struggles. The stranger does not tighten his grip, neither does he let go. He looks into Gavin's eyes and says, "This is going to happen. And you will thank me for it."

The woman lays the towel on the table, puts the first-aid kit to one side and takes up the bolt cutter. It is an old and dirty object, wholly at variance with everything else in the house, the metal surface scratched and dented from years of use, black oil in its joints and crevices.

"The index finger on your right hand," says the stranger.

There is nothing he can do. He curls his three other fingers into his palm and points upwards like John the Baptist in a Renaissance painting. He closes his eyes. He feels the cold weight of the metal as the woman fits the jaws around his finger between the knuckle and the first joint. There is no blade as such. It is sheer pressure which will do the work, the two plates sliding across one another.

She says, "I'll be as quick as I can."

He feels her adjust her position, a little rock from side to side as if preparing for a golf swing. She takes a quick, deep breath and squeezes hard. The big teeth slice through the skin but come to a halt at the bone. It is a harder job than she expected. She changes the position of her feet and shifts her hands a little farther down the handles so as to get more leverage then puts all her effort into a second squeeze. This time there is a cracking crunch as the metal shears through the bone. It is surprisingly loud. It sounds more like a thigh bone breaking. He opens his eyes.

The finger end falls onto the hand towel and blood pours from the stump. For a couple of seconds there is no pain. Then there is more pain than he has felt in his life. He feels sick with it. The stranger lets go of his uninjured hand, picks up the severed finger and throws it to the dog who catches it and trots away to chew it in the corner of the room by the snowy window.

The woman takes a length of bandage from the first-aid kit,

wraps it round the stump of Gavin's finger as a tourniquet and knots it tight. The endorphins start to come online. The pain is replaced by a giddy nausea and the room recedes a little. The woman folds a wad of dressing over the end of his finger and secures it with a strip of plaster round his palm. She adds a second dressing and secures it in the same way. The stranger wipes the blood from the table with the hand towel and drops it into the waste bin. The woman replaces the contents of the first-aid kit and puts it back in the drawer together with the bolt cutter. She returns with two pills in the palm of her hand and a small cup of coffee. "Paracetamol. It's the best we can do, I'm afraid."

He puts the pills into his mouth and washes them down.

"And now," says the stranger, "it is time for us to leave."

For a moment he thinks that they are talking about their own departure, that he will be left alone in this beautiful house, but they do not move and he realises that it is he who will be leaving. "Where am I going?"

"Come on. It's getting late."

They give him the shoes he has been wearing for the last seven months. They give him the coat has been wearing for the last seven months. Neither has been cleaned. They smell vile and he is amazed that he could have become inured to this.

He is ushered out of the front door and into the rear seat of a black BMW. The snow continues to fall thickly and steadily. He is starting to feel his hand again. The stranger climbs into the driver's seat and only as they are pulling away does he realise that the woman is not coming with them. In spite of what has just happened he feels both guilty for not having said goodbye and desperately sad that he may never see her again.

§

It is impossible to work out where they are going. Through the windscreen he can see the constantly expanding funnel of illuminated flakes, the occasional lit window, the occasional glare of headlights from a car passing them in the opposite direction, then darkness again. They drive through a village, then another. He is no longer aware of anything outside the car. He has run out of endorphins. The pain in the stump of his severed finger is overwhelming and he must use all his energy to hold his hand as still as he can while the car bumps and twists along these country roads. He is crying. He has never cried with pain before.

He has no real sense of how long they are in the car. After a period that might be anything between half an hour and two hours they come to a halt. He had assumed that he was being taken back to the train line where the stranger had found him, but he can see lit windows on both sides of the street.

The stranger turns the engine off, gets out, comes round and opens the door. "We're here."

Gavin wipes his eyes with the back of his hand and climbs out. It is blisteringly cold. There are three or four inches of snow on the ground and he is surprised that they have driven so swiftly and with no obvious problems.

The stranger shuts the car door behind him. "Follow me."

Partly it is the injury, partly it is the darkness and the obscuring snow, but he does not realise where he is until he sees that he is being led through the gates of the Rookery. He wants to turn and walk away. He does not want to see his family. He does not want to tell them what has happened to him over the previous year. It is entirely possible that they think he is dead. But he cannot turn and walk away. He knows that the stranger will not let him back in the car and he knows that he cannot survive a night out here without asking for someone's help.

"Look," says the stranger.

They are standing on the lawn now. In front of them are the French windows, lit up, uncurtained. He takes a couple of steps forward and thinks, at first, that his parents must have sold the house because what he sees is an old man making his way to the dining table using a walking frame. He wonders if he has been away for a fairy-tale number of years and it is his parents who are long dead. Then the man sits down and Gavin realises that he is looking at his father. Either the fall he had earlier in the year was more serious than he realised or something else has happened to him in the intervening months. He seems half the size and twenty years older.

Gavin takes another step towards the house. His mother sits at the head of the table in the seat his father used to occupy. Leo sits on one side of her, Sarah on the other. His sister seems uncharacteristically subdued. A teenage girl sits beside her, willowy, dark. He guesses that this must be Ellie. It has been two years since he last saw her. Sofie and Anya are having an animated conversation, but he cannot see David, nor can he see a place set for him.

A veil of snow swings between him and the house, breaking his concentration and reminding him how cold he is and how much his finger is hurting. He turns to find that the stranger has vanished. He is alone. He looks down at his hand and sees that the bandage is now soaked with blood which is dripping onto the snow at his feet. He needs to see a doctor. He needs warmth. He needs help of many kinds.

He turns back to the house. Another gust of wind. He takes a deep breath. He steps onto the little paved area between the potted shrubs. The intruder light clicks on. He knocks twice on the glass. As one his family turn to look at him.

THE GUN

Daniel stands in the Funnel, a narrow path between two high brick walls that join the playground to the estate proper. On windy days the air is forced through here then spun upwards in a vortex above the square of so-called grass between the four blocks of flats. *The Wizard of Oz* in stained concrete. Anything that isn't nailed down becomes airborne. Washing, litter, dust. Grown men have been knocked off their feet. A while back there was a story going round about a flying cat.

Except there's no wind this morning, there hasn't been any wind for days, just an unremitting mugginess that makes you want to open a window until you remember that you're outside. The end of August, a week since the family holiday in Magaluf where he learnt the backstroke and was stung by a jellyfish, a week till school begins again. He is ten years old. Back at home his older sister is playing teacher and his younger brother is playing pupil. Helen is twelve, Paul seven. She has a blackboard and a little box of chalks in eight colours and when Paul misbehaves she smacks him hard on the leg. His mother is doing a big jigsaw of Venice on the dining table while the tank heats for the weekly wash.

He can see the white socks of a girl on the swings, appearing, disappearing, appearing, disappearing. It is 1972. "Silver Machine" and "Rocket Man." He cannot remember ever having been this bored before. He bats a wasp away from his face as a car door slams in the distance, then steps into the shadow of the stairwell and starts climbing towards Sean's front door.

§

There will be three other extraordinary events in his life. He will be sitting at dusk on the terrace of a rented house near Cahors with his eight-year-old son when they see a barn on the far side of the valley destroyed by lightning, the crack of white light appearing to come not from the sky but to burst from the ground beneath the building.

He will have a meeting with the manager of a bespoke ironworks near Stroud whose factory occupies one of three units built into the side of a high railway cutting. Halfway through the meeting a cow will fall through the roof and it won't be anywhere near as funny as it sounds.

On the morning of his fiftieth birthday his mother will call and say that she needs to see him. She will seem calm and give no explanation and despite the fact that there is a large party planned for the afternoon he will get into the car and drive straight to Leicester only to find that the ambulance has already taken her body away. Talking to his father the following day he will realise that he received the phone call half an hour after the stroke which killed her.

Today will be different, not simply shocking but one of those moments when time itself seems to fork and fracture and you look back and realise that if things had happened only slightly differently you would be leading one of those other ghost lives speeding away into the dark.

§

Sean is not a friend as such but they play together because they are in the same class at school. Sean's family live on the top floor of Orchard Tower whereas Daniel's family live in a semi-detached house on the approach road. Daniel's mother says that Sean's family are a bad influence but she also says that television will damage your eyes if you sit too close and that you will die if you swim in the canal. In any case Daniel likes their volume, their expansiveness, their unpredictability, the china greyhounds on either side of the gas fire, Mr. Cobb's green BMW which he polishes and T-Cuts lovingly on Saturday mornings. Sean's older brother, Dylan, works as a plasterer and carpenter and they have a balcony which looks over the ring road to the woods and the car plant and the radio mast at Bargave, a view which moves Daniel more than anything he saw from the plane window between Luton and Palma because there is no glass and when you lean over and look down you feel a thrilling shiver in the backs of your knees.

He steps out of the lift and sees Sean's mother leaving the flat, which is another thing that makes Daniel envious, because when his own mother goes to the shops he and Paul and Helen have to accompany her. *Try and keep him out of trouble.* Mrs. Cobb ruffles his hair and sweeps onwards. She is lighting a cigarette as the silver doors close over her.

Sean's jumbled silhouette assembles itself in the patterned

glass of the front door and it swings open. *I've got something to show you.*

What?

He beckons Daniel into Dylan's bedroom. *You have to keep this a total secret.*

Daniel has never been in here before. Dylan has explicitly forbidden it and Dylan can bench-press 180 pounds. Daniel steps off the avocado lino of the hall onto the swirly red carpet of the bedroom. The smell of cigarettes and Brut aftershave. It feels like the bedroom of a dead person in a film, every object heavy with significance. Posters of *Monty Python* and *The French Connection*. *Jimmy Doyle Is the Toughest.* A motorbike cylinder head sits on a folded copy of the *Daily Express*, the leaking oil turning the newsprint waxy and transparent. There is a portable record player on the bedside table, the lid of the red leatherette box propped open and the cream plastic arm crooked around the silvered rod in the centre of the turntable. *Machine Head. Thick as a Brick. Ziggy Stardust.*

You have to promise.

I promise.

Because this is serious.

I said.

Sean tugs at the pine handle of the wardrobe and the flimsy door comes free of the magnetic catch with a woody clang. On tiptoe Sean takes down a powder-blue shoe box from the top shelf and lays it on the khaki blanket before easing off the lid. The gun lies in the white tissue paper that must have come with the shoes. Sean lifts it from its rustling nest and Daniel can see how light it is. Scuffed pigeon-grey metal. The words REMINGTON RAND stamped into the flank. Two cambered grips are screwed to either side of the handle, chocolate brown and cross-cut like snakeskin for a better grip.

Sean raises the gun at the end of his straightened arm and rotates slowly so that the barrel is pointing directly into Daniel's face. *Bang*, he says softly. *Bang*.

§

Daniel's father works at the local pool, sometimes as a lifeguard, more often on reception. Daniel used to be proud of the fact that everyone knew who his father was but he is now embarrassed by his visibility. His mother works part-time as a secretary for the county council. His father reads crime novels, his mother does jigsaws which are stored between two sheets of plywood when the dining table is needed. Later in life when he is describing his parents to friends and acquaintances he will never find quite the right word. They aspired always to be average, to be unremarkable, to avoid making too much noise or taking up too much space. They disliked arguments and had little interest in the wider world. And if he is often bored in their company during his regular visits he will never use the word *boring* to describe them because he is genuinely envious of their rare ability to take real joy in small pleasures, and hugely grateful that they are not demonstrating any of the high-maintenance eccentricities of many of his friends' retired and ageing parents.

§

They walk across the living room and Sean turns the key before shunting the big glass door to one side. They step into heat and traffic noise. There is a faint brown smog, as if the sky needs cleaning. Daniel can feel sweat running down the small of his back.

Sean fixes the pistol on a Volvo travelling in one direction then follows an Alfa Romeo going the other way. *We could kill someone and they'd never find out who did it.* Daniel explains that the police would use the hole in the windscreen and the hole in the driver's body to work out exactly where the shot came from. *Elementary, my dear Watson*, says Sean.

Let's go to the woods.

Is the gun loaded?

Course it's loaded, says Sean.

§

The woods rise up on the other side of the ring road, a swathe of no-man's-land between town proper and country proper. People park their cars at the picnic area by Pennington on the far side of the hill and walk their dogs among the oak and ash and rowan, but the roar of the dual carriageway and the syringes and the crushed lager cans dissuade most of them from coming down its northern flank.

§

They wait on the grass verge, the warm shock waves of passing lorries thumping them and sucking at their clothes. *Go*, shouts Sean and they sprint to the central reservation, vaulting the scratchy S-shaped barrier, pausing on the ribbon of balding grass then running across the second carriageway to the gritty lay-by with its moraine of shattered furniture and black bags of rubbish ripped open by rats and foxes. All that bacteria breeding in the sun. There is an upturned pram. They unhook the clanky gate where the rutted track begins. Sean has the gun in a yellow Gola bag thrown over his shoulder.

They pass the scrapyard with its corrugated-iron castellations. They pass the Roberts' house. A horsebox with a flat tyre, a floodlight roped to a telegraph pole. Robert Hales and Robert Hales and Robert Hales, grandfather, father and son, all bearing the same name and all living under the same roof. The youngest Robert Hales is two years above them at school. He has a biscuity unwashed smell and bones that look slightly too big for his skin. He used to come in with small animals in a cake tin. Stag beetle, mouse, wren, grass snake. Donnie Farr grabbed the last of these and used it to chase other children round the playground before whipping its head against one of the goalposts. Robert pushed Donnie to the ground, took hold of the fingers of his left hand and bent them backwards until two of them snapped.

The curtains in the Roberts' house are closed, however, and there is no red van parked outside so they walk on towards the corner where the path narrows and turns into the trees. Slabs of dusty sunlight are neatly stacked at the same angle between the branches. The bubbling runs of a blackbird's call. An empty pack of pork scratchings trodden into cracked and powdery earth. Luckily the junkies and lager drinkers don't have a great deal of stamina and if you walk for ten minutes the litter thins out and if it weren't for the smell of exhaust fumes you could imagine that the roar of traffic was a great cataract pouring into a ravine to your left.

They find a clearing that contains the last few broken branches of a den they built earlier in the summer where they drank Babycham and smoked six menthol cigarettes and were violently sick. *Let's do it here.* Sean finds a log to use as a shooting gallery and Daniel is sent in search of targets. He climbs the boundary fence and roots around among the hawthorn bushes which line the hard shoulder, coming back with two empty beer bottles, a battered plastic oil can and a muddy teddy bear with both arms missing. He feels exhausted by the heat. He imagines standing on the lawn at home, squeezing the end of the hose with his thumb and making rainbows in the cold falling water. He arranges the objects at regular intervals along the log. He thinks about the child who once owned the teddy bear and regrets having picked it up but doesn't say anything.

Sean raises the gun and moves his feet apart to brace himself. Daniel sees the pad of Sean's forefinger flatten as he begins to squeeze the trigger. A deep, cathedral quiet. The traffic stops. The blackbird no longer sings. He can hear the shuttle of his own blood.

He is not aware of the shot itself, only the loose rattle of scattering birds. He sees Sean being thrown backwards as if a big animal has charged and struck him in the centre of his chest mid-leap. The oil can, the bottles and the bear are still standing.

Oh my God. Sean gets to his feet. *Oh my God.* He begins dancing. He has clearly never done anything this exciting in his life. *Oh my God.*

A military plane banks overhead. Daniel is both disappointed and relieved that he is not offered the second shot. Sean breathes deeply and theatrically. He braces himself again, wipes the sweat from his forehead with the sleeve of his T-shirt and raises the gun. This time the noise is breathtakingly loud. It seems obvious to Daniel that many, many people will have heard it.

What are you doing? It is the youngest Robert Hales.

They jump, both of them, but Sean recovers his composure quickest. *What do you think we're doing?*

You've got a gun. Despite the heat, Robert is wearing a battered orange cagoule.

Duh.

Let me have a go.

Yeh, right, says Sean.

I want a go, says Robert. He steps forward. He is taller than Sean by a good six inches.

Just as he did in the bedroom, Sean lifts his arm until the gun is pointing directly at Robert's face. *No way, José.*

Daniel realises that Sean may kill Robert. He is excited by this possibility. He will be a witness to a crime. People will respect him and feel sorry for him.

Robert doesn't move. Five, maybe ten seconds. *The Good, the Bad and the Ugly.* Daniel can't tell if Robert is terrified or utterly unafraid. Finally he says, *I'm going to kill you*, not in the way kids say it to one another in the playground but in the way you say, *I'm going to the shop.* He walks away without looking back. Sean aims at him till he vanishes. The two of them listen to the fading crunch of twigs and dry leaves under his trainers. *Spastic.* Sean lets his arm slump. *Bloody spastic.* He walks up to the teddy bear and places the barrel in the centre of its forehead. Daniel thinks how similar they look, the bear and Robert, uninterested, staring straight ahead. But Sean can't be bothered to waste another bullet. *Shit.* Robert's appearance has made the adventure seem mundane. Sean throws the gun into the Gola bag. *Let's go.*

They walk back through the woods, taking the long route that loops up the hill and comes out on the far side of the scrapyard, avoiding the Roberts' house altogether. Gnats and dirty heat. Daniel has dog shit on his left shoe which he has not been able to scrape off completely.

§

His sister, Helen, was unexpectedly born breech. The cord became trapped while her head was coming out and she was deprived of oxygen. Daniel is not told about this until he is sixteen. He knows only that there is a light in her eyes which stutters briefly sometimes then comes back on. He knows only that she has trouble with numbers, counting objects, telling the time.

She will leave school at sixteen with no qualifications, living at home and working in a furniture warehouse, then in a greengrocer's. She will change doctors and get better drugs. Ethosuximide. Valproic acid. The petit mal will stop. She will be easily confused but she will be plump and blonde and pretty and people will like her instinctively. She'll meet Garry at a night club. Overweight, thirty-five, detached house, owner of a taxi firm, a big man in a small world. They will marry and it will take Daniel a long time to realise that this is a happy ending.

§

The noise is nothing more than a brief hiss followed by a clatter of foliage. Crossbow? Catapult? Then a second shot. It is the oddest thing, but Daniel will swear that he saw it before he heard it, before Sean felt it even. A pink stripe appears on the skin just above Sean's elbow. He yelps and lifts his arm. *Bastard.*

They squat on the path, hearts hammering. Sean twists his arm to inspect the damage. There is no bleeding, just a red weal, as if he had leant against the rim of a hot pan. Robert must be somewhere farther down the hill. The hole in the windscreen, the hole in the driver's body. But Daniel can see nothing without lifting his head above the undergrowth. The best plan would be to run away as fast as they can so that Robert is forced to aim between the trees at two moving targets, but Sean is taking the gun out of the bag. *I'm going to get him.*

Don't be stupid.

And what's your brilliant idea?

Another hiss, another clatter. They duck simultaneously. For a couple of seconds Sean looks frightened. Then he doesn't. *This way.* He starts to commando-crawl through a gap in the brambles.

Daniel follows him only because he doesn't want to be alone. Sean holds the gun in his hand as he crawls. Daniel thinks how easy it would be for him to pull the trigger accidentally. Cracked seed cases, dry leaves and curls of broken bark. They drag themselves between the gnarly trunks. Born and bred in a briar patch. He tries to pretend that they are in a film but he can't do it.

They are moving in the wrong direction, away from the scrapyard. And this is Robert's back garden. He will know every inch of the wood. Daniel scratches his cheek on a thorn and squeezes his eyes shut until the pain dies away so that he doesn't cry out. He touches his face. Blood on his dirty fingers.

They find themselves under a low dome of branches just big enough for them to lie stretched out, a place where an animal might sleep, perhaps. Improbably, they hear the sound of an ice-cream van, far off.

No fourth shot.

What do we do now?

We wait, says Sean.

What for?

Till it's dark.

Daniel looks at his watch. At six his mother will call Sean's flat, at seven she will ring the police. He rolls onto his back and narrows his eyelids so that the light falling from the canopy becomes a shimmer of overlapping circles in white and yellow and lime green. The smell of dog shit comes and goes. Is this is a safe place or a trap? He imagines Robert looking down at the two of them lying there under the brambles. Fish in a barrel. The way Donnie wept when his fingers snapped.

After twenty minutes the tension begins to ease. Perhaps this was what Robert intended after all, to scare them then go home and sit in front of the TV laughing. Forty minutes. Daniel hasn't had anything to drink since breakfast. He has a headache and he can feel little gluey lumps around the edge of his dry lips. They decide to run for it. They no longer believe that Robert is waiting for them, but the running will amplify the excitement of their escape and recapture a little of their injured dignity.

And this is when they hear the footsteps. A crackle, then silence, then another crackle. Someone is moving gingerly through the undergrowth nearby, trying not to be heard. Each heartbeat seems to tighten a screw at the base of Daniel's skull. Sean picks up the gun and rolls onto his stomach, elbows braced in the dirt. Crackle. Daniel pictures Robert as a native hunter. Quiver, loin-cloth, arrow in the notch, two crooked fingers holding the bow-string taut. The steps move to the right. Either he doesn't know where they are or he is circling them, choosing his direction of approach. *Come on*, says Sean to himself, turning slowly so that the gun points constantly towards the direction of the noise. *Come on*.

Daniel wants it to happen quickly. He doesn't know how much longer he can bear this before jumping up and shouting, *Here I am!* like Paul used to do during games of hide-and-seek.

Then everything goes quiet. No steps. No crackle. Midges scribble the air. The soft roar of the cataract. Sean looks genuinely frightened now.

A stick snaps behind them and they twist onto their backs just as the silhouette springs up and shuts out the dazzle of the sun. Sean fires and the gun is so close to Daniel's head that he will hear nothing for the next few minutes, just a fizz like rain on pylon wires.

He sees straightaway that it is not Robert. Then he sees nothing because he is kicked hard in the stomach and the pain consumes him. When he uncurls and opens his eyes he finds himself looking into a face. It is not a human face. It is the face of a roe deer and it is shockingly big. He tries to back away but the brambles imprison him. The deer is running on its side, wheezing and struggling in vain to get to its feet. A smell like the camel house at the zoo. Wet black eyes, the jaws working and working, the stiff little tongue poking in and out. Breath gargles through a patch of bloody fur on its neck. It scrabbles and twitches. He can't bear to look but can't make himself turn away. The expression on its face. It looks like someone turned into a deer in a fairy tale, crying out for help but unable to form the words.

Two minutes. Three. It's weakening visibly, sinking into the cold black water that lies just under the surface of all we do. That desperate hunger for more time, more light. Whenever Daniel hears the phrase *fighting for your life* this is the picture that will come back to him.

Sean hoists his leg over its body and sits on the deer's chest. He presses the end of the barrel to the side of its head and fires. *Bang . . . bang . . . bang . . . bang . . .* Each shot sending the deer's body into a brief spasm. The gun is finally empty. A few seconds of stillness then a fifth spasm. It stops moving. *Oh yes*, says Sean, letting out a long sigh, *Oh yes*, as if he has been dreaming about this moment for a long time.

Fingers of gluey blood start to crawl out from under the head. Daniel wants to cry but something inside him is blocked or broken.

Sean says, *We have to get it back.*

Back where?

To the flat.

Why?

To cook it.

Daniel has no idea what to say. A part of him still thinks of the deer as human. A part of him thinks that, in some inexplicable way, it is Robert transformed. A fly investigates one of the animal's eyes.

Sean stands up and stamps the brambles aside, snapping their stems with the heel of his trainers so they don't spring back. *We can skin it.*

He tells Daniel to return to the lay-by to fetch the pram they saw beside the rubbish bags. Daniel goes because he needs to be away from Sean and the deer. He walks past the scrapyard. He wants to bump into Robert, hoping that he will be dragged back into the previous adventure, but the curtains are still closed and the house is silent. He removes the loop of green twine and opens the clangy gate. There is a brown Mercedes in the lay-by. The driver watches him from the other side of the windscreen but Daniel cannot make out the man's face. He turns the pram over. It is an old-fashioned cartoon pram with a concertina hood and leaf-spring suspension. The rusty handle is bent, the navy upholstery is torn and two of the wheels are tyreless. He drags it back through the gate, closing it behind him.

§

It's a trick of the light, of course. Time is nothing but forks and fractures. You step off the kerb a moment later. You light a cigarette for the woman in the red dress. You turn over the exam paper and see all the questions you've revised, or none of them. Every moment a bullet dodged, every moment an opportunity missed. A firestorm of ghost lives speeding away into the dark.

Perhaps the difference is this, that he will notice, that he will come to picture things in this way when others don't, that he will remember an August afternoon when he was ten years old and feel the vertigo you feel walking away unharmed from a car crash. Or not quite unharmed, for he will come to realise that a part of himself peeled away and now exists in a parallel universe to which he has no access.

§

When they lift the deer onto the pram it farts and shits itself. It doesn't smell like the camel house now. Daniel is certain that it would be easier to drag the body but says nothing, and only when the track flattens out by the scrapyard and they are finally free of the roots and the sun-hardened ruts does the pram finally begin to roll a little.

The man is sitting against the bonnet of his Mercedes, as if he has arranged himself for a better view of the second act. He has shoulder-length black hair, a cheap blue suit and a heavy gold bracelet. Sean shuts the gate and reattaches the loop of green twine. The man lights a cigarette. *Lads*. It's all he says. The smallest of nods. No smile, no wave. He will recur in Daniel's dreams for years, sitting there at the edge of whatever else is going on. Cigarette, gold bracelet. *Lads*.

They stand at the side of the carriageway. Hot dust, hot metal. Daniel sees drivers glance at them, glance away then glance back again. *Three, two, one*. The pram is less stable at speed and less inclined to travel in a straight line and they reach the central reservation accompanied by a hiss of air brakes and the angry honk of a lorry that comes perilously close to hitting them in the fast lane.

Clumsily, they heave the deer and the pram over the barrier. This takes a good deal of time and the strip of yellow grass is not wide. *Police*, says Sean, and Daniel turns in time to see the orange stripe of a white Rover slide past, lights and siren coming on as it goes up the hill. It will turn at the roundabout and come down the other carriageway. They have a minute at most.

Now, yells Sean, and the relief Daniel feels when they bump over the kerb of the service road and heave the pram up the bank through the line of stunted trees into the park makes him whoop. *The Warrens*, says Sean, panting, and they keep their momentum up past a gaggle of rubbernecking children on the climbing frame and into the network of walled paths round the back of the estate. They stop by the peeling red lock-ups and wait. No siren. No squeal of tyres. Daniel's head pulses. He needs to lie down in the dark.

They push the pram across the parched quadrangle to Orchard Tower. An elderly lady watches them, transfixed. Polyester floral dress and varicose veins. Sean gives her a jokey salute. *Mrs. Daley*.

The double doors are easy but it takes some juggling to get

the pram and the deer into the lift and they leave a great lick of blood across the mirror that covers one of the side walls. Sean puts his finger into it and writes the word MURDER in capital letters on the glass at head height. The lift bumps to a halt, the chime goes and the doors open.

§

Later when he tells the story to people they won't understand. Why didn't he run away? His friend had a loaded gun. He will be repeatedly amazed at how poorly everyone remembers their childhoods, how they project their adult selves back into those bleached-out photographs, those sandals, those tiny chairs. As if choosing, as if deciding, as if saying *no* were simply skills you could learn, like tying your shoelaces or riding a bike. Things happened to you. If you were lucky you got an education. If you were lucky you weren't abused by the guy who ran the five-a-side. If you were very lucky you finally ended up in a place where you could say, *I'm going to study accountancy . . . I'd like to live in the countryside . . . I want to spend the rest of my life with you.*

§

It happens fast. The door opens before Sean can put his key into the lock. Dylan is standing there in dirty blue dungarees, phone pressed to one ear. He says, calmly, *Cancel that, Mike. I'll talk to you later,* and puts the phone down. He grabs a fistful of Sean's hair and swings him into the hallway so that he skids along the lino and knocks over the little phone table. He puts his foot on Sean's chest and yanks at the bag, ripping it open and breaking the strap. He takes out the gun, checks the chamber, shunts it back into place with the heel of his hand and tosses it through the open door of his room onto his bed. Sean sits up and tries to back away but Dylan grabs the collar of his T-shirt and hoists him up so that he is pressed against the wall. Daniel doesn't move, hoping that if he stands absolutely still he will remain invisible. Dylan punches Sean in the face then lets him drop to the floor. Sean rolls over and curls up and begins to weep. Daniel can see a bloody tooth by the skirting board. Dylan turns and walks towards the front door. He runs his hand slowly across the deer's flank five or six times, long, gentle strokes as if the animal is a sick child. *Bring it in.*

They wheel the pram across the living room and out onto the balcony. Dylan gives Daniel a set of keys and sends him downstairs to fetch two sheets from the back of his van. Daniel feels proud that he has been trusted to do this. He carries the sheets with their paint spatters and the crackly lumps of dried plaster back upstairs. Dylan unfolds them, spreads them out on the concrete floor and lays the deer in the centre. He takes a Stanley knife from his pocket, flips the animal onto its back and scores a deep cut from its neck to its groin. Gristle rips under the blade. He makes a second cut at ninety degrees, a crucifix across the chest, then yanks hard at one of the angles in the centre of the crucifix so that the corner of furred skin rips back a little. It looks like a wet doormat. Daniel is surprised by the lack of blood. Under the skin is a marbled membrane to which it is attached by a thick white pith. Dylan uses the knife to score the pith, pulling and scoring and pulling and scoring so that it comes gradually away.

Sean steps onto the balcony holding a bloody tea towel against his face like a mask. Daniel cannot read his expression. Turning, Daniel sees the sandy slab of the car plant rippling slightly in the heat coming off the road. A hawk hangs over the woods.

His headache is coming back, or perhaps he has simply begun to notice it again. He wanders inside and makes his way to the kitchen. There is an upturned pint mug on the drying rack. He fills it with cold water from the tap and drinks it without taking the glass from his lips.

He hears the front door open and close and Mrs. Cobb shouting, *What the bloody hell is going on?*

He goes into the living room and sits on the brown leather sofa, listening to the slippery click of the carriage clock on the mantelpiece, waiting for the pain to recede. There are framed school photographs of Sean and Dylan. There is a wall plate from Cornwall that shows a lighthouse wearing a bow tie of yellow light and three gulls, each made with a single black tick. The faintest smell of dog shit from the sole of his shoe. Sean walks down the corridor carrying a full bucket, the toilet flushes and he comes back the other way with the bucket empty.

He dozes. Twenty minutes, maybe half an hour. The sound of a saw brings him round. It takes a while to remember where he is, but his headache has gone. So strange to wake and find the day going on in your absence. He walks out onto the balcony. Dylan is cutting the deer up. The legs have been sawn off and halved, hoofs in one pile, thighs in another. Carl from next door has come round and is leaning against the balcony rail smoking a cigarette. *I'll have a word at the chippy. They've got a chest freezer out the back.* Sean is no longer holding the tea towel against his face. His left eye is half closed by the swelling and his upper lip is torn.

Get rid of that, will you? Dylan points to a yellow plastic kids' bathtub. Lungs, intestines, glossy bulbs of purple.

He and Sean take a handle each. As they are leaving Dylan holds up the severed head and says to Carl, *What do you reckon?*

Over the fireplace? But it's the bathtub that unsettles Daniel, the way it jiggles and slops with the movement of the lift. MURDER in capital letters. The inside of a human being would look like this. The dazzle of the sun blocked out. Thinking for a moment that it was Robert.

He says, *How are you?*

Sean says, *Fine.*

Some kind of connection has been broken, but it feels good, it feels like an adult way of being with another person.

They put the bathtub down and lift the lid of one of the big metal bins. Flies pour out. That wretched leathery stink. They hoist the tub to chest height as two teenage girls walk past. *Holy shit.* A brief countdown and they heave the bathtub onto the rim. The contents slither out and hit the bottom with a great slapping boom.

Upstairs the oven is on and Mrs. Cobb has put a bloody haunch into a baking tray. Carl is helping her peel potatoes with a lit cigarette in the corner of his mouth. Dylan drinks from a can of Guinness. *Come here*, he says to Sean. Sean walks over and Dylan puts an arm around him. *If you ever do anything like that again I'll fucking kill you. Understand?* Even Daniel can hear that he is really saying, *I love you.* Dylan gives Sean the half-finished can of Guinness and opens another one for himself.

Your mum rang, says Mrs. Cobb. *Wondering where you were.*

Right. He doesn't move.

Because it has nothing to do with the gun, does it? Right now, this is the moment when time fractures and forks. If he speaks, if he asks to stay, everything will be different from this point on. But he doesn't speak. Mrs. Cobb says, *Go on. Hop it, or your mum will worry.* And however many times he turns her words over in his mind he will never be able to work out whether she was being kind to his mother or cruel to him. He doesn't say goodbye. He doesn't want to risk hearing the lack of interest in their voices. He walks out of the front door, closes it quietly behind him and goes down via the stairs so that he doesn't have to see the blood.

§

Forty years later he will go to his mother's funeral. After-wards, not wanting to seem callous by heading off to a hotel, he will sleep in his old bedroom. It will make him profoundly uncomfortable, and when his father says that he wants things back to normal as soon as possible, he takes the hint with con-siderable relief and leaves his father to the comfort of his routine. The morning walk, the *Daily Mail*, pork chops on Wednesdays.

There are roadworks on the way out of town and by chance he finds himself diverted along the stretch of ring road between the flats and the woods. It comes back so vividly that he nearly brakes for the two boys running across the carriageway push-ing the pram. He slows and pulls into the lay-by, grit crunching under the tyres. A rusted oil drum half full of rainwater, a pink sofa with wedges of soiled yellow foam poking from slashes in the arms and the back. He gets out of the car and stands in the same thumping draught that comes off the lorries. Freakishly the gate is still held shut by a loop of green twine. It scares him a little. He steps through and shuts it behind him.

The scrapyard is still there, as is the Roberts' house. The cur-tains are closed. He wonders if they have been closed all these years, Robert Hales and Robert Hales and Robert Hales, the same person, growing old and dying and being reborn in the stink and the half-light.

That cathedral silence before the first shot. The stag beetle. Planks of butter-yellow light stacked among the trees.

He stoops and picks up a jagged lump of broken tarmac. He imagines throwing it through the front window, the glass crazing and falling. The loose rattle of scattering birds. Light flooding in.

A stick cracks directly behind him. He doesn't turn. It's the deer. He knows it's the deer, come again.

He can't resist. He turns slowly and finds himself looking at an old man wearing Robert's face. His father? Maybe it's Robert himself. What year is it?

The man says, *Who are you?* and for three or four seconds Daniel has absolutely no idea.

THE WOODPECKER
AND THE WOLf

Every time she wakes she is convinced for a couple of seconds that when she opens her eyes she will be looking up at the mobile of wooden animals which hung over her bed in the house in Gloucester where she spent the first seven years of her life—hippo, lion, monkey, snake, eagle. Then she opens her eyes and she sees the air vent with its halo of beige stain and the four cables running across the ceiling which Mikal has duct-taped to the panels. The air smells faintly of sweat and hot plastic and human waste. In the wall space she can hear the water pumps ticking over.

Day 219. She sits up and rubs her eyes. Her back is sore. She lowers herself to the floor and sits against the bed with outstretched legs. She holds her right foot with her left hand for ten seconds then holds her left foot with her right hand for ten seconds. She sits back and feels the knotted muscles loosen. She listens until she is certain that it's unoccupied then she steps into the corridor and goes to the toilet. She comes back to the room, takes off her pants and vest and rubs herself down with the damp orange cloth. She gets back into her pants and vest, massages Epaderm into her heels and elbows, takes her testosterone and brushes her teeth. Then she zips herself into her green worksuit and heads over to North 2 to get breakfast.

§

Suki and Arvind are sitting at the table eating granola, drinking coffee and staring at tablets. Arvind looks up. "Good morning, Clare."

She has never found Arvind attractive but he has skin so smooth and flawless it looks like suede and sometimes she wants to reach out and stroke the back of his neck. She asks what the news is from home.

"Baby girl." Arvind rotates the screen to show a picture of his sister holding a tiny, damp person in a crocheted yellow blanket. "Leyla."

"Uncle Arvind. Congratulations."

"Thank you, though it required very little effort on my part." He looks at his niece. "Nine pounds six ounces."

"Is that big?"

"I have absolutely no idea."

"That's pretty much a Thanksgiving turkey," says Suki without looking up. They are all small but Suki is the smallest by some margin, and moves so lightly on her feet that Clare sometimes catches her out of the corner of her eye and thinks there is a teenage girl here with them, which spooks her every time. Suki has black belts in judo and karate. Clare guesses that she is still in the middle of *Angels & Demons*.

"Also, there's been a coup in Guatemala," says Arvind, "and Brad Pitt is dead."

"Are you serious?"

"I'm serious."

"Overdose?"

"Cancer."

"Were we expecting this?"

"The world was, I think, unprepared," says Arvind. "Though I am not always on top of celebrity gossip."

"We should have a memorial night," says Suki, again without looking up. *"Ocean's Eleven, Fight Club, Twelve Monkeys."*

"Happy Feet Two," says Arvind. "He voiced Will the Krill according to a very comprehensive obituary I have been reading." He is looking at the little girl he will never be able to hold in his arms. He puts his hand across his mouth, riding out a lump in his throat perhaps. He turns the screen off and Leyla vanishes.

Suki finally looks up. "Have you seen Jon, by the way?"

"I've only just got up," says Clare. "Is there a problem?"

"He must be having a lie-in." Suki returns to her Dan Brown. "I'll prod him later."

Clare pours water onto some powdered apple and spreads cream cheese onto a rye cracker. She sits and stares through the scratched porthole at five thousand acres of pink rock under a washed-out, gull-grey sky. There are five or six dust devils in the distance, twenty, thirty metres tall. The Endurance impact crater, Margaritifer Sinus quadrangle. She thinks, every time, how ironic it is that they chose to name the place after Shackleton's ship, abandoned and crushed by pack ice in the Weddell Sea.

In truth she misses being en route, sealed inside a tiny metal bead on the longest string in the world, slipping through the great tide of radiation at two hundred degrees below zero. It was her reason for coming, those childhood fantasies of being at sea with Magellan or Frobisher, hunting the Northwest Passage, anchored off the Celebes, hunkering below decks while the hull rolled, a hundred cold fathoms below and nothing from the crow's nest, the way it made her feel, the belonging of not belonging, so that she was not afraid when Suki's epilepsy started, or the port-forward adjuster blew and set them spinning for two weeks, because that was the cost of stepping over the edge of the known world, and if you didn't embrace it then why were you here?

In truth, if she were writing the script they would have died during the landing, entering the atmosphere nose first, shredding the parachute, hitting the ground at a hundred, a hundred and fifty, no flames, no suffocation. Bang. Over and done with. Because what do you do when the most extraordinary thing has happened and you are still alive? You hunker down and don't complain. After all, it was one of the reasons they'd been chosen, wasn't it, their ability to accept, to be patient, to endure.

She remembers the garden in Painscastle the year before her mother went into care, those two hours of stillness and silence she needed between hoisting that tiny body into bed and returning to sleep in her own bed. Late spring, Orion setting, Cassiopeia almost gone, Jupiter with its pinprick moons, Mars rising on the great Ferris wheel of the ecliptic, the red of the iron oxide visible even at that distance. Information pouring like rain down through the dark. The desire to be somewhere else, which is never satisfied by being somewhere else, however far you go, though you have to go a very long way indeed to figure that one out.

She scoops up the morning's data. She takes it all down twice then meets up with Per in South 2 for the handover.

"Greetings, co-worker." He looks directly into her eyes for three or four seconds. "You're still sleeping badly."

"I need to ski for longer."

"Then ski for longer." Per has a birthmark on his neck precisely where the bolt would be if he were Frankenstein's Monster. His blond buzz cut has grown into a blond ponytail. In one of the early training runs there was a fire. Everyone assumed it was real, that something had gone terribly wrong. Per sealed Shona and Kurt inside a module to stop it spreading. Shona wept openly assuming she was about to die. They were gone by the end of the week. If the shit really hits the fan Clare wants Per nearby, on her side of the airlock.

"Water throughput?" says Per.

"Two hundred and five litres."

"Backups?"

"A good. B good."

"UV sterilisation?"

"We're up and running again."

"Thank God for that," Per says, "the chlorine is disgusting."

"Oxygen 21.85 percent, nitrogen 77.87, CO_2 0.045."

"Internal radiation?"

"Top 10.5 milirads, bottom 9.5."

"Humidity?"

"Twenty-three percent," says Clare. "I dropped the night temperature a couple of degrees."

"Don't want people getting too comfortable. And how is the weather out there?"

"Minus 12.2°C and rising. Winds 4 to 8 kph. Visibility between 18 and 20 km."

"So, people, it is shaping up to be a fine summer's day." Per leans back. "Enjoy your drive-time commute. Stay safe. And here is some classic Bruce Springsteen to kick off the programme, the appropriately titled 'Radio Nowhere' from 2007's *Magic* album."

§

The second crew are en route aboard the *Halcyon*, 408 days into their journey—Joe Deller, Annie Chen, Anne-Marie Harpen, Thanh Thuy, Kees Van Es. They don't seem real yet. Perhaps it's self-preservation, perhaps it's the two-way light-time of thirty minutes, perhaps it's those two weeks of radio silence when the earth was behind the sun. None of them use the word "home" anymore. It has become a fictional place, despite the daily ebb and flow of information. So here they come, these five new people, like characters walking out of a fairy-tale forest, no one knowing if they are good or evil.

§

She goes to West 1 and strips down to pants and vest. She wipes the headphones clean, puts them in and scrolls through her playlist till she finds Kylie's *Impossible Princess*. She presses play, steps onto the machine and turns the resistance up to 64.

Gravity here is 0.4 G. But after two weightless years on the *Argo* it felt like being poured onto the Wall of Death in a fairground. It seems normal now. She no longer notices the bounce in everyone's step, the thin legs, the puffy faces. But on the increasingly rare occasions when she watches a DVD she is surprised by the speed at which everyone moves, like Charlie Chaplin or the Keystone Cops. A couple of months back Suki broke her ankle tripping over a chair. They still don't know if the bone loss plateaus. They're the guinea pigs on this one. Fifteen minutes, twenty. She cheats and drops the resistance a little. The trick is not to ask why you are doing anything, the trick is simply to persist. Twenty-five, thirty. *I should be so lucky.* She is sweating heavily.

Arvind says he misses baths, the sensation of lowering yourself into ridiculously hot water. It's showers for her. One in particular keeps coming back. They were on holiday in Portugal. The name of the resort escapes her, as does the year, her poor memory being one of those disabilities which become skills in the right context. But the beach is clear in her mind, the wooden diving platform, the jellyfish like Victorian lampshades, Peter in his green Speedo. They're in the hotel room afterwards, wind moving the balcony curtains, those cool terra-cotta tiles underfoot, the tightness on her salty, almost-burnt skin. Standing naked in the falling water. What is it about that moment which calls her?

§

After lunch she goes to find Mikal. They're doing an EVA later in the day to work on the Long Array, not much more than a slow walk for a kilometre and a half carrying two titanium poles and a rock drill, but a hundred ways to die en route. On her first outing her oxygen supply failed after forty metres. She lost consciousness halfway back and Per saved her life by dragging her to the airlock.

They now have a 73-point checklist to work through before they call in Per and Jon to get suited and booted. They take their helmets out of the lockers and lay them on the table. They take our their thermal underwear and lay it on the table.

"Suki tells me Jon is not feeling well," says Mikal. "So if you're thinking of having a heart attack it might be wise to postpone it till tomorrow."

"A heart attack would be a good way to go, don't you think?" says Clare.

"Not in the immediate future, I hope."

Per and Suki are, in the best possible way, psychopaths. They have retained pretty much every piece of information they've been given and they have never been visibly tired or frightened, but Clare has absolutely no idea what is going on in their minds. She suspects, sometimes, that for long periods there is nothing going on in their minds, that they sleep like sharks, on autopilot, shutting down half their brain at a time. Arvind pays for his buoyancy with periods of darkness which he tries hard to keep from the rest of them, so that Clare holds him at a distance for fear of becoming infected, as they all do. Jon, the crew's doctor, is constantly positive, a whipper-up of good cheer, and while she enjoys playing backgammon with him or helping him swab down one of the units she is uncomfortable with his relentless need for activity, for noise, for distraction. But she can sit in a room with Mikal for hours and his silent presence puts her at ease in the way that dogs and horses once put her at ease. He has a piratical beard, bends every rule a little and treats his previous life as a deep well of entertaining stories. They have sex sometimes. She never used to like it much, one of the reasons her relationship with Peter faltered. She doesn't like it much now, but the testosterone which stops her bones turning to powder gives her discomfiting dreams unless she relieves her raised libido every now and then. Of all times this is the one she finds hardest, when they are lying together afterwards, the way he runs his hand through her hair, the way three years and three hundred million kilometres seem like a curtain she could step through.

They take out their boots. "There was a beech wood just below the sawmill," says Mikal. "It was the most astonishing place in spring. Yellow rapeseed to one side, bluebells coming up through the dead leaves." They visually check the airtight joints at the ankles, knees and pelvis, rotating each one through 360 degrees. "I was chased by a forester once. A huge man. He had a gun. It was tremendously exciting."

Suki appears in the doorway, noiselessly as always. There is a look on her face that Clare has never seen before. "You need to come."

§

"I have pain moving from my stomach down to my right iliac fossa." Jon is finding it hard to speak. "I have no appetite. I've been vomiting. I have a temperature of forty-one and I have rebound tenderness. I think it's fairly obvious without doing a white blood cell count."

"Antibiotics?" asks Per.

"I'm taking them."

"When do we have to make a decision?"

"Now would be good," says Jon.

Everyone looks at Clare. She's never done an appendectomy.

Per turns back to Jon. "Tell her everything she needs to do. Suki, get into a blue suit, sterilise West 2, put new air filters in. Arvind, set up the equipment. Mikal, we need references, photos, notes, diagrams. Jon, morphine or ketamine?"

Everyone else leaves the room and Jon and Clare are alone. He says, "Well, this is an adventure."

§

She did military medical in Florida, four years of college compacted into six months. No time for surgery. In 403 days they would be joined by Dr. Annie Chen. In the end all you could do was to rank the conceivable emergencies in order of likelihood, draw a red line where time and money and the capacity of the human brain came to an end and hope you encountered nothing on the far side.

"Sofanauts" was the word they coined, people willing to be fired into space on top of a 700-tonne firework then spend the rest of their lives playing Scrabble and cleaning toilets. You had to get pretty close to the Venn diagram to see where those two circles overlapped.

She had very little to tie her down. Her parents were dead. Three years with Peter convinced her that she did not possess a talent for intimacy. He wanted children but the rough end of her father's anger had warned her against the dangers of that particular relationship.

She had two degrees in physics and a job as a lab technician. People told her that she should be more ambitious but it didn't seem like something one could change. Less sympathetic people said that she was detached and uninterested. Then she found her niche. Vasco da Gama, Shackleton, Gagarin. Was it stupid to hope that your name might be remembered in four hundred years' time?

§

Jon lies on his back with his right arm tucked up out of the way. He is intubated and Mikal is hand-ventilating him. She stands on his right, Suki on his left, both of them masked and blue-suited. Laid out on a second table are scalpels, six retractors, a couple of clamps, an electrocauter, suture, needles, saline and antiseptic gel. Behind the instruments are two tablets, one showing images of the skin and muscles in the abdomen, the other showing the notes she made from Jon's instructions. Before he was anaesthetised Jon drew a 4 cm diagonal line on his own abdomen with a Sharpie to show her where to begin cutting. She washes the area and swabs it with green gel.

Suki's and Mikal's eyes are unreadable above their masks. Through the one porthole she can see the layered shale slopes of Mount Sharp and the featureless carbon dioxide sky. She ratchets her focus down. Be calm. Pause before every new action. Detail, detail, detail.

Mikal says, "You can do this."

She picks up a 12-blade scalpel and cuts into the abdominal wall. The blood starts to flow. Suki hooks the tube into the lower end of the wound to pump it out. Clare can see the three layers of which the flesh is composed: the outer skin, the fatty layer of Camper's fascia and below that the membranous Scarpa's fascia. She cauterises the bleeding from the bigger blood vessels. It smells like bacon frying. The heart monitor chirps. 78 bpm. Mikal squeezes and releases the clear plastic ball. She makes a second incision and refers back to the diagram. She has reached the upper layer of stomach muscle. The parallel fibres run northwest to southeast. This is where the hard part begins. She makes an incision along the fibres, pushes two clamps into the slit and uses a retractor to crank it open. She is surprised by the force she has to exert and the fact that the muscle doesn't rip. The resulting hexagonal hole is shockingly small.

Under the muscle she can see the peritoneum. She takes hold of it carefully with the Metzenbaum scissors and cuts into it making an even smaller hole. Mikal asks if she needs any help. She tells him she doesn't. She hears the snappiness in her voice. She stops and takes three long, slow breaths. Twenty-four minutes, but doing it right is more important than doing it fast.

She checks her notes. She has to find the ascending colon and the longitudinal muscles around it. She scrolls through the pictures. Nothing seems to correlate. She is going to have to move the colon around using clamps. She is unsure of how much pressure she can apply before the glossy membrane tears. Gently pinching, she moves it to the left, shifting the clamps one over the other in turn as if she is hauling on a wet rope. Then she moves to the right in the same way. She can see them now, the taenia coli. She follows them downwards and there it is. The inflammation is all too visible.

Arvind comes in, masked and blue-suited and takes over from Mikal who leaves the room.

Clare uses the rounded metal end of a clamp to guide the appendix gently up and out through the hole. She puts a clamp on the junction between the appendix and the colon, squeezing it shut until it catches on the first notch and holds, then a second clamp beside it. There is an artery in that little isthmus of flesh around which she is going to tie the sutures. She stretches her hands and fingers to loosen them. Suki gives her the first length of suture. She threads it round the neck of flesh between the clamps and ties it tight with a reef knot. She cuts the loose ends away. She ties a second suture next to it. To make absolutely sure she ties a third. Slowly she releases the clamp on the appendix side of the suture.

She hadn't thought to ask Jon what the appendix contained. Pus, presumably, but how liquid, and under what pressure? She asks Suki to soak several swabs in antiseptic gel and pack the opening to protect the peritoneal cavity. She uses a new scalpel to cut through the pinched flesh between the sutures and the clamp.

It is tougher than she expects and when it finally gives she slips and slices through one of the swabs right into the muscle.

"Fuck."

She waits and breathes. She examines the fresh wound. She hasn't punctured the peritoneum. Luckier still, the swollen appendix has come away with no leakage. She drops it into a tray then cauterises the bunched flesh where it was attached.

She releases the second clamp. The sutures hold. She is going to wait for five minutes. She wants to be absolutely certain. There is no noise except the hush and crumple of the air bag. Four minutes, four minutes thirty seconds, five minutes. She rinses the wound with saline. She pulls the two sides of the cut peritoneum together and clamps them. Suki threads a curved needle and hands it to her. She stitches, moves the clamp, stitches again and moves the clamp. When she has finished she prods the peritoneum on either side of the wound. The stitches are not tidy but they hold. She washes them with saline.

She clamps and stitches the muscle. She clamps and stitches the fasciae. She clamps and stitches the skin. She washes the wound with saline.

It has been three and a half hours.

Suki says she'll clean up and keep an eye on Jon.

Arvind says, "That was an extraordinary piece of work."

Clare steps outside, removes her gloves and lowers her mask. Mikal comes up to her and puts his arms around her. Per is standing beside them. It is the first time Mikal has shown her physical affection in front of another person. "You were heroic."

§

Jon dies the following morning. Suki has brought him some warm oatmeal and a weak coffee. He hoists himself up the bed so that he can eat and drink more easily and this must be the moment when the sutures break. He asks for Clare. Suki doesn't understand what is happening.

He tells Clare that it is his fault. He should have told them earlier that he was feeling ill. The sheet under him is red. He asks for morphine. Everyone is in the room now. Arvind, Mikal, Per. Between the pain and the growing fog there are five minutes of clarity.

Per stands up straight and sticks out his chest. "I would like to say on behalf of all of us—"

Jon says, "Oh, do fuck off."

Arvind laughs and catches himself.

Jon lies back and closes his eyes. "I want to listen to some music."

"What music?" asks Mikal.

"Bluegrass," says Jon.

He is unconscious by the time Mikal returns. Mikal puts the music on anyway. No one knows what else to do. There is nothing in the Protocol which deals with this situation. Leaving the room seems wrong, talking seems wrong, but standing quietly doing nothing makes it seem prematurely like a funeral. Suki holds Jon's hand for a while but he does not respond so she drops it again. Arvind stares out of the window so that no one can see his face. Jon dies listening to "My Lord Keeps a Record" by Carl Story and his Rambling Mountaineers.

§

Per says, "Let's concentrate on the small things."

They strip Jon's body, plug it and wrap it in the bloody sheet. Recycling is so axiomatic that Clare cannot help thinking how wasteful it is to discard an object containing so much fluid and so many calories. They lay him in the airlock ready for the morning. They don't want to be outside with night falling.

Mikal and Clare tidy Jon's room. They fold the clothes, put them away and make the bed. Clare opens Jon's Ark and takes out a crucifix of palm fronds, a fossil trilobite and a green toy Ferrari with one tyre missing. She arranges them beside Jon's little zoo of origami animals. In the bottom of the Ark she finds a dog-eared and faded photo of a young woman aged eighteen or nineteen lying naked on a bed. She is dark-skinned with shaggy coal-black hair, big breasts, utterly at ease. There is an open bottle of red wine on the carpet and the bottom of a film poster Clare cannot identify above the headboard. She puts it back in the box and they seal the room to save energy.

§

They bury Jon the following morning. They have no vehicle so Mikal and Arvind have to carry him slung between them. The EVA suits make it hard to get up after a fall so they move slowly and rest often. It takes them twenty-five minutes to reach the site a couple of hundred metres south of the base which has already been quietly earmarked as a graveyard. They return for spades. The soil is not as deep as they had hoped. They lay Jon in a shallow trough. They have been outside for more than two hours by this time. Per tells them to return to the base but they insist on completing the job, gathering stones and building a long, low cairn so that Jon's body is not uncovered by the wind. When they return they have been outside for more than five hours. They are exhausted.

Per says, "I know that this is a difficult situation but we mustn't allow emotion to undermine discipline."

Mikal and Arvind remove their suits and everyone eats lunch together.

Arvind says, "I would like to recite a poem."

Per says, "That would be acceptable. If no one has any objections."

Arvind stands up. "*Maranare tuhu mamo shyamo saman meghaba-ran tujha, megha jotajuta, raktakamalkara, rakta adharaputa . . .*"

Suki asks what the poem is.

"It is Tagore," says Arvind. He does not offer a translation or a title. Clare suspects that he is trying to show more grief than the rest of them.

Mikal tells stories about Jon, how he played noughts and crosses on the *Argo* with floating grids of rye crackers, the monitor he made to predict Suki's fits, his God-awful singing voice.

Per says, "I think it would be a good idea if we were to carry on with this afternoon's timetable as usual."

Suki says, "We have years ahead of us. Perhaps we should each of us decide how best to spend the rest of the day."

§

They write reports for Geneva and give video testimonies. They are not allowed to discuss these with one another in advance. They are given pre-prepared scripts to learn and perform for a media package. They are encouraged to edit these to make them seem more personal. They take psychological tests which have been devised for them in the event of the death of a crew member.

§

Previously when she tired of company she retired to her room. Conversely when she felt lonely she sought the others out. Now she hungers for some indefinable third option. She has become the crew doctor. She tells Mikal that she does not want to have sex. He asks if he can simply hold her. As he is doing so she wonders if she was frightened of loving Peter too much, if that was why the relationship failed. Loving someone too much, not loving someone enough. Was it possible to mistake one of those for the other?

One evening Per is absentmindedly humming "My Lord Keeps a Record" to himself as he prepares his supper. Arvind says, "What the fuck are you doing?" She has never heard Arvind be anything less than courteous. Per has no memory of where the tune comes from. Arvind calls him a robot. Per puts his hand high on Arvind's chest but not quite around his neck. He says, "This mission is more important than you or your feelings."

Clare says, "We are all upset. We just express it in different ways."

After a pause Per takes his hands off Arvind and says, "You are right, of course."

She gives Arvind diazepam, 6 mg a day with a slow taper. She makes him increase his exercise regime by 50 percent. She sees him every evening to assess his mood. He is allowed to record and receive more videos to and from his extended family in New Haven and Chennai.

Per asks to talk to her in private and says that now might

be a good moment to share with her the contents of the Kent Protocol. She says that Arvind will get better. It was a temporary aberration. She will read the Protocol if and when it becomes necessary.

Life refinds its equilibrium. Per, Mikal, Suki and Arvind take turns doing EVAs to the Long Array. Clare is no longer allowed to take part in potentially dangerous activities. Instead she measures heart rates and blood pressure and lung capacity and muscle tone and bone mass and visual acuity. She gives reaction tests and scans for tumours. She reads Neil Gaiman. She reads George R. R. Martin. Christmas comes and goes and the fact that none of them are practising Christians prevents the party atmosphere thickening to something more sombre. Arvind finishes his course of Valium and seems stable.

§

It is early February when the *Halcyon* is lost. There is a brief audio message from Anne-Marie Harpen to Geneva saying that they have detected heightened oxygen levels and will be performing a 95 percent electrical shutdown while they find the leak. Contact is never resumed. They wake the black box from Geneva. An hour after Anne-Marie's message the internal temperature rose rapidly to unsurvivable levels and remained there for seventeen minutes. There is no subsequent electrical activity anywhere on the main vessel. If anyone has managed to survive in a sealed section they will be taking their Moxin to avoid a longer, less comfortable death. There is no change of trajectory, so the ship is still heading in their direction. Nine months later, on 4 or 5 September, if it strikes the atmosphere at the right time of day they will see it burn up overhead like a shooting star.

§

They watch a video of the non-denominational services of remembrance in Geneva and Florida then perform their own more modest version. Arvind does not quote Tagore. Once more they are given pre-prepared scripts to learn for media circulation.

There is a third crew waiting to travel and another ship, the *Sparrowhawk*, ready to take them but the launch will only be authorised after a report has identified the reason for the loss of the *Halcyon* and the fault has been rectified.

The *Halcyon* was carrying more solar panels, new air filters, a range of medical supplies, a 3D printer and half a ton of ABS blocks. The five of them must now catalogue everything they possess and work out the rates at which they are allowed to consume these things. Per and Suki collate the figures. There will be no more EVAs. Daily food intake is reduced by 10 percent and the ambient temperature is lowered by three degrees. East 2 is sealed off and the dining area in North 2 is narrowed to make space for the gym equipment. She and Suki move into a single room as do Per and Mikal.

They have more time on their hands. Per exercises for three hours a day. Squats, press-ups, pull-ups. He skis sometimes while they are trying to eat a meal only a couple of metres away.

Suki learns German. Arvind, who worked in Stuttgart for seven years, carries on conversations with her as if they are both residents of a German town of his own invention called Stiller am Simssee. *"Tut mir Leid, ich bin zu spät da mein Fahrrad einen Platten hatte."*

"Komm in mein Haus. Mein Vater wird es reparieren können."

Mikal watches old thrillers, *North by Northwest, The French*

Connection, Serpico. He sits in quiet corners practising mindfulness. He says, "Are you OK, Clare? I worry about you."

Floods in Bangladesh kill over 10,000 people, though the real number will never be known. Fukushima is finally enclosed in a vast box of concrete, half above ground, half below. Over Arvind's shoulder Clare reads a headline saying "Fate of *Halcyon* Still a Mystery." She thinks of Frank Wild and his men hiding under their boats on Elephant Island eating seal and penguin while Shackleton travelled in search of help.

An alarm goes off. The internal pressure is dropping unexpectedly. They gather in North 1, seal off all the other units and reopen them in turn until they track down the leak to South 2. Per suits up with Mikal and the two of them go inside. It takes three days and five visits to locate and mend a broken valve inside a wall panel.

Arvind says, "It is not a real emergency."

She fears that he is losing his balance again. "Arvind . . ."

"It is a piece of theatre," he says, "designed to keep us on our toes."

This possibility has never occurred to her before. She would like to tell Arvind that he is being ridiculous but how can she prove it?

§

A commission sits in The Hague to discuss the fate of the *Halcyon* and hears expert testimony from a long string of physicists, engineers and systems analysts.

§

She asks Mikal for sex. She would dearly love to get drunk. She wants to take a hammer and smash things. These feelings are tangled in a knot which she can neither understand nor undo. She makes noises when Mikal is inside her. He puts a hand over her mouth so that no one hears and she bites him hard, drawing blood. She has orgasms for the first time, and in the minutes afterwards, when she floats untethered in the dark, she sees brief visions of her past life. Pear-tree blossom in the Painscastle garden, Tokyo from the air, the neat line of hair which ran down from Peter's belly button.

§

One of the transmitters fails. There is no spare capacity for personal audio and visual. Until it is mended they can communicate with their families by text only.

Mikal watches *Marathon Man*, *The Night of the Hunter*, *The Long Weekend*.

"*Es sind Sommerferien und ich bin sehr gelangweilt*," says Arvind.

"*Morgen werde ich dich zum segeln auf dem See mitnehmen*," says Suki.

He says, "The messages from my sister, they are not real."

"Arvind," says Clare, "what are you talking about?"

"They are being written by the same group of people who write our video scripts. They are amusing. Humour has never been my sister's strong suit. The news, too. I find it increasingly unconvincing. For example, we ourselves do not feature."

She urges Arvind not to say these things to Per. He touches her arm as if it is she who is having problems. "Do not worry, Clare. All is well and all manner of things shall be well."

Per does the Paris Marathon on the running machine in North 1 at precisely the same time as it is being run 300 million kilometres away. He completes the course in three hours forty-two minutes.

She is ill. She cannot identify specific symptoms but she knows that something has changed inside her body. She runs all the tests she can think of but finds nothing. She does one final check to be certain. She is pregnant. She did not think that this was possible on her drug regime. She does not tell Mikal. She falsifies her weekly obs to Geneva. She cannot have a child here but the thought of killing it is unthinkable.

§

Per asks to talk to her in private. He sits on the end of her bed. He appears calm but many minutes pass before he is able to speak. He says, "I don't know why I am doing this."

"Doing what?"

"This." He leans over and touches the wall of her unit in a way that is surprisingly tender. "Honour, pride, duty, a love of one's country, one's family, the desire to be remembered well. I no longer know what any of these things mean."

She says, "The emails from our families, Per. Are they fake?"

He does not answer for a long time.

"And the news?"

"The commission has been dissolved," he says. "They have no idea why the *Halcyon* was lost. There will be no third flight. It's too risky." He puts his hands over his nose as if he is breathing through a mask. "We are coping with the situation remarkably well according to the newspapers. We understand that money is not unlimited, that technology is not perfect, that our safety was never guaranteed. We are going nobly to our deaths."

She says, "Perhaps you should show me the Kent Protocol."

"Oh, I don't think that will be necessary."

§

They find him next morning in South 2, on all fours, his head pressed to the floor as if he is not dead, just listening to something underground.

"Moxin." Mikal hands Suki the empty blister pack.

Arvind appears behind them. "Now that I was not predicting."

Clare leads everyone to South 1 where Per has written his log-in code on the control desk with a permanent marker.

The CAPCOM's video is four weeks old. "These things are out of my hands, Per. We'll keep pressing but this may need a change of government. I'm not meant to voice an opinion but they have fucked you over. And you won't find many people in the building who think differently."

The ban on EVAs seems pointless now and no one wants the body inside so Mikal and Arvind suit up. They decide not to take it to the burial site. They do not feel about Per as they felt about Jon. Suki protests but she is unable to wield the power she inherited on Per's death. They lay him beside the hopper, into which they put the hair and nail clippings, where he cannot be seen from any of the windows.

Suki sends a report. She says that Per is dead. They know about the commission. They know they have been abandoned. CAPCOM's reply comes back in light time plus four hours.

CAPCOM releases them from all protocols and says that they

will try to provide whatever assistance is needed. There is a pause. "I'm afraid we can't tell your families."

"Fuck," says Mikal.

Clare stops the video.

"Our families will have guessed already," says Arvind.

"I don't understand," says Suki.

"Are you reassured by your frankly unconvincing emails from home?" asks Arvind. "I doubt that our families are reassured by the frankly unconvincing emails they will be getting from us."

Clare says, "I'm pregnant."

There is a long silence.

"How did that happen?" says Suki.

Mikal says, "I'm so sorry."

§

They watch *Double Indemnity*, *The Wages of Sin*, *Paan Singh Tomar*.

Mikal draws a timeline. "Let's assume there are no accidents. Let's assume consumption and depreciation continue at the present rate. This is the approximate date beyond which we will not survive. And this is the last date for a second crew to set out if it is to have a chance of reaching us in time."

Suki has a rotten tooth. Clare extracts it under local anaesthetic.

CAPCOM sends them real news again. Wildfires burn out of control in California. The Cardinals win the World Series. Everest is closed to foreign climbers.

She assumed that the desire for sex would vanish with her pregnancy but the opposite seems to be true. She is becoming a stranger to herself. When Mikal says he is not in the mood she slaps him.

Arvind says, "Do you want to keep learning German?"

Suki says, "When we get home I am going to move to Stiller am Simssee. I am going to buy a little apartment. I am going to eat stollen and walk in the mountains and read the detective novels of Friedrich Dürrenmatt."

Arvind says, "Stiller am Simssee does not exist."

"Oh," says Suki. "I misunderstood."

Mikal says, "You cannot have a child. We cannot have a child. This is insane."

Clare's nausea recedes. She plays *Skyrim* on her own and backgammon with anyone who's willing. There is a sandstorm. It is the fiercest they have experienced. It howls outside, the hard carcinogenic grains rasping against the walls. Contact with Geneva is degraded and intermittent. Then it fails completely. They cannot find a fault. It may be outside, but they cannot go outside until the dust dies down.

Mikal says, "The *Mignonette* sank en route to Sydney in 1883. The four crew members managed to escape in a lifeboat with two tins of turnips. They were seven hundred miles from land. They ate a turtle and drank their own urine but couldn't catch any rainwater. After three weeks the cabin boy Richard Parker passed into a coma. Tom Dudley and Edwin Stephens stabbed him in the neck with a penknife and ate him and drank his blood."

"Why are you telling us this?" asks Arvind.

She is woken from sleep by Jon hammering on the walls asking to be let in. He is cold and lonely. She does not tell anyone about this.

During her weekly scan Clare spots what she thinks is the beginning of a tumour in Suki's left breast.

Mikal says, "I love you."

She says, "I think you are just frightened."

"I'm frightened and I love you."

"I need you not to be frightened." Her belly is visibly swollen now.

§

After six weeks the sandstorm dies with freakish speed over a single morning. The silence for which they have been longing is unsettling, the sound of nothing and no one and nowhere. They cannot re-establish contact with Geneva. Mikal and Arvind do an EVA but can find nothing wrong with the transmitters. EVAs are energy-hungry. Each one shortens their remaining lives by eight days. They vote against a second. Unless a ship falls from the sky there will be no more contact. Mikal says, "Los Angeles may burn and we will never know."

Suki suggests that they reduce their daily calorie intake, down to a thousand for Arvind and Mikal, down to eight hundred for Clare and Suki herself.

Mikal says, "Clare is pregnant."

"So we should give up food for someone who will never be born?" says Suki.

Mikal says, "We should kill a child so that you can live a month longer?"

Arvind stands and leaves the room. Clare thinks, he is play-ing the long game, he is preserving his energy, he will last the longest.

They can smell ammonia on one another's breath.

An alarm goes off. There is a structural problem of some kind in North 2. The stresses of the storm perhaps. They do not have the strength to suit up and run ultrasound checks so they simply seal it off.

No one is exercising anymore. Suki falls again and breaks her ankle. Clare offers her as much pain relief as she wants.

She can feel the baby moving. She scans herself. It is a boy. She dares not give it a name.

They watch *Ocean's Eleven*, *The Princess Bride*, *The Bridges of Madison County*. Clare stays in another room, reading or playing games. She cannot bear to see pictures of earth.

Arvind says, "I miss the sensation of wet grass under my feet."

Clare says, "For Christ's sake, Arvind."

§

Suki takes Moxin. They reopen North 2, put her inside and reseal it.

§

There was a group of five skinny brown boys who spent every afternoon on the wooden diving platform. She and Peter ate chickpeas with cow's feet and vegetables in the café at the top of the beach.

"Eu gostaria Orangina, por favor?"

She was stung by a jellyfish on the second day and had to keep her foot in a bucket of ice for the rest of the evening. Peter told her about Atlit Yam, the oldest stone circle in the world, built circa 7000 BC, underwater near Haifa. He told her about the Hurlers on Bodmin Moor, the Merry Maidens, the Nine Ladies, the Twelve Apostles. They lay on the bed naked in the afternoon. Beams of dusty sunlight, the sound of splashing outside and tinny Brazilian pop from Jordão's cheap speakers. Then she got the phone call from the hospital saying that her mother had suffered a stroke.

§

Mikal has diarrhoea. She gives him Imodium and Dioralyte but he remains badly dehydrated. He has a headache that will not go away.

§

Neither of them has the strength to move Mikal's body.

§

Arvind says, "Death, you are no different to me than my lover with your cloud-coloured skin, and your hair a mass of dark cloud, your hands like blood-red lotus, and your lips the colour of blood." She says, "What is that?" "Tagore," he says. *"Maranare tuhu mamo.* Do you not remember?" She puts her hand on the smooth skin on the back of his neck and waits till it goes cold.

§

She has no sense of how long her labour lasts. Every time she thinks that death would be easier than this she remembers the baby and she manages to find the strength from somewhere. Jon sits on the far side of the room. His face is grey. She thinks he might be a doctor and this reassures her. She drags herself to the medicine cupboard and finds a plastic bottle of liquid morphine. She takes a sip. Not too much or the baby will die inside her and rot. Is that how it works? She knew these things once.

A contraction, then a contraction, then a contraction. It is like putting her hand into a flame, taking it out then putting it in again. She prays. She remembers that there is no one to pray to, that there is no one for hundreds of millions of kilometres, no life of any kind. The thought is a gale sweeping through the empty rooms of her head, slamming doors and smashing windows. Another contraction. If only she could let this happen to her. If only she didn't have to push.

Lights flash behind her closed eyelids, like the flashes they see at night, the remnant particles of supernovae giving up their energy to the retina. Then there is an animal on the floor and it is moving. She lifts her vest and lays it against her breast. The world vanishes and there is darkness for a period. Then she opens her eyes and expects to see the hippo and the lion and the monkey and the snake and the eagle but sees instead that she is lying in a pool of blood in the corner of a room with aluminium and plastic walls and there is a baby in her arms.

§

It is easier to think about someone else's welfare instead of her own. She wraps the baby in towels. He cries. She comforts him. She eats two portions of everything for the first five days, reducing her intake only when she can feel her strength returning. She cannot bear to eat the placenta, not yet at any rate, so she freezes it. There are more supplies now that everyone is dead.

The bodies of Mikal and Arvind are decomposing. She drags them into the corridor and seals it. She is living in a single room now.

She watches nature films. If there are no human beings it

no longer causes her pain. It is just a beautiful planet far away. Gelada monkeys eating grass in the Ethiopian highlands. Marine iguanas. A pride of lions bringing down a female elephant. When the baby will not be comforted she holds him and walks in circles until he sleeps. He looks into her eyes and holds her finger and something like a smile passes over his face. She remembers that Mikal is his father. She remembers how they ran through the beech wood below the sawmill, the bluebells coming up through the dead leaves. It seems like such a long time ago. She knows that this will not last forever. If the power fails, if the oxygen fails there is nothing she can do. There is a blister pack of Moxin on the shelf.

§

Two grad students in Seattle solve the mystery. It was a freak surge of solar wind which knocked out the oxygen sensors on the *Halcyon*. They run a simulation and run it again and run it again. Fitting a shield takes two weeks. The *Sparrowhawk* is launched a month later. Serendipitously it has to spend only thirty-six hours in orbit waiting for the best slingshot opportunity of the past two years. The journey is estimated to take fourteen months.

The launch happens only two months after the sandstorm takes out the station's transmitters.

There are six astronauts on board—Mina Lawler, Vijay Singh, Giulia Ferretti, "Bear" Jonson, Mary D. Eversley and Taylor Paul. Two months into their journey there is still no communication from Endurance. It is assumed that everyone is dead. The best-case scenario is that the station lost power and they will have to bury the bodies, clean up and fix whatever is broken. The worst-case scenario is that those bodies have been sitting inside a warm, functioning station for fifteen months.

They monitor the surges in the solar wind with some trepidation but there is no recurrence of the previous problem. Only during descent does the mission skirt the edge of disaster when one of the parachutes fails. The landing is uncomfortable but the lander remains intact.

They overshoot the station by twelve hundred metres. It is not important. They are in no rush to perform six funerals. When everything else is up and running, when they've carried out a few shorter EVAs, they will head over and take a look.

§

She is woken by a tremor passing through the rock below the station. She wonders if it is a seismic shift, or simply a hallucination. It is getting progressively harder to tell whether events are happening inside or outside her head.

In the morning there is no doubt. Through the sand-scratched window, in spite of her failing eyesight she recognises the shape instantly. She looks into the baby's face and says, "We're going to be saved." She is unable to stop herself weeping.

But no one comes, not on the first day, not on the second, not on the third. She wonders if something terrible has happened, if there is no one alive in the lander. She can think of no way of signalling to them, either physically or electronically. Ten days go by. She and the baby are weak and getting weaker. Previously he cried when she couldn't feed him enough. Now he is silent. She is looking through a milky fog that will not clear. Her joints hurt.

It is the last thing she does. She gathers the remaining solid state light sticks. She waits for darkness to fall and tapes them to the window. She can do no more. She lies down with Michael on the mattress and pulls the blanket over the two of them.

§

They run the tape again. Is it lens glare? Reflected sunlight? They wait an hour. It is still there, visible through both windows. Vijay thinks he can see a shape but it is fading in the growing daylight. They take a photograph, increase the contrast and blow it up. Mina says, "Dear God in heaven." The words HELP ME are spelled out in broken light sticks in the triangular window. Light sticks shine for two days max. Someone is alive in there.

Taylor asks Geneva to override protocol. This will be their first EVA. Bear Jonson and Mina Lawler volunteer. It takes nine hours to prepare. Before the EVA begins Bear and Mina sleep for two hours. Vijay prepares his own suit in case there is an emergency. They have three hours of daylight left.

The terrain is smooth. It takes them only thirty minutes to reach the old base. To the right they can see the rocky barrow under which Dr. Jon Forrester is buried, to the left the raking sun glinting off the titanium poles of the uncompleted Long Array. They circle the chunky double spider of units. In a recess at the rear lies a body so fiercely abraded by the sandstorm that it is now a skeleton. Taylor, Giulia, Vijay and Mary watch all of this on the headcam feeds.

Most of the windows in the base are dark and a temperature reading indicates that these units have been sealed off and depressurised. Only one unit seems to be in use. There is a low light in the window to which the now-dead glow-sticks remain attached but the sand which scoured the corpse has scoured the glass, too, and they can see very little through it. There is something which might be a body on the infrared. Afterwards both Bear and Mina will confess to an irrational conviction that whoever—or whatever—is inside is not one of the six original crew, perhaps not even human.

They return to an adjacent unit. As on all the doors there is a central crank for last-resort use. They try to turn it with the steel rod they have brought for the purpose, first Bear then Mina, but they are wary of slipping and falling or, worse, ripping one of the EVA suits. After twenty fruitless minutes Taylor says, "Just hit the thing with a damn rock." Bear does this and they hear the dull chime of the whole structure ringing. He bangs it again. The crank gives a little. He bangs it a third time, puts the rock down and they are now able to turn it with their gloved hands alone. Finally the door swings open and they step inside.

There is a body on the floor, gaunt, leathery, mummified. It is tiny with thick black hair and must therefore be Suki Camino. They close the door behind them and seal it. They power up and the overhead lights come on, so the generators are working. They check the internal pressure. They start to pump the CO_2 out and let the air in from the rest of the station. There has been no response whatsoever to their grandstand entrance. If there is anyone still alive on the far side of the second door they must be either unconscious or remaining deliberately silent. Might this be a trap of some kind?

A soft pop and the door opens.

Clare Hogg and the baby are lying on a soiled mattress. The baby is not moving, Clare is barely conscious. There was no simulation which included this scenario.

Over the intercom Taylor says, "Oh, Jesus."

Giulia says, "People, do something, OK?"

Mina ignores Taylor's instructions and removes her helmet. The air smells of urine and sweat and something dense and sugary she doesn't recognise. She takes her gloves off and picks the baby up. It is limp but warm. It is covered in its own shit and has sores and rashes all over its body. It is a boy. Bear keeps his helmet and gloves on. He rolls the woman into the recovery position. Her hair is knotty and rat-tailed. She appears unable to see clearly or understand what is being said to her. She cannot talk. She claws the air vaguely in search of her baby. There is an unopened blister pack of two Moxin on the floor, a couple of arm's lengths away from the mattress. Mina wraps the baby in a clean blanket and holds it close.

Bear finds some powdered banana. They decant their own water supplies to create a paste. The woman eats it but Mina has to remove the needle from a syringe and squirt the paste into the baby's mouth. It chokes then swallows then coughs it all up. She repeats the process.

It is too complex and dangerous to bring Clare and the baby back to the lander. Bear runs checks. The base is functioning normally despite the lack of external communications. Vijay walks twelve hundred metres carrying a bag of medical supplies. Night is falling. For the last ten minutes of the journey he is not visible from the lander. Bear finds two more corpses in one of the adjacent units. Mikal Galkin and Arvind Sangha. Judging by its appearance Mikal must be the baby's father. Vijay puts the woman and the baby on glucose and saline drips.

§

She calls them "Mikal" and "Suki" and "Per." She says that someone has taken her baby away. They say, "Here is your baby." They ask her what the baby's name is. She doesn't know. Vijay washes the baby and covers it in Epaderm. She says she wants to go and stand in the garden. They explain that there is no garden.

They say, "You are very lucky to be alive." They say, "Clare, can you tell us what happened?"

She says, "We were walking by the sawmill. There were bluebells."

She breastfeeds her baby. She refuses to let go of him. They give her beef noodles and rye bread and apple juice. She says, "I want to talk to Mikal." They say that they will explain everything once she is feeling better. Her baby cries. They say, "This is a good sign."

§

She walks to the lander. It is the hardest exercise she has ever done. The baby is strapped to her torso inside an EVA suit five sizes too large. Jon and Bear walk on either side of her, holding her upright.

§

She remembers that Mikal is dead. She remembers that she watched Arvind die lying on the floor in front of her. She remembers that Per and Jon and Suki are dead. She remembers the fire on the *Halcyon*. She listens to bluegrass. She listens to Kylie. She listens to Mozart. She has her photograph taken with the baby. Taylor says, "You're famous."

§

After three months they are well enough to travel home. The craft is tiny and fully automated. There is nothing she will have to do. She and the baby will be alone for nineteen months. It does not matter. Other people do not seem real to her.

The ascent to orbit is terrifying but short. The baby screams. They circle for a week until the heavens are aligned then three short bursts of flame set them off on their great sleigh ride through the dark.

She must exercise. She puts on her belt, straps herself down and walks on the track. Two hundred metres, five hundred, a kilometre, two. She and the baby sleep in the bulkhead where the shields are thickest to minimise the effect of radiation on the baby's tiny body. He floats in the air. He laughs. She wonders if his legs will ever develop the strength to walk. There are voices on the radio. She worries about her mind. She ate so little for so long. Has she suffered some kind of irreparable brain damage? He stares at her face, smiles in response to her smile, laughs in response to her laugh. He follows objects as they float past. She does not count time. They have the universe to themselves. The constellations are their toys. She tells him their names. Eridanus, Cepheus, Draco. He sleeps less now, eats solid food, explores constantly. She must watch him all the time to prevent him breaking or stealing things. He says, "Mamma, Mamma . . ." They eat dried pear and stollen and fish fingers. Nineteen months. It seems too short. She wishes the two of them could stay here forever on this endless silent sea.

§

They land twenty-four kilometres northwest of Baikonur. The re-entry capsule is not made for a tiny child. In the last twenty minutes of descent she sits him on her lap and straps the two of them together with loop after loop of electrical tape. He screams and struggles. They will experience 4G when they hit the ground. They've been living in microgravity for a year and a half. Already she can feel her body becoming heavy. She uses the last of the tape to fix the baby's head to her chest so that his neck doesn't snap. She can do nothing about the effect of the impact on his brain.

The noise and the vibration are now indescribable. Is something wrong? She finds it hard to believe that this is how it is meant to be. There is a double crunch, audible even above the roaring, and the craft bucks violently as the two red-hot heat shields are jettisoned and appear briefly in the tiny window before ripping away to burn up above them. There is a bang. It is like jumping from a roof and hitting concrete. She thinks they have hit the ground but it is only the parachute opening. In the final second the touchdown rockets go off under the capsule to soften the landing. Again she thinks she has hit the ground. Then they hit the ground. She blacks out.

§

When she comes round she has no idea where she is. She can hear a child crying. She doesn't understand why her arms are so heavy. The child is strapped to her chest. She wants to release him but she needs to cut the tape so as not to rip his hair out. She remembers that there is a knife in one of her trouser pockets. She twists her head to reach it but knows immediately that she has broken her neck. She gently rotates her head back to its original position.

She must lie perfectly still. The child is screaming. She says, "I'm sorry. I'm so sorry. Someone will come and help us."

But someone does not come. Out of the corner of her eye she can see a triangle of colourless sky through sooty glass. They are on land and it is daytime. That is all she knows. She can't even be sure what country she is in. After all that she has survived, after so many deaths, after the hundreds of millions of kilometres it seems possible that she may die after taking the very last step of the journey.

The child is weakening, his cries getting quieter and quieter. Perhaps he is the one who will survive. If she could give her own life in order for that to happen she would do it willingly.

And then they come. First the thundering purr of helicopters, then the rumble of the big amphibious trucks. Doors banging, footsteps and dull voices outside in Russian and English. They call her name. She is meant to have opened the hatch from the inside so they will have to cut the seals. She sees the sparkfall of oxyacetylene torches beyond the glass.

The door falls away and the smells roll in. Dust and grass and exhaust fumes—and it is this which makes her weep. There are faces above her. She holds up her hand. "Stop. My neck is broken." A plastic collar moulded for precisely this eventuality is slipped around her neck and locked into place. Someone is cutting the child free. A scoop is slid down the back of her seat and she is lifted gently out of the capsule.

The light and the noise and the sheer scale of the world are shocking. Cameras flash and radios crackle. There are so many people. The child is being carried alongside her. He is completely limp. Then she sees him scrunching his eyes against the light. He is alive. It is the gravity which is holding him down.

There are too many things around her changing too quickly. Everything inside her body feels wrong. Her head aches and spins.

She vomits. Someone wipes her with a wet cloth. The paramedics carry her up the ramp into the nearest amphibious vehicle. The scoop is locked down and the engine starts up. She reaches out and holds the child's hand.

It is strange to be travelling so slowly over this bumpy ground after the silent glide of space. People are talking to her but she doesn't have the energy to respond. They find an unmetalled road and the bumping softens. Later there is tarmac under the wheels and the low singing of the big rubber tyres. Her head is fixed in one position. She can't see a window. She can feel the weight of her tongue, her feet, her hands, her intestines. A doctor slides a needle into her arm and attaches a cannula.

The truck slows and turns into the Cosmodrome.

§

She assumes at first that she is dreaming.

"Clare . . . ?"

Even when she opens her eyes it takes some time before she trusts what she is seeing. He has a beard now, trim, black. He has put on a little weight but it gives him an authority he didn't have before.

"Peter?" He squeezes her hand. "You waited for me."

She lies in bed for two days. She eats chicken soup and scrambled egg. The nausea recedes and she is able to sit up. The child sits in a car seat with sheepskin under him to prevent him getting pressure sores. As often as she can she lifts him out and holds him under his arms and puts his feet on the floor and bounces him up and down. He seems unsure what to do with his legs.

Peter stays in Hotel Tsentralnaya in Baikonur. The shower doesn't work and the restaurant is closed.

She lifts little weights. She walks to the other side of the room and back. She eats lamb and bread. She drinks a glass of wine. She sits outside in the sun for ten minutes, for twenty minutes. The sky makes her agoraphobic. She loves wind. She loves rain. She meets journalists. They are allowed to ask only certain questions and cannot stay for longer than fifteen minutes. She has her photograph taken holding the child. He is not walking. He seems to be in pain. But he is alive and they are together and there was a time when she dared not hope for these things.

Peter comes in every day for an hour. He holds Michael in his arms. He seems unconcerned that this is another man's child. His generosity overwhelms her. She does not deserve this.

§

They fly to Moscow on a military Antonov. There are more interviews at the airport. She says, "There are some things I cannot talk about." She says, "More than anything I would like to be left alone." She says, "Death, you are no different to me than my lover with your cloud-coloured skin, and your hair a mass of dark cloud." They say, "You must understand that Miss Hogg is still very tired. I'm afraid that we must end the interview now."

She cuts her hair and dyes it blonde. She buys a summer dress. She has not worn one since she was a girl.

They fly to Munich. The child is still not walking. It will take time. They hire a silver BMW and drive south on the E52 towards Salzburg, the Bavarian Alps rising in front of them. They turn north after crossing the Inn. Cresting the hill, the lake catches her by surprise, ten kilometres of cold blue light and a flock of sails all tilted at the same angle.

A sign beside the road says STILLER AM SIMSSEE.

They drive through the centre of the town. There are cobbles and awnings. There is the Hotel Möwe am See and the Westernacher Gästehaus. A whole skinned pig hangs outside a butcher's shop. They take Rasthausstraße down to the water's edge and follow the curve of the shore. Peter pulls up outside a small block of apartments facing the water. White walls, balconies in chocolate-coloured wood and a roof like a black hat four sizes too large.

She lifts the sleeping child from his car seat and puts him over her shoulder. Peter retrieves a key from his pocket and lets them into a hallway empty except for six wooden pigeonholes of post, a vase of paper tulips and a framed sepia photograph of the lakefront at the beginning of the last century. The stairs echo under their feet. Peter takes the child. Three flights. She has to wait and get her breath back after each one.

They step into the apartment. He doesn't turn the lights on. He closes the door behind them. The darkness is almost complete. The cool air smells of beeswax and vanilla. "Stand there." She hears a triple squeak of rusty handles and hinges being turned and the shutters are swung open. It does not matter what is in the room. It is merely a frame for this extraordinary view. She walks out onto the balcony. The flotilla is spread out now, white sails tacking one by one around a yellow buoy. It flows over her, this greenery, this life, this light. Peter stands beside her holding the sleeping child. She runs her fingers over the grain of the wooden rail, every line a summer long gone. She looks beyond the lake to the mountainside forests where it was cut down fifty, a hundred, two hundred years ago.

There is something wrong with all of this but she cannot put her finger on what it might be.

Peter says, "Tomorrow afternoon we will go sailing on the lake."

BREATHE

She leaves the institute, takes the Red Line to Davis and walks back home. She stands in the empty house and feels sick in the pit of her stomach. And then it comes to her. There is nothing keeping her here anymore. She can go, just go, leave everything behind. She packs two bags, leaves the keys in the mailbox and takes a taxi to Logan where the next BA departure has a last-minute seat in club class going for a song. An omen maybe, if she believed in such things.

She nurses an espresso in Starbucks and imagines the sour little woman from Fernandez & Charles standing in the living room wondering what the fuck to do with the exercise ball and the Balinese shadow puppet and the armchairs from Crate and Barrel. On the table to her right two Mormons sit side by side, strapping farm boys in black suits, Elders Thorsted and Bell, the names on their badges as big as signs on office doors. On her left an ebony-skinned man in an intricately embroidered white djellaba is reading a book called *The New Financial Order*. There are four messages on her phone. She pops the back off, drags the SIM

card out with her fingernail and flips both phone and card into
the waste bin.

Her flight comes up and she boards. A glass of complimen-
tary champagne, pull back from the stand, a short taxi, those big
turbines kick in and she is lifted from the surface of the earth. An
hour later she is eating corn-fed chicken, wild-mushroom sauce
and baby fennel as night streams past outside. She falls into a
deep sleep where she dreams not the old dream of crashing and
burning but a new dream of cruising forever in the radiation and
the hard light and the deep cold and when she wakes they are
banking over the reservoirs of Hertfordshire on their descent into
Heathrow.

The train clatters north from Euston. The deep chime of the
familiar. Chained dogs in scrapyards, level crossings, countryside like a postcard, all her history lessons written on the landscape, Maundy money and "Ring a Ring o' Roses." She should
have called ahead. At least this way she can creep up on the place
from downwind, see what it looks like when it doesn't know she's
watching then turn round and move on if that's what feels right.

She gets out of the taxi and stands on Grace Road, looking
across the big grass triangle that sits at the centre of the estate,
tower blocks on two sides, a row of shops on the third, a playground in the centre, the kind of place which must have looked
fantastic as an architectural model before it got built and real
human beings moved in.

There is a Nisa Local, there is chip shop called the Frying
Squad. Between the two is the Bernie Cavell Advice Centre. Two
boys are doing BMX stunts on the big rock in the centre of the
pedestrian precinct which they used to call the Meteorite. She

turns left and walks past Franklin Tower, the smell from the bins still rancid in the December chill.

17 Watts Road. A shattered slate lies on the path in front of the house. It's mid-afternoon but behind the dirty glass all the curtains are closed. The bell isn't working. She raps the letter box, waits then raps it again but gets no reply. Something passes through her. Despair or relief, she can't tell. She crouches and looks through the slot. It is dark and cold in the hallway, some faint urinous scent.

"Mum . . . !" Briefly she is nine again, wearing a green duffel coat and those crappy socks which slid down under your heel inside your Wellingtons. She raps the letter box for a third time. "Hello . . . ?"

She checks that no one is watching then breaks the glass with her elbow, the way it's done in films. She reaches through the broken pane and feels a shiver of fear that someone or something is going to grab her hand from inside. She slips off the safety chain and turns the latch.

The smell is stronger in the hallway, damp, unclean. There is a fallen pagoda of post on the phone table and grey fluff packs out the angle between the carpet and the skirting board. Here and there wallpaper has come away from the damp plaster. Can she hear something moving upstairs or is it her imagination?

"Mum . . . ?"

The only light in the living room is a thin blade of weak sun that cuts between the curtains. She stops on the threshold. A body is lying on the floor. It is too small to be her mother, the clothes too ragged. She has never seen a corpse before. To her surprise what she feels, mostly, is anger, that someone has been squatting in her mother's house and that she now has to sort out the resulting mess. She covers her nose and mouth with her sleeve, walks around the room and crouches for a closer look. The woman is older than she expects. She lies on a stained mattress, knotted grey hair, dirty nails, a soiled blue cardigan and a long skirt in heavy green corduroy. Only when she recognises the skirt does she realise that she is looking at her mother.

"Oh Jesus."

She wants to run away, to pretend that she was never here, that this never happened. But she has to inform the police. She has to ring her sister. She crouches, waiting for her pulse to slow and the dizziness to pass. As she is getting to her feet, however, her mother's eyes spring open like the wooden eyes of a puppet.

"Holy fuck!" She falls backwards, catching her foot and cracking her head against the fire surround.

"Who are you?" says her mother, panicking, eyes wide.

She can't speak.

"I haven't got anything worth stealing." Her mother stops and narrows her eyes. "Do I know you?"

She has to call an ambulance but her mind has gone blank and she can't remember the emergency number in the UK.

"It's Carol, isn't it?" Her mother grips the arm of the sofa and lifts herself slowly onto her knees. "You've changed your hair." She gathers herself and stands up. "You're meant to be in America."

"I thought you were dead."

"I was asleep."

"You were on the floor." The back of her head is throbbing.

"I was on the mattress."

"It's the middle of the day."

"I have trouble with the stairs."

Dust lies thick on every horizontal surface. The framed Constable poster is propped beneath the rectangle of unbleached wallpaper where it used to hang, the glass cracked across the middle.

"I thought you hated us," says her mother. "I thought you were going to stay away forever."

This is the room where she and Robyn ate tomato soup and toast fingers in front of *Magpie* and *Ace of Wands*. This was where they played Mousetrap and threw a sheet over the coffee table to make a cave. "What happened?"

"I was asleep."

"To the house. To you."

"Your father died."

"And then what?"

There was a lime tree just beyond the back fence. It filled the side window and when the wind gusted all the leaves flipped and changed colour like a shoal of fish. The window is now covered with a sheet of plywood.

"How did you get in?" says her mother.

"Mum, when did you last have a bath?"

"I spent forty-three years looking after your father."

"I can actually smell you."

"Enough housework to last a lifetime."

"Does Robyn know about all this?"

"Then I no longer had to keep him happy. Not that I ever succeeded in keeping your father happy."

"She never said anything."

"I prefer not to go out. Everyone is so fat. They have electric signs that tell you when the next bus is coming. I should make you a cup of tea." And with that she is gone, off to make God alone knows what bacterial concoction.

Carol picks the papier-mâché giraffe from the windowsill and blows the dust off. She can still feel the dry warmth of Miss Calloway's hands wrapped around her own as they shaped the coathanger skeleton with the red pliers, coffee and biscuits on her breath from the staffroom at break. "Come on, squeeze."

§

She asks the woman behind the till in the Nisa for the number of a local taxi firm and rings from a call box. Sitting on a bench waiting for the cab she remembers the street party they held to celebrate the wedding of Charles and Diana in July of 1981, everyone getting drunk and dancing to Kim Wilde and the Specials on a crappy PA in the bus shelter. *This town . . . is coming like a ghost town.*

There were trestle tables down the centre of Maillard Road but no timetable beyond a rendition of "God Save the Queen" and a half-hearted speech by a local councillor which was rapidly drowned out by catcalls. The atmosphere became rowdier as the day went on, the older people dispersing around nightfall when the air of carnival turned sinister. She remembers a woman sitting on the grass and weeping openly. She remembers Yamin's terrifying older brother having sex with Tracey Hollywood on the roundabout while his mates whooped and spun it as fast as they could. She remembers the Sheehan twins firing rockets across the field until the police arrived, then starting up again when they left. For months afterwards you would find little plastic Union Jacks and lager cans and serviettes bearing pictures of the royal couple wedged into the nettles at the edge of the football pitch and stuck behind the chicken-wire fence around Leadbitter's Bakery.

She remembers how Helen Weller's brother jumped from a

seventh-floor balcony in Cavendish Tower one Christmas while high on mushrooms, equipped only with a Spider-Man bedsheet. She remembers Cacharel and strawberry Nesquik and Boney M singing "Ra Ra Rasputin." She remembers how her father would stand at the front window staring out on all of this and say, *Look on my works, ye mighty, and despair.* Only many years later did she realise that he hadn't made the phrase up himself, though whether he was pretending to be Shelley or Ozymandias she still doesn't know.

§

Robyn is taking wet washing from the machine. The dryer churns and rumbles. Through the half-opened concertina doors Carol can see the children watching *Futurama.* Fergal, Clare and Libby. She can never remember which girl is which. There are crayon pictures in cheap clip frames. There are five tennis rackets and a space hopper and a dead rubber plant and two cats. The clutter makes Carol feel ill. "Jesus, Robyn, how did you let it happen?"

"I didn't let anything happen."

"I'm pretty certain she'd wet herself."

"So you got her undressed and put her into the bath and helped her into some clean clothes?"

Robyn has put on two stone at least. She seems fuzzier, less distinct.

"Six years. Shit, Carol. Why didn't you tell us you were coming?"

"She's my mother, too."

"Christmas cards, the odd email." Robyn slams the washing-machine door and hefts the laundry basket onto a chair.

"Let's not do this."

"Do what? Draw attention to the fact that you waltzed off into the sunset?"

"Why didn't you tell me?"

"You never asked."

"Asked what? 'Has Mum gone crazy?'"

"She's not crazy and you never asked about anything."

The argument is unexpectedly satisfying, like getting a ruler under a plaster and scratching the itchy, unwashed flesh. "This is not about scoring points. This is about our mother who is sleeping on the floor in a house full of shit."

"You didn't come back when Dad was dying."

"We were in Minnesota. We were in the middle of nowhere. I didn't get your message till we got back to Boston. You know that."

"You didn't come to his funeral."

Carol knows she should let it go. Her life has exceeded Robyn's in so many ways that her sister deserves this small moral victory, but it niggles, because the story is true. She remembers it so clearly. There were eagles above the lake and chipmunks skittering over the roof of the cabin. Every room smelt of cedar. Down at the lakeside a red boat was roped to a wooden quay. She can still hear the putter of the outboard and the slap of waves against the aluminium hull. "How often does she get out?"

"I pop in on Tuesdays and Thursdays after work and do her a Sainsbury's shop on Saturday morning."

"So she never goes out?"

"I make sure she doesn't starve to death." Robyn looks at her for a long moment. "How's Aysha, Carol?"

How can Robyn tell? This X-ray vision, her ability to home in on a weakness. Is it being a mother, spending your life servicing other people's needs? "Aysha's fine. As far as I know."

Robyn nods but doesn't offer any sisterly consolation. "Secondaries in his lungs and bone marrow. They sewed him up and sent him to the hospice."

"I know."

"No, Carol. You don't know." Robyn picks out three pairs of socks and drapes them over the radiator below the window. "He collapsed in the bathroom, his trousers round his ankles."

"You don't need to do this."

"The doctor was amazed he'd managed to keep it hidden for so long." She takes a deep breath. "I've always pictured you sitting in the corner of the kitchen with your hands over your ears while the phone rings and rings and rings." The dining table is covered in half-made Christmas cards, glitter glue and safety scissors and cardboard Santas. "Sometimes people need you," says Robyn. "It might be inconvenient and unpleasant but you just do it."

§

She books into the Premier Inn and eats a sub-standard lasagne. Her body is still on Eastern Standard Time so she sits in her tiny room and tries to read the Sarah Waters she bought at the airport but finds herself thinking instead about her father's last days, that short steep slope from diagnosis to death.

Lake Toba in Sumatra used to be a volcano. When it erupted 70,000 years ago the planet was plunged into winter for a decade and human beings nearly died out. The meteorite that killed the dinosaurs was only six miles across. The flu epidemic at the end of the First World War killed 5 percent of the world's population. Some fathers told their little girls about Goldilocks and Jack and the Beanstalk, but what use were stories? These were facts. We were hanging on by the skin of our teeth and there was nowhere else to go in spite of the messages you might have picked up from *Star Trek* and *Doctor Who*. She remembers Robyn weeping and running from the room.

He left school at sixteen then spent thirty years building and decorating. Damp rot, loft conversions, engineered wood flooring. He liked poetry that rhymed and novels with plots and pop science with no maths. He hated politicians and refused to watch television. He said, "Your mother and your sister believe the world's problems could be solved if people were polite to one another."

Which is why he didn't want her to leave, of course. He was terrified that she'd get far enough away to look back and see how small he was, a bullying, bar-room philosopher not brave enough to go back to college for fear he might get into an argument with people who knew more than he did.

Pancreatic cancer at fifty-seven. "All that anger. It turns on you in the end," was Aysha's posthumous diagnosis and for once Carol was tempted to agree with what she'd normally dismiss as hippy bullshit.

Sometimes, on the edge of sleep, when worlds overlap, she slips back forty years and sees the sun-shaped, bronze-effect wall clock over the fireplace and feels the warmth of brushed cotton pyjamas straight from the airing cupboard and her heart goes over a humpbacked bridge. Then she remembers the smell of fried food and the small-mindedness and her desperation to be gone.

She presses her forehead against the cold glass of the hotel window and looks down into the car park where rain is pouring through cones of orange light below the streetlamps. She is back in one of the distant outposts of the empire, roughnecks and strange gods and the trade routes petering out.

She abandoned her mother. That hideous house. She has to make amends somehow.

She climbs into bed and floats for eight hours in a great darkness lit every so often by bright little dreams in which Aysha looms large. The dimples at the base of her spine, the oniony sweat which Carol hated then found intoxicating then hated once more, the way she held Carol's wrists a little too tight when they were making love.

They met at an alumni fund-raiser about which she remembered very little apart from the short, muscular woman with four silver rings in the rim of her ear and a tight white T-shirt who materialised in front of her with a tray of canapés and a scowl, after which all other details of the evening were burned away.

She had the air of someone walking coolly away from an explosion, all shoulder roll and flames in the background. A brief marriage to the alcoholic Tyler. RIP, thank God. Three years on the USS *John C. Stennis*—seaman recruit E-1, culinary specialist, honourable discharge. A mother who spoke in actual tongues at a Baptist church in Oklahoma. Somewhere in the background, the Choctaw Trail of Tears, the Irish potato famine and the slave ports of Senegambia if Aysha's account of her heritage was to be believed, which it probably wasn't, though she had the hardscrabble mongrel look. And if the powers that be had tried to wipe out your history you probably deserved to rewrite some of it yourself. She was self-educated, with more enthusiasm than focus. Evening classes in philosophy, Dan Brown and Andrea Dworkin actually touching on the bookshelf, a box set of Carl Sagan's *Cosmos*.

Two months later they were in the Hotel de la Bretonnerie in

the Marais, Aysha's first time outside the States unprotected by
fighter aircraft. Aysha had gone sufficiently native to swap Marl-
boro for Gitanes but she was sticking to the Diet Coke. They were
sitting outside a little café near the Musée Carnavalet.

Aysha said, "Thank you."

"You don't owe me anything," said Carol.

"Hey, lover." Aysha held her eye. "Loosen up."

§

The following morning she hires a Renault Clio and drives
to the house via B&Q and Sainsbury's. Her mother is awake but
doesn't recognise Carol at first and seems to have forgotten their
meeting of the previous day, but perhaps the back foot is a good
place for her to be on this particular morning. Carol dumps her
suitcases in the hall, turns the heating on and bleeds the radiators
with the little brass key which, thirty years on, still lies in the
basket on top of the fridge. The stinky hiss of the long-trapped
air, the oily water clanking and gurgling its way up through the
house.

"What are you doing?" asks her mother.

"Making you a little warmer."

She rings a glazier for the broken window.

"I've changed my mind," says her mother. "I don't like you
being here."

"Trust me." She can't bring herself to touch the dirty cardigan. "It's going to be OK."

The noises are coming from the built-in cupboard in the bedroom she and Robyn once shared. Scratching, cooing. She shuts
the landing door, opens the windows and arms herself with a
broom. When she pulls the handle back they explode into the

room, filling the air with wings and claws and machine-gun clatter. She covers her face but one of them still gashes her neck in
passing. She swings the broom. "Fuck . . . !" They bang against
the dirty glass. One finds the open window, then another. She hits
a third and it spins on the ground, its wing broken. She throws
a pillow over it, stamps on the pillow till it stops moving then
pushes pillow and bird out of the window into the garden.

She boards up the hole in the wall where they have scratched
their way in, takes two dead birds to the bin outside then stands
in the silence and the fresh air, waiting for the adrenaline to ebb.

Back inside, the radiators are hot and the house is drying out,
clicking and creaking like a galleon adjusting to a new wind. A
damp jungle smell hangs in the air. Plaster, paper, wood, steam,
fungus.

"This is my home," her mother says. "You cannot do this."

"You'll get an infection," says Carol. "You'll get hypothermia.
You'll have a fall. And I don't want to explain to a doctor why I
did nothing to stop it happening."

She puts the curtains into the washing machine. She drags a
damp mattress down the stairs and out onto the front lawn. Half
the slats of the bed are broken so she takes it apart and dumps
it on top of the mattress. She has momentum now. The carpet
is mossy and green near the external wall so she pulls it up and
cuts it into squares with blunt scissors. The underlay is powdery
and makes her cough and coats her sweaty hands with a brown
film. She levers up the wooden tack strips using a claw hammer.
She adds everything to the growing pile outside. She sweeps and
hoovers till the bare boards are clean, then takes the curtains out
of the washing machine and hangs them over the banisters to dry.

She sponges the surface of the dining table and they eat lunch together on it, a steak-and-ale puff-pastry pie and a microwaved bag of pre-cut vegetables. Her mother's anger has melted away. The lunchtime TV news is on in the background. *"Who Wants to Be This* and *Get Me Out of That,"* says her mother. "All those women with plastic faces. Terrorists and paedophiles. We called it 'interfering with children.' Frank, who worked in Everley's, the shoe shop, he was one. I'm certain of that." She stares into her plate for a long time. "A woman drowned herself in the canal last month. That little bridge on Jerusalem Street? Jackie Bolton. It was in the paper. You were at school with her daughter. Milly, I think her name was." Carol has no memory of a Milly. "I'd go out more if I still lived in the countryside. There was a flagpole by the pond in the centre of the village. They put it up for the coronation. Your uncle Jack climbed all the way to the top and fell off and broke his collarbone."

Carol must have heard the story twenty times. It is oddly comforting.

Her mother leans over and takes Carol's hand. "I thought I might never see you again."

Her skin has a sticky patina, like an old leather glove. "We need to get you into the bath."

She is compliant until halfway up the stairs when she looks through the banisters and sees the uncarpeted boards in the bedroom. "You're selling the house."

"Don't be ridiculous." Carol laughs. "It's not mine to sell." She doesn't say how little she thinks it would fetch, in this state, on this road.

"That's why Robyn hates you being here."

"Jesus Christ, Mum." Carol is surprised by how angry she feels. "I could be in California, I could be working, but I'm stuck here on a shitty estate in the middle of nowhere trying to turn this dump back into a house before it kills you."

"You thieving little . . ." She slaps Carol's face with her free hand, loses her footing and for a second she is falling backwards down the stairs until Carol grabs her and hauls her upright.

"Shit." Carol's heart is hammering. In her mind's eye her mother is lying folded and broken by the front door. She loosens her grip on the bony wrist. "Mum . . . ?"

Her mother doesn't reply. She is suddenly blank and distant. Carol should take her downstairs and sit her on the sofa but she might not get this chance again. She puts her hands on her mother's arms and guides her gently up the last few steps.

She removes her mother's shoes and socks. She peels off the soiled blue cardigan and unzips the dirty green corduroy skirt. Both are heavily stained and patched with compacted food. She takes off her mother's blouse, unclips the grey bra and kicks all the clothing into the corner of the room. Her mother's skin is busy with blotches and lesions in winey purples and toffee browns, the soft machinery of veins and tendons visible under the skin where it is stretched thin around her neck, at her elbows, above her breasts. The smell is rich and heady. Carol tries to imagine that she is dealing with an animal. She takes off her mother's slip and knickers, perches her on the rim of the bath, lifts her legs in one by one then lowers her mother into the hot, soapy water. She flips the corduroy skirt over the pile of discarded clothing so she can't see the brown streaks on the knickers then sits on the toilet seat. She'll bin them later. "Hey. We did it."

Her mother is silent for a long time. Then she says, "Mum filled a tin bath once a week. Dad got it first, then Delia, then me." She is staring at something way beyond the wall of dirty white tiles. "There was a sampler over the dining table. Gran made it when she was a girl. 'I saw an angel come down from heaven, having the key of the bottomless pit and a great chain in his hand.' The angel locks the dragon in a pit for a thousand years. After that he must be 'loosed a little season.'" She looks at Carol and smiles for the first time since she arrived. "Are you going to wash my hair?"

§

Carol makes them each a mug of coffee. Now that her mother is clean the room looks even more squalid. Old birthday cards, a china bulldog with a missing leg, mould in the ceiling corners, one of those houses cleared out post-mortem by operatives in boiler suits and paper masks.

They hear the click and twist of a key in the front door. Robyn is in the hallway. "There's a pile of stuff outside."

"I know."

She steps into the living room and looks around. "What the hell are you doing, Carol?"

"Something you should have done a long time ago."

"You can't just ride in here like the fucking cavalry." Robyn silently mouths the word *fucking*.

"What's going on?" says her mother.

"There were pigeons in the bedroom," says Carol.

"How long are you staying?" asks Robyn. "A week? Two weeks?"

"Carol?" says her mother. "What are you two arguing about?"

"Jesus," says Robyn. "Fucking up your life doesn't mean you can take over someone else's instead." This time she says the word out loud.

"Carol gave me a bath," says her mother.

"Did you hurt her?"

It is too stupid a question to answer.

"Aysha rang me." Robyn holds her eye for a long time. "Sounds like you left a trail of destruction in your wake."

Carol assumes at first that she has misheard. Aysha talking to Robyn is inconceivable.

"She wanted to check you hadn't killed yourself or been sectioned. I'm giving you the highlights. Some of the other stuff you probably don't want to hear."

"How did she get your number?" asks Carol.

"I presumed you'd given it to her in case of emergencies. Her being your partner."

There is something barbed about the word *partner* but Carol isn't sure who or what is being mocked.

"We'd have come to the wedding," says Robyn. "I like weddings. I like America."

"What are you both talking about?" says her mother.

"I'm taking Mum out for dinner," says Carol, though the thought had not occurred to her until that moment.

Robyn stands close enough so that their mother can't hear. "She's not a toy, Carol. You can't do this. You just can't."

Then she is gone.

§

"There's too much going on."

Carol looks around the half-empty Pizza Express.

"Too much noise," says her mother. "Too many people."

There is a low buzz of conversation, some cutlery-clatter. Rod Stewart is singing "Ruby Tuesday" faintly from the speaker above their heads. She rubs her mother's arm. "I'm here and you're safe." She wonders if her sister's apparent care disguises something more sinister, her mother's supposed fear of the outside world a fiction Robyn uses to keep her in the house. But her mother is becoming increasingly agitated and when the food arrives she says, "I really don't feel very well."

"Come on. That pasta looks fantastic. When was the last time you had a treat?"

Her mother stands up, knocking a water glass to the floor where it shatters. Carol grabs her mother's arm but there is no way she can hang on to it without making the scene look ugly. She lets her mother go, puts thirty pounds on the table, runs for the door and finds her sitting at a bus stop, crying and saying, "Why did you bring me here? I want to go home."

When they pull up outside the house her mother says, "I don't want you to come inside."

She could throw her bags into the car and go, to London, to Edinburgh, to anywhere in the world, leaving her mother to live the narrow and grubby life to which she has become addicted. But the phrase *anywhere in the world* gives her that queasy shiver she's been experiencing on and off since Aysha left, the sudden conviction that everything is fake, the fear that she could step through any of these doors and find herself on some blasted heath with night coming down, the world nothing more than a load of plywood flats collapsing behind her. "I'm staying. I don't want to leave you on your own."

"One night."

§

She lies in a sleeping bag on the blow-up mattress, orange streetlight bleeding through the cheap curtains, sirens in the distance. It is thirty years since she last slept in this room. For a brief moment those intervening years seem like nothing more than a vivid daydream of escape. She'd got into Cambridge to read Natural Sciences, driven in equal parts by a fascination with the subject and a desperation to put as much distance as possible between herself and this place. A doctorate at Imperial and a postdoc in Adelaide. Jobs in Heidelberg, Stockholm . . . working her way slowly up the ladder towards Full Professor. Four years max in any one country had been the rule. Out of restlessness, partly, though it was true that she ruffled feathers, and ruffled feathers were easier to live with if they were on a continent where you no longer lived.

She is not a team player, so she has been told on more than one occasion, usually by men who were quite happy to stab someone else in the back so long as the victim wasn't a member of whatever unspoken brotherhood they all belonged to. But she has run successful groups and the grants have followed her and in the end the world doesn't give a damn about a few cuts and bruises if it gets a firmer grip on ageing or diabetes, or a clearer picture of how one cell swallowed another and ended up flying to the moon.

Boston was her fourth position as a group leader, running a lab working on the mammalian target of rapamycin complex. Two years in, however, Paul Bachman became the institute's new director and everything started to turn sour. He brought with him a blank cheque from Khalid bin Mahfouz and instead of supporting the existing faculty went on a global hiring spree. Enter the Golden Boys who deigned sometimes to attend faculty meetings or listen to sub-stellar visiting academics but only as a favour. Paul himself had a house in Bar Harbor and a yacht called *Emmeline* and a younger wife with a breathtakingly low IQ. Feeling at home wasn't Carol's strong suit but under the new dispensation she started to feel like a junior member of the golf club.

In other circumstances she'd have put out feelers, quietly letting colleagues elsewhere know that she had itchy feet. But she'd just met Aysha and, to her astonishment, they were sharing a house, so she knuckled down and put up with the Cinderella treatment.

Eighteen months later, out of nowhere, Aysha said she wanted to get married. Because that's what loving someone meant, apparently, gathering your families and friends from the four corners of the globe, dressing up, making public vows, getting a signed certificate. Like you hadn't proved it already by putting up with the subterfuge and the vilification. Carol didn't understand. The straight world shut you out for two thousand years, the door opened a crack and you were meant to run in and curl up by the fire like grateful dogs. What was wrong with being an outsider? Why this desperate urge to belong to a world which had rejected you?

A year later she and Aysha were no longer sharing a house because . . . the truth was that she was still not entirely sure. It was the kind of puzzle there was no point trying to solve, the kind of puzzle you didn't have to solve if you sloughed off all the human mess every few years, trimmed your life down to a few suitcases and headed off for a new skyline, new food, a new language.

Two months of panic and claustrophobia came to an end when Daniel Seghatchian from Berkeley threw her a lifeline, asking if she'd come over and give a chalk talk, meet the faculty, meet the postdocs. Just getting off the plane in California was a relief. Space and sunlight and opportunity. The Q&As were tough but they felt like the respectful aggression meted out to a worthy opponent and by the end of three days the position seemed pretty much in the bag.

She wonders now if the whole thing had been a trap of some kind. Is that possible? Or was it merely her blindness to the allegiances and loyalties and lines of communication upon which others built whole careers?

Her first morning back in Boston she was summoned by Paul who asked what she had against the institute. He didn't explain how he'd heard the news so quickly. Only later did she realise that he wasn't asking her what they could do to persuade her to stay. He was giving her enough rope to hang herself. He listened to her diatribe and if she had been a little less exhausted by three days of non-stop thinking she might have asked herself why he seemed untroubled, pleased even. He waited for her to finish then leaned back in his chair and said, "We'll miss you, Carol." And only walking away from his office, thinking back to this obvious lie, did she wonder what unseen wheels were turning.

Three days later she got a call from Daniel Seghatchian saying that there was a problem with funding.

"Three minutes of grovelling," Suzanne said, sitting in her office that lunchtime. "You won't really mean it. Everyone else will know you don't really mean it. Paul will know you don't really mean it. Or, shit, maybe you will mean it. Either way, you go through a little ceremony of obeisance. Kneel before the king. Ask for a pardon. He loves all that stuff."

Why had that seemed such an impossible thing to do?

After talking to Suzanne she went to the regular meeting with her three postdocs working on the PKCα project. They were in the room that looked onto the little quadrangle with the faux-Japanese garden. Minimal concrete benches, rectangular pond, lilac and callery pear, wind roughening the surface of the water. She was finding it hard to concentrate on what was being said. She was thinking about the last walk she took on Head of the Meadow Beach in Provincetown with Aysha. She was thinking about the humpbacks out on the Stellwagen Bank. Three thousand miles a year, permanent night at forty fathoms, cruising like barrage balloons above the undersea ranges.

Suddenly the room was full of water. Shafts of sunlight hung like white needles from the surface high above her head. Darkness under her feet, darkness all around. Ivan was talking but his voice was tinny and unreal as if he were on a radio link from a long way away. "Breathe," he was saying. "You have to breathe." But she couldn't breathe because if she opened her mouth the water would rush in and flood her lungs.

§

Finally, despite these churning thoughts she passes into shallow sleep until she comes round just after three on the tail end of a scratchy, anxious dream in which she hears someone entering the house. Unable to sleep without reassuring herself she gets out of bed and goes downstairs to find the living room empty and her mother gone. She runs into the street but it is silent and still. She puts her shoes on, checks the garden then jogs once round the estate's central triangle calling, "Mum . . . ? Mum . . . ?" as if her mother is a lost dog.

A pack of hooded teenage boys cycle past, slowing to examine her, then sweeping silently onward. She comes to a halt at the junction of Eddar and Grace Roads where the taxi dropped her off forty-eight hours ago. A scatter of lights still burn in Cavendish and Franklin Towers like the open doors in two black Advent calendars. The cherry-red wing tip of a plane flashes slowly across the dirty, starless sky. A dog is barking somewhere. *Yap . . . yap . . . yap . . .* It is a couple of degrees above freezing, not a good night for an old woman to be outside.

She returns to the house and as she puts the key into the lock she remembers her mother's story of Jackie Bolton drowning herself in the canal. She puts the key back into her pocket and starts to run. Harrow Road, Eliza Road. A milk float buzzes and tinkles to a halt on Greener Crescent. She is flying, the surface of the world millpond-smooth while everyone sleeps. A fox trots casually out of a gateway and watches her, unfazed. Jerusalem Road. She stops on the little bridge and looks up and down the oily ribbon of stagnant water. Nothing. "Shitting shit." She walks down the steps onto the gravelled towpath and sees her mother standing on the little strip of weeds and rubble on the far side of the canal. It is like seeing a ghost. The blankness of her mother's stare, the black water separating them.

"Don't move."

She runs down the towpath to a decayed cantilever footbridge. She heaves on the blocky, counterweighted arm and it comes free of the ground, the span bumping down onto the far side of the little bottleneck in the stream. She steps gingerly across the mossy slats, squeezes round a fence of corrugated iron and kicks aside an angry swirl of barbed wire.

She comes to a halt a little way away, not wanting to wake her mother abruptly. "Mum . . . ?"

Her mother turns and narrows her eyes. "You've always hated me."

"Mum, it's Carol."

"I know exactly who you are." It is a voice Carol has not heard before. "But I look at you and all I see is your father."

Her mother is tiny and cold and she is wearing a thick skirt and a heavy jumper which would become rapidly waterlogged. How long would it take? And who would know? The thought passes through her mind and is gone.

Her mother's glare holds firm for several seconds then her face crumples and she begins to cry. Carol takes her hand. "Let's get you home."

§

The registrar says they are keeping her in overnight. Carol leaves a message for Robyn. On the ward her mother is unconscious so she drinks a styrofoam cup of bitter coffee in the hospital café, doing the quick crossword in *The Times* to distract herself from something gathering at the edge of her imagination. Whales cruising in the dark, right now, just round the corner of the world. The sheer size of the ocean, crashed planes and sunken ships lost until the earth's end. Serpentine vents where everything began. Images from a magazine article she'd read years ago of the *Trieste* six miles down in the Mariana Trench, steel crying under the pressure, a ton of water on every postage stamp of metal.

Robyn sits down opposite her.

"She walked out of the house in the middle of the night."

"Sweet Jesus, Carol. You've only been here two days."

She stops herself saying, "It wasn't my fault," because it probably is, isn't it? She can see that now.

"You're just like Dad. You think everyone else is an idiot."

"She's going to be OK."

"Really?"

"She had a shock. She's exhausted."

"You can't just decide how you want things to be, Carol. That's not how the world works." She sounds more exasperated than angry, as if Carol is a tiresome child. "Some people's minds are very fragile."

§

The doctor is plump and keen and seems more like a schoolboy prodigy than a medical professional. "Dr. Ahluwalia." He shakes their hands in turn. "I will try to be quick and painless." He takes a pencil from his pocket and asks Carol's mother if she knows what it is.

She looks at Carol and Robyn as if she suspects the doctor of being out of his mind.

"Humour me," says Dr. Ahluwalia.

"It's a pencil," says her mother.

"That is excellent." He repockets the pencil. "I'm going to say three words. I want you to repeat them after me and to remember them."

"OK."

"Apple. Car. Fork."

"Apple. Car. Fork."

"Seven times nine?"

"My goodness, I was never any good at mental arithmetic."

"Fair enough," says Dr. Ahluwalia, laughing gently along with her.

Carol can see her mother warming to this man and is suddenly worried that she can't see the trap which is being laid for her. Her mother tells the doctor the date and her address. "But you'll have to ask my daughter for the phone number. I don't ring myself very often."

Dr. Ahluwalia asks her mother if she can repeat the phrase "Do as you would be done by."

"Mrs. Doasyouwouldbedoneby." Her mother smiles, the way she smiled in the bath. "I haven't heard that name for a long time." She drifts away with the memory.

"Mum . . . ?"

Dr. Ahluwalia glances at Carol and raises an eyebrow, the mildest of rebukes.

"Mrs. Doasyouwouldbedoneby," says her mother, "and Mrs. Bedonebyasyoudid."

Dr. Ahluwalia asks her mother if she can make up a sentence. "About anything."

"It's from *The Water Babies*," says her mother. "We read it at school. Ellie is very well-to-do and Tom is a chimney sweep." She closes her eyes. " 'Meanwhile, do you learn your lessons, and thank God that you have plenty of cold water to wash in; and wash in it too, like a true Englishman.' " She is happy, the bright pupil who had pleased a favourite teacher.

"Excellent." Dr. Ahluwalia takes a notepad from his pocket and draws a pentagon on the top sheet. He tears it off and hands it to her mother. Every page is inscribed with the words *Wellbutrin—*

First Line Treatment of Depression. "I wonder if you could copy that shape for me."

She seems unaware of how little resemblance her battered star bears to its original but Dr. Ahluwalia says, "Lovely," using the same bright tone. "Now, I wonder if you can tell me those three objects whose names I asked you to remember."

Her mother closes her eyes for a second time and says, slowly and confidently, "Fire . . . clock . . . candle . . ."

§

The empty house scares her. Carol tries reading but her eyes keep sliding off the page. She needs something trashy and more-ish on the television but she can't bring herself to sit in a room surrounded by so much crap so she starts cleaning and tidying and it is the sedative of physical work that finally comforts her. She ties the old newspapers in bundles and puts them outside the front door. She stands the mattress against a radiator in the hall to air and dry. She puts the cushion covers on a wool cycle and dusts and hoovers. She cleans the windows. She rehangs the Constable poster and puts a new bulb into the standard lamp.

She finishes her work long after midnight then goes upstairs and falls into a long blank sleep which is broken by a phone call from Robyn at ten the following morning saying that she and John will bring their mother home from hospital later in the day.

She digs her trainers from the bottom of her suitcase and puts on the rest of her running gear. She drives out to Henshall, parks by the Bellmakers Arms and runs out of the village onto the old sheep road where their father sometimes took them to fly the kite when they were little. It's good to be outside under a big sky in clear, bright air away from that godforsaken estate, the effort and the rhythm hammering her thoughts into something small and simple. Twenty minutes later she is standing in the centre of the stone circle, just like she and Robyn did when they were girls, hoping desperately for a sign of some kind. And this time something happens. It may be nothing more than a dimming in the light, but she feels suddenly exposed and vulnerable. It's not real, she knows that, just some trait selected thousands of years ago, the memory of being prey coded into the genome, but she runs back fast, a sense of something malign at her heels the whole way, and she doesn't feel safe until she gets into the car and turns the radio on.

§

She paces the living room, a knot tightening in the base of her stomach. She dreads her mother coming home in need of constant care and Robyn saying, "You've made your bed, now lie in it." She dreads her mother coming home in full possession of her senses and ordering her to leave. She dreads the car not turning up at all and afternoon turning to evening and evening turning to night. And then there is no more time to think because her mother is standing in the doorway saying, "This is not my house."

"Don't be silly." Carol shows her the papier-mâché giraffe. "Look."

"This is definitely someone else's house." She seems very calm for someone in such a disconcerting situation.

Robyn steps round her mother and into the room. "What did you do, Carol?"

"I cleaned and tidied."

"This is her home, Carol. For fuck's sake."

"You can't make me stay here," says her mother.

"Mum . . ." Carol blocks her way. "Look at the curtains. You must remember the curtains. Look at the sideboard. Look at the picture."

"Let me go." Her mother pushes her aside and runs.

Robyn says, "Are you happy now?"

Carol can't think of an answer. She's lost confidence in the rightness of her actions and opinions. She feels seasick.

"I hope you have nightmares about this," says Robyn, then she turns and leaves.

§

She drives to the off-licence and returns with a bottle of vodka and a half-litre of tonic water. She pours herself a big glass and sits in front of the television, scrolling through the channels in search of programmes from her childhood. She finds *The Waltons*. She finds *Gunsmoke*. She watches for two hours then rings Robyn.

"I don't think I want to talk to you."

"I'm sorry."

"No you're not, Carol. I don't think you know the meaning of the word."

It strikes her that this might be true. "Where's Mum?"

"Back on the ward. They still had a bed, thank God."

"And what's going to happen to her?"

"You mean, what am I going to do now that you've smashed her life to pieces?"

Was it really possible to destroy someone's life by giving them a bath and cleaning their house? Could a life really be held together by dirt and disorder?

"Have you been drinking?"

She can't think of a reply. Perhaps she really is drunk. The line goes dead.

§

She returns to the television. *Columbo*, *Friends*. It is dark outside now and being drunk isn't having the anaesthetic effect she hoped. She watches a documentary about the jungles of Madagascar. She sleeps and wakes and sleeps and wakes and somewhere in between the two states it becomes clear how much she loved Aysha, how much she still loves her, and how it is the strength of those feelings which terrifies her. Then she sleeps and wakes again and it is no longer clear.

She comes round with a grinding headache and sour sunlight pouring through the gap in the curtains. She rifles through the kitchen drawers and finds some antique ibuprofen and washes down two tablets with tonic water. She remembers how the cleaning and tidying of yesterday calmed her mind. So she takes a collection of planks from the broken bed in front of the house and stacks them in the centre of the lawn at the back, then breaks the rusty padlock from the shed door with a chunk of paving stone. Inside, everything is exactly as her father left it, concertinas of clay pots, jars of nails and screws, balls of twine, envelopes of seeds (Stupice early vine tomatoes, Lisse de Meaux carrots . . .), a fork, a spade . . . The lighter fuel is sitting in a little yellow can on the top shelf. She sprinkles it on the pyramid of wood and sets it alight. When it is blazing she drags the mattress outside and folds it over the flames. Through a gap in the fence a tiny woman in a pink shalwar kameez and headscarf is watching her, but when Carol catches her eye she melts away. There were twins there once, two scrawny boys with some developmental problem. Donny and Cameron, was it? Their mother worked in the Co-op.

The mattress catches. The smell is tart and chemical, the smoke thick and black. She takes the sofa cushions outside and adds them to the pyre. Then, one by one, the dining chairs. She hasn't been this close to big unguarded flames since she was a child. She's forgotten how thrilling it is. And out of nowhere she remembers. It was the one public-spirited thing her father did, building and watching over the estate's bonfire in the run-up to Guy Fawkes Night. Perhaps being an outsider was a part of it. Ferrymen, rat catchers and executioners, intermediaries between here and the other place. Or perhaps her father was simply scary enough to stop the more wayward kids starting the celebrations with a can of petrol in mid-October. She remembers how he drove out to the woods behind the car plant and brought back a bag of earth from the mouth of a fox's den then built the fire round it so that the scent would keep hedgehogs and cats and mice from making a home inside. It is a tenderness she can't remember him ever showing to another human being.

She goes back inside the house. Someone is knocking at the front door. Then they are knocking on the front window. Shaved head, Arsenal shirt. "You're a fucking headcase, you are. I'm calling the council."

She burns the poster, the glass shattering in the heat. She hasn't sweated like this in a long time. It feels good. She burns the ornaments and the knick-knacks and the bundles of newspapers. She stares into the heart of the fire as light drains slowly from the sky.

It starts to rain so she goes indoors. She rips up the carpet and the tack strips just like she's done upstairs. She cuts the carpet into squares and throws them into the garden. The black wreckage of the bonfire steams and smokes. She sweeps and hoovers the floorboards. The TV and the curtains are the only remaining objects in the room.

She is too tired to do any more work but she is frightened of silence. She makes herself a large vodka and tonic. She sits with her back against the wall and scrolls through the channels until she finds a band of white noise in the mid-eighties. She turns the volume up so that the room is filled with grey light and white noise. She lies down and closes her eyes.

§

The phone is ringing. She has no idea what time it is. She lies motionless just inside the border of sleep, like a small animal in long grass waiting for the circling hawk to ride a thermal to some new pasture. The phone stops.

She dreams that she is a little girl standing in the stone circle. She dreams that she is flying over mountains. She dreams that she is looking down into a pit containing a dragon. She hears someone saying, over and over, "The fire, the clock and the candle," but she doesn't know what it means.

§

"Carol . . . ?"

She opens her eyes and sees that dawn is coming up.

"Carol . . . ?"

The TV screen fizzes on the far side of the room. Her hip and shoulder hurt where they were pressed against the hard, wooden floor. Why does the person calling her name not come through to the living room to find her? She gets slowly to her feet, flexing her stiff joints. She squats for a few seconds until the room stops swaying.

"Carol . . . ?"

She thinks about slipping out the back door but it seems important that she doesn't run away. Has she perhaps run away on a previous occasion with dire consequences? She can't remember. Steadying herself with a hand on the wall she steps into the hall but sees only two blank rectangles of frosted daylight hanging in the gloom.

"Carol . . . ?"

She turns. An old man is standing in the kitchen doorway. He is wearing pyjamas and there is a battered yellow tank strapped to an old-fashioned porter's trolley at his side. He presses a mask to his face and takes a long, hissy breath. "It's good to see you." His voice is raspy and small. She half recognises him and this reassures her somewhat but she has no idea where she has seen him before and doesn't want to appear foolish by asking.

He presses the mask to his face, takes a second hissy breath, drapes the rubber tube over the handle of the trolley and rolls it past her towards the front door. He stops on the mat and holds out his hand. "Come."

She is nervous of going with this man but the thought of staying here on her own is worse. She takes his hand. He opens the door and Carol sees, not the houses on Watts Road but long grass and foliage shifting in a breeze. He takes another breath through his mask and bumps the trolley wheels over the threshold. They step into cold, clear winter light. He leads her slowly down a cinder path into a stand of trees. She can feel how weak he is and how much effort he is making not to let this show. She moves closer so that she can share more of his weight without this being obvious. He takes nine steps then stops to breathe through the mask, then eight more steps, then another breath.

They are among the trees now, dancing submarine light and coins of sun like fish around a reef. The trees are birch, mostly, bark curling off the creamy flesh like wallpaper in a long-abandoned house. She wonders what will happen when the oxygen runs out. The tank is clearly very old, the yellow paint so chipped that it has become a map of a ragged imaginary coastline.

They enter a large clearing. It is hard to see precisely how big the clearing is because it is occupied almost entirely by a great mound of logs and branches and sticks, woven like a laid winter hedge in places and in other places simply heaped up higgledy-piggledy. The whole edifice rises steeply in front of them, curving away so that it is impossible to tell whether the summit is fifty or a hundred and fifty feet high.

The man squeezes her hand and moves gingerly forward again. They enter a narrow corridor in the structure, like the tunnel leading to the burial chamber of a pyramid. He is her father, she remembers now. There is something not right about him being here but she doesn't know what. She is tired, her head hurts and she slept badly. Perhaps that is the problem.

Her eyes become accustomed to the low light and she can make out the monumental fretwork of beams and branches which surrounds them. Here and there shafts of sunlight cut across the bark-brown gloaming. Little twigs crunch underfoot and the poorly oiled wheels of her father's trolley squeak. There is dust in the air and the smell of fox.

Now they are standing in the central chamber, a rough half-dome of interwoven sticks some eight or nine feet high, the tonnage above their heads supported by a central column as thick and straight as a telegraph pole.

"Carol . . . ?"

The voice is muffled and distant. It is a woman's voice and it is coming from outside. Only now does she realise that it was not her father who was calling her name when she woke. Was she wrong to follow him? He takes a little yellow can from his pocket, unscrews the top and pours the contents all over his pyjamas. The smell is potent and familiar but Carol can't give it a name and there is not enough light to read the writing on the label.

"Carol . . . ?" The voice is more urgent now.

Her father puts the can back into his pocket and lifts something from the other pocket. Only when he spins the flint does she realise what it is. The flame leaps the gap between his hand and his pyjama jacket, spreading quickly across his torso, climbing upwards over his face and digging its long violet fingers into his hair.

"Carol . . . ? For God's sake . . ."

She spins round looking for the corridor down which they came. It should be easy to spot for the latticed dome of sticks is now lit up in the jittery light but she can see no opening. Has the wood collapsed, blocking off her exit? Could such a thing happen without her hearing or feeling it?

If she were a cat or a dog or a rabbit she might be able to squirm her way out but the gaps between the branches of which the structure is made are too small for a human being. She grabs a long pole in the least dense part of the pyre and starts to pull but as she does so she feels a great shifting in the spars above. She tries doing the same thing on the opposite side of the chamber but it has the same effect. She turns back to her father. His face is alight now, flesh spitting like meat on a barbecue, lips gone, teeth snapping in the heat. The wood above his head is ablaze and the flames are running like excited children outwards and upwards through all the airways in the great wooden maze.

"Carol . . . ?"

She can feel her hands and face blistering. She is going to die in here. Her father takes a couple of frail steps in her direction and lifts the oxygen mask towards her face. "Breathe. Trust me. Just breathe."

THE BOYS WHO LEFT HOME
TO LEARN FEAR

I did not intend to tell our story here. This notebook was meant for notes of a technical nature only. I assumed that we would be able to give our individual accounts at our own pace and in our own words when we returned home, but I am now the only person who can tell those stories and unless a miracle comes to pass I will not be returning home.

There are people who will find some of what I have written distressing. I offer them my sincere apologies but I cannot dissemble. Leaving a true record of recent events is the sole remaining ambition I may be able to achieve.

I have one personal request of whoever finds this book. Please ensure that a copy of this one page at least is forwarded to Christina Murchison, formerly of Dundonald Street in Edinburgh's New Town in Scotland, if she is still living. I care for her more deeply now than I have ever done. She will be my final thought. My greatest fault was to give insufficient weight to her misgivings.

I have lost track of the passing of days so I can no longer be certain of dates. Nevertheless I know that our final troubles began just over a week ago when we heard a faint roar and spied sunlight directly ahead of us. Emerging from the trees we found ourselves at the edge of a deep gorge of schist and migmatite. The far bank, where the jungle continued, stood some sixty feet away. Between the two banks the sides of the gorge fell sheer and slick to rapids which tumbled and foamed on jagged rocks. Downstream a rainbow hung in the spray.

After a month of laborious progress through dense, unvarying jungle I felt drunk with space and light and had to sit down while my head spun. It was now a fortnight since the death of Nicholas's brother, and images of Christopher's last hours had haunted me ever since, but this panoramic view of our one, shared sky connected me to other people and other places and thereby lifted my spirits a little. I only hoped that it might do something similar for Nicholas himself.

Bill attached a pan to the end of a rope and lowered it to the water, measuring the drop at two hundred feet and retrieving a gallon of liquid which tasted better than champagne. Edgar and Arthur then hacked their way through the undergrowth along the edge of the gorge in one direction while Nicholas hacked his way through the undergrowth in the opposite direction. They returned after an hour having discovered no easier crossing point. I built a fire and set myself to brewing tea and skinning and roasting one of the little monkeys we had caught the previous afternoon, and Bill applied his mind to the problem of engineering a bridge.

His solution, like his solutions to all of our previous practical problems, was elegant and efficient. We felled and trimmed two ungurahui trunks, lashed ropes around one end of each, heaved them upright, threw the ropes over a high branch then cantilevered them across the gorge beside one another to make a rudimentary bridge.

The monkey was gamey and fibrous but we were in a jovial mood so it mattered little. We finished our meal, repacked our equipment and began our crossing. Bill insisted that he be our canary and go first. The oily wood bounced a little but held firm and he gained the far side to universal applause. I followed him and was granted, midway, the most extraordinary view upriver to smoky, mauve highlands as if I were a bird suspended on the very air. I felt the giddiness coming back and dared not turn round to take in the opposing view. Edgar shouted out to me to "get a bloody move on, man" and I completed the journey looking only at my feet. I was followed in turn by Arthur and Edgar, leaving only Nicholas on the other side.

When he was halfway across, however, the left-hand trunk cracked and split. As he dropped he threw his arms around the right-hand trunk and clung to it as the broken spar separated into two sections which fell beneath him into the rapids, bouncing several times, booming loudly upon each impact, before lodging themselves between the wet rocks.

Every detail of the following minute is imprinted sharply upon my memory—the wood bending like a bow under Nicholas's weight, his feet circling as if by sheer force of will they might conjure steps from the empty air. To my shame I stood motionless not knowing what to do. Arthur, however, threw his own pack to the ground, urged Nicholas to hang on, climbed astride the remaining trunk and began shifting himself out over the drop. Were he unburdened Nicholas might have been able to inch towards us, hand over hand, but he was carrying a heavy pack. It was Arthur's intention, I believe, to cut the straps with his clasp knife. He did not arrive in time. The two men were still some ten feet apart when Nicholas's remaining strength failed him. He looked towards us with what appeared to me to be an expression of embarrassed apology, his fingers loosened and gravity took him. I cannot help but wonder whether, if his brother had still been alive, he might not have clung to life a little longer.

He seemed to fall very slowly. Perhaps it was a trick of the mind but I have a very clear memory of sketching out the elements of the letter we would have to write to his grieving parents during the one or two seconds of his terrible descent.

I assumed that he would be swept instantly away but he struck a large, flat boulder which lay midstream dividing the current. He came to rest in a sitting position so that if you had not seen what went before you might have thought he was simply taking a rest while crossing the river, except that his thigh was folded sideways just above the knee. He did not move for half a minute and I hoped earnestly that he was dead for it was not possible to survive a wound of that nature this far from civilisation (his brother had died from an infection contracted after being scratched by a thorn, an injury which would have been utterly unremarkable in England). Then he began to move, rubbing his face and looking around like a man waking from a doze, surprised at where he had slumbered.

Bill untied the rope from the remaining ungurahui and looped it around the nearest palm. Edgar asked him what he was doing and Bill replied, "What does it look like I'm doing?"

Edgar told him not to be a fool.

"So we are to stand here and watch him die?" asked Bill.

Edgar drew his handgun and I thought for one awful second

that he intended to shoot Bill for his insolence, but he did not point the gun at Bill. Instead he turned towards the gorge where Nicholas sat swinging his head slowly from side to side in the manner of an injured bear.

Arthur cried out, "No!," but Edgar did not pause. The shot was perfect. Nicholas seemed to shudder as the bullet entered the top of his head, then he rolled sideways off the rock, the foam was briefly pink and he was gone.

No one spoke. The echoes of the shot died away until there was only the roar of the river and some nameless bird calling from deep in the jungle like a rusty wheel being turned. Edgar slotted his handgun back into its leather holster and refastened the buckle.

"Dear God in heaven," said Arthur.

"It would have ended in no other way," said Edgar. "Better that it was swift." His voice did not waver. I heard neither sorrow nor regret, though Nicholas was a man he had called a friend for many years. "Perhaps one of you would like to say a prayer to mark his passing."

After a pause Arthur slowly removed his hat, took a deep breath then proceeded to recite Psalm 39 in its entirety and, as far as I could tell, without a single error. "I will take heed to my ways: that I offend not in my tongue. I will keep my mouth as it were with a bridle: while the ungodly is in my sight . . ."

When he had finished I asked him how he had been able to remember the words so perfectly. He said, "I wish I could forget them. My sister died of scarlet fever two years ago. I attend her funeral every night in my dreams."

"We should keep moving," said Edgar. "We have only three more hours of daylight left to us," and I had the unsettling sensation that he had removed a mask he had been wearing for many years.

§

I began our expedition thinking that Edgar's ambition, his sangfroid, his bravery and self-belief were admirable. I see now that it is possible to demonstrate these qualities to such a degree that they become an illness, dangerous both to oneself and to those around one. I came to understand that he had never possessed any genuine interest in the professed purpose of our travels and that if we were to find Carlysle and his men still alive deep in the jungle it would please him only if this involved some further adventure, such as rescuing them from violent aboriginals. The entire expedition was for him simply an arena in which he might try his courage and strength to their limits, and the greater our difficulties the more he relished them. He reminded me of no one so much as the eponymous hero of "The Boy Who Left Home to Learn Fear," one of the fairy tales collected by the Brothers Grimm which I had read as a boy.

I realise now that when Arthur and I had rooms on the same staircase as Edgar at Oxford we did not really know him. In truth it would be more accurate to say that we were simply two among many people who were in awe of him. His not being an intellectual did not matter because he was the kind of man who made other men wonder whether being an intellectual was perhaps a little shameful. I can vividly recall the five framed *Punch* cartoons of his uncle, all of them featuring a globe, spinning on the man's finger, crushed beneath his foot, served to him on a plate or subjugated in some other symbolic manner. Edgar talked repeatedly of his intention to surpass his uncle in some way and none of us doubted that he would succeed. He was almost comically handsome. He had a scar down the side of his face which he had acquired falling downstairs when he was four years old but he carried himself with such martial dignity that everyone thought of it as a duelling wound, even those of us who were party to the secret. He had been awarded Blues in both rugby and fives and was, in short, one of those men who take it for granted that they are liked and admired, that wealth and opportunity will flow naturally to them and that this is simply the nature of the world. Consequently they never learn how to make a compromise or earn respect, they never need to imagine how the world might appear from the point of view of another person, they never truly love and they are never truly loved.

I did not understand these things until two weeks ago.

§

The following morning, after a night of shallow and restless sleep, while Edgar was relieving himself and Arthur was shaving, Bill asked if he might discuss something with me. Bill was the only non-university man among us and we rarely shared small talk so I feared bad news.

He sat close enough that Arthur might not overhear. "I fear that Mr. Soames has lost his mind and we're here only so long as we're useful to him."

I was shocked to hear him talking about Edgar in this manner.

"I no longer think we can trust him."

I reminded Bill that whether he trusted Edgar was neither here nor there. He was, ultimately, an employee. I softened my rebuke a little by adding, "The drop was two hundred feet. The rope was two hundred and twenty. There was insufficient slack to form a belay and a cradle."

"Did he know that?" asked Bill.

I said, "You would both have died. You may dislike him but you owe him your life."

Bill, I realised, was testing the ground in case he fell foul of Edgar. Might I be an accomplice, a co-conspirator? I found his presumption distasteful. I asked him what he would have done in Edgar's shoes.

"I would have discussed the matter at least," said Bill, "before putting a bullet through a man's head as if he were no more than a racehorse with a broken leg."

I said that democracy was not necessarily the best model for governing an expedition of this kind.

"So we submit to a tyrant?" said Bill.

"When your name is on the front page of *The Times* I suspect that you will not care greatly about what kind of dispensation we were briefly living under."

Bill got to his feet. "I have spoken out of turn. Forgive me. I did not mean to place you in a difficult position." He turned and walked away.

§

A few days after Nicholas's death our compass readings began to go awry. Divining true north by means of the stars, however, a process which involved Arthur ascending tall trees, monkey-like, at night to broach the canopy, we were able by degrees to make our way towards the epicentre of the magnetic disturbances.

Shortly after breakfast one morning Edgar called for us to

come and look at a boot which he had found lodged at head height in a mass of creepers and vines choking a rubber tree. He took it down and turned it over in his hand, wiping away with his hat some of the feathery lime-green mould which had gathered on the putrid leather.

Edgar spread his outstretched hand along the sole to gauge the size. "It must have belonged to the boy." He put the boot back into the crevice between the vines as if he were a shop assistant and a customer had decided not to make a purchase. "Let us press on. If our luck holds we may find the cave by nightfall."

Later during the morning, as the two of us were walking together, Arthur said, "There is a possibility, of course, that they killed one another."

I said that after all this time, in this heat and this humidity, even if we were to find the bodies their manner of death would be exceedingly difficult to ascertain.

"You would be surprised," said Bill who was walking behind us. "I've seen many corpses in my time. They are more eloquent than you might expect."

I cast my mind back to the asylum, to Nat Semperson sitting in the director's library, November rain lashing the casement and the panes rattling in their leads. His morning dose of laudanum had been postponed in the hope that this might sharpen his mind, the director explained; even so he very much doubted that we would be told a comprehensible story. Semperson rarely spoke, he continued, and remained as feeble-minded as he had been when the HMS *Cadogan* deposited him at Falmouth. He often cried out in his sleep and seldom slept a whole night without waking.

Edgar asked what had happened to Lord Carlysle and the

rest of the men. What point had they reached on their journey through the jungle? Were they still alive when he last saw them? If not, how had they met their end? Semperson watched the rain and seemed blind to Edgar's presence and deaf to his questions.

"He sometimes talks about a terrifying creature," said the director. He had the air of a ringmaster, I thought, thumbs hooked into his waistcoat, a voice slightly too big for the room. I wondered how much of the story was concocted for our benefit in the hope of a second monetary donation. "He claims sometimes to have seen it approaching across the fields. Sometimes he is certain that it has broken through the doors and that we must arm ourselves."

Edgar pulled up a chair and sat in front of Semperson so that he was able to look directly into the man's eyes. He explained that we were planning to travel to Jamanxim in search of Carlysle and the rest of his party. "The family will not rest easy until they know the whereabouts of their son. We will spend sixteen weeks in the jungle. If there are predictable dangers I would like to be forewarned. I do not wish our party to come to a similar end."

"To my knowledge," said the director, "he has never spoken of what happened to his companions."

After a long pause Edgar got to his feet and replaced his chair. "This is a great disappointment."

Only I knew how great. Carlysle's family would fund an expedition only if there were dependable evidence. Semperson was our last hope. We would now be forced to return to London and, within the month, Edgar would reluctantly take up the job at his great-uncle's bank which he no longer had a justifiable reason for postponing.

Struck by a sudden inspiration I asked the director if I might borrow a sheet of paper and a fountain pen. I removed the tea set, placed them on the tray and placed the tray in Semperson's lap. He looked at them with his head cocked to one side the way a dog does when it is listening to a faint and distant noise.

"Children learn to talk before they learn to write," said the director. "I strongly suspect that we lose those faculties in the reverse order."

But Semperson had taken up the pen in the shaking fingers of his right hand.

"Go on," I said gently.

In my memory the room fell silent though this cannot be true for the storm did not abate until the evening, a fire was crackling busily in the grate and the tall-case clock ticked loudly in syncopation during our entire visit. Semperson's pen began to move. The director, Edgar and I stood as still as if we were watching a stag enter a glade, knowing that it might bolt at the slightest disturbance.

He drew for five minutes then laid his pen down.

"If I may . . . ?" Semperson did not respond so Edgar picked up the paper, carried it to the table and set it down in order that we might both inspect it. Whether Semperson had once drawn well I do not know. He now drew like a child. On the left-hand side of the paper was a map showing a tiny village, a forking river, two cataracts and a range of jagged mountains. Midway between the river and the peaks he had sketched a large X in the manner of a boy playing a game of buried treasure. In the centre of the paper was a separate drawing of a hill with a lopsided elliptical hole in its flank and a group of rudimentary figures in the opening which made me think of the Pied Piper stealing away the town's children. On the right-hand side of the paper was a third drawing, a sketch of a monster—part man, part bear, part lizard—so preposterous that it made me laugh out loud. The whole was signed in the bottom left-hand corner.

Edgar took from his travelling bag the slim volume belonging to the Royal Geographical Society. He opened it at the bookmark and laid it beside Semperson's sketch. The maps were not identical but they were close enough to make the hairs stand up on the back of my neck.

"And how do we navigate through the jungle?" said Edgar. "This is a vast area."

"There is a natural lodestone in the cave," said Semperson. His voice was small and timid. "Your compass will become useless as you draw near. The effect extends for some twenty miles about. It is quite extraordinary."

"What happened to Carlysle?"

Semperson said no more. His eyes became vacant and I saw that he was weeping.

"If you gentlemen are finished," said the director, stepping between the two men, "then I will give Mr. Semperson his laudanum."

"I think we have what we need," said Edgar. "Thank you, Dr. Fairweather. Thank you, Mr. Semperson."

The director handed his patient a small willow-patterned cup of suspension. While Semperson drank it I leaned close to Edgar. "I doubt the Carlysles will pay a thousand pounds on the evidence of a map drawn by the man who also believes that this higgledy-piggledy manticore stalks the Gloucestershire countryside."

Edgar folded the paper neatly, took the paper-knife from the desk and ran it along the fold, excising the monster. "I have no memory of the animal to which you are referring." He laid the creature on the hot coals and it became briefly incandescent before it was swallowed by the flames. "Gentlemen, you have been generous with your time. We must bid you good day."

§

We found the cave towards the end of the afternoon. The trees thinned, the earth gave way to rock and we walked up a shallow slope to find ourselves on a low, stony plateau some five or six acres in size. At the far end the granite rose vertically, and cut into this cliff was a hole shaped almost exactly like the lopsided parabola in Semperson's drawing. We had taken the picture literally, however, and misread the scale by a factor of eight or more. Hazlemere House would have sat comfortably within its maw.

We could see the sides of the moss-covered vault receding into the dark but they did not narrow noticeably and beyond a hundred and fifty yards all light was swallowed up. The air emerging from the interior was fetid and chill and seemed unwilling to mix with the warm vapour rising from the jungle and as we moved around we passed in and out of rank, wintery currents.

I walked to the edge of the plateau and looked out across the jungle, the uninterrupted green canopy blurring in the vaporous distance. The space should have offered me some relief but I felt nothing of the dizzying elation which had overtaken me on the bridge over the gorge. I could hear no animal cries of any kind, nor any birdsong, not even the buzzing of insects.

Arthur and Bill returned from a brief reconnaissance having found the dark star of a long-dead fire burnt into the rock. Edgar appeared only vaguely interested. It was the cave itself which had now captured his imagination, to which end he suggested that he and I make a short foray inside to gauge its size and ascertain whether it was the lair of any creatures against which we should protect ourselves overnight.

I armed myself with a machete, Edgar clipped his handgun to his belt and we stepped into the dark. The temperature dropped rapidly as we made our way down a gradual slope in the dying light and I was soon shivering in my sweat-soaked shirt. If we paused we could hear only the occasional splash of water dripping from the roof onto the wet floor. Here and there a sour, chemical smell became particularly intense and I found it difficult to shake the suspicion that some beast was only inches away, shrouded completely by the near-absolute dark. Our weapons, I realised, would be of little use against such invisible adversaries.

We were clearly in a chamber of extraordinary size. The echoes coming from the walls on either side of us were like those one might hear in an empty cathedral, but we could hear no similar echoes returning from walls ahead. I pictured the trees above and thought that one might correctly refer to this as the underworld.

After a quarter of an hour or so Edgar suggested that we save our resources for the morning and when we turned we saw, suspended in a great, starless dark, a droplet of bright green light within which tiny figures moved and I had the uncanny sensation that this was the world in its entirety and that I was looking upon it from the moon.

We re-entered the day to find Bill holding a broken shovel with a bent and rusted head. He and Arthur had also found a rudimentary cross, but a good deal of dense undergrowth would need to be cleared before we knew where to begin digging in search of a grave, if indeed there was one.

Edgar announced that Bill and I would do this in the morning while he and Arthur undertook a proper exploration of the cave. In the meantime we would pitch camp on the rock. A brief silence fell and I realised that I was not alone in the unease I felt about the place. Bill suggested that we spend the night instead in a clearing through which we had passed some twenty minutes before arriving at the cave, but Edgar replied that if we were to be attacked in the night he would rather see our assailants coming across a hundred yards of open ground than dropping from an overhanging branch. He untied his pack, extracted his canvas, poles and mosquito net and the subject was closed. We headed off to the tree line to find rocks and logs with which to hold our guy ropes down.

After we had erected our own shelters Bill and I built a fire and plucked and roasted the large flightless bird we had trapped the previous night. The sparse flesh was surprisingly good despite a strong aftertaste of aniseed. We followed it with several chunks of Quiggin's mint cake, watery coffee and two shots each of the ten-year-old Glenturret which Arthur had brought, wrapped in a blanket at the base of his pack, to celebrate the midpoint of our journey.

I felt unwell on account, I assumed, of so much rich food after weeks of meagre fare, and was therefore in no mood for conversation. I offered my apologies and slipped away to the edge of the rock with my battered Ovid whose fine pages were now speckled with mould. I found it difficult to read, however. So I put the book down and watched the sky. Night fell fast at this latitude, and while I would be denied the spectacle of the sunset by the position of the hill into which the cave was cut, I would, in compensation, be able to see the Milky Way in all its glory for there was no trace of cloud and, apart from our fire, no other light for three or four hundred miles.

I was beginning to discern the faintest points of light against the darkening indigo of the eastern horizon when I became aware that Edgar, Arthur and Bill had fallen silent. Something was about to happen but I was ignorant of how I knew this. There was a brief pause, then a faint susurration from the mouth of the cave, like the long receding of a wave on a gravel beach. An object of great size was moving swiftly towards us out of the subterranean dark. I briefly considered running but no one else had moved and I was unwilling to be judged unmanly. The susurration became a roar and I could feel a cold, ammoniac wind being driven from the cave's mouth by the mass of whatever was speeding behind it. The fire, I recall, began to burn with a fierce green light. The noise continued to rise in volume until it was almost unbearable, at which point the very darkness inside the cave erupted into the surrounding air and the sky went black. I pressed myself to the ground, covered my head with my hands and felt something like hail pummel my exposed back.

I have no clear memory of how long I lay in this position, only that after a period the noise and the smell abated somewhat. I opened my eyes, got to my knees and saw Arthur standing in the light of a fire that was glowing once more with a reassuring orange flame, exclaiming, excitedly, "Bats. Dear God in Heaven. Bats."

We walked over and saw, strung between his hands, a furry body the size of a field mouse at the junction of two segmented, translucent wings. "Some near-cousin of *Tadarida brasiliensis*," he said, "plucked from the air by my own hands." The struggling animal possessed the face of one of the demons in the illustrated Bible which had given my younger brother nightmares when we were children. "There was, after all, some point to those tedious afternoons at deep square leg."

"*Arthura brasiliensis*," said Bill. "You'll go down in history."

"*Tadarida arthuriensis*," replied Arthur. He broke the neck of the creature with a sharp twist and dropped it into his pocket. "*Brasiliensis* is the adjective. And you may call me greedy but I'd prefer a more substantial memorial."

"A bat would suit me just fine," said Bill. "A flower, a tree . . ."

I returned to my bed, lay down and watched the Via Galactica reveal itself, the sky so clear and dark that I was able to discern the colours of individual stars, each one burning with the light of a different spectrum according to the peculiar combination of elements which fuelled its monstrous furnace. I fell finally into a doze and was woken, as was everyone else, by the return of the bats just before dawn.

§

While we were eating breakfast I rolled up my trousers and discovered a raised purple lump on my left calf. The cotton duck of my trousers had not been punctured so it must have been the bite of some creature, perhaps one of the brown spiders through whose webs we had been walking repeatedly over the last couple of days. I showed the lesion to Arthur, the only one of us with any medical knowledge now that Nicholas was gone. He advised me to wait and see if the swelling and discoloration went down before risking any further intervention.

He and Edgar then prepared themselves for their journey

underground, donning all their clothes against the cold and equipping themselves with the remaining rope, two belay devices, the two handguns, a machete, water, food and both our oil lamps.

"We shall press ahead for two hours at most," said Edgar. "Then we will return. If after four hours we have not reappeared you must decide whether to search for us or attempt the journey home alone." There was relish in his voice as if he might enjoy playing any of the roles in such a scenario.

We wished the two men luck, bid them goodbye, gathered the spade and the machetes and made our way to the cross which Bill and Arthur had discovered the previous day so that we might dig for bodies and find some clues as to the fate of our predecessors. I was very grateful indeed not to be entering the cave. I was convinced that something would go wrong and the fact that my sense of impending doom was without foundation made it no easier to bear. If Bill and I were lucky enough to uncover Carlysle's body, however, and identify it by means of his signet ring, for example, we might soon be heading home.

I was unnaturally tired and after half an hour of labour Bill suggested that I sit to one side and resume the work when I felt stronger. By this time we had uncovered two graves. Bill put down his machete, picked up the antique spade and began to excavate the second of these. Within a very short time he struck a human femur. Digging more carefully now he rapidly produced a skull complete with a jawbone and a nearly complete set of teeth. Sinews and muscle were stretched around the whole like ageing strings of India rubber. He brushed the earth away and handed it to me. It seemed fake, a theatrical prop or a desktop memento mori.

I remained incapable of significant manual labour. Bill said that there was no hurry and that my exhausting myself would be to no one's advantage. Within half an hour I was handed a second skull, this one incomplete, the dome shattered and absent on the left-hand side of the head. These dead men were the reason we had made this laborious and fatal journey yet I could summon little interest. Bill returned after a few minutes carrying a handful of broken fragments. He laid them out like a jigsaw and fitted them together, the final shape mirroring the hole in the skull I still held in my hand. "He was killed by a heavy blow to the head."

I asked Bill how he could be certain of this.

"If a man were to fall from a cliff he would crack his skull at most. To do this you would need to hold him down and stave his head in with a rock."

"Then he was killed by one of his own party."

"Or someone was already here and did not want company."

"And it was they, perhaps, who buried the bodies and spirited away the expedition's equipment."

Something had caught Bill's eye. He picked up one of the machetes and began cutting back a mass of vines and creepers which had climbed the side of the rock before petering out for lack of damp soil. He pulled back the foliage and I could see letters scratched into the rock. I got slowly to my feet and walked over so that I could read the inscription.

φυγῇ φυγῇ
νωθὲς πέδαιρε κῶλον,
ἐκποδὼν ἔλα

"I assume you can tell me what it means," said Bill.

I confessed that my Greek was poor but that the word repeated in the first line almost certainly meant "flee," from the same root as "fugue" and "fugitive." As for the meaning of the second and third lines I had little or no idea.

Bill looked at the sun. "Four hours have passed."

I had become so preoccupied by the graves, the skulls and the inscription that I had forgotten about Edgar and Arthur. We made our way back up onto the top of the rock, Bill striding comfortably ahead, the muscles in my legs protesting at the incline. Our little camp was empty and the two men were nowhere to be seen. My premonition had been correct.

"So," said Bill. "We have a decision to make."

It had not occurred to me that Bill might take Edgar's instructions literally. For a moment I was tempted. Then my senses returned. "There is no decision to make."

We dressed as warmly as possible. There were no more lamps so I lit a fire while Bill hammered and split the ends of two staves of firewood to make brands. We took up a machete each, oiled and lit the brands then entered the cave.

The walls, illuminated now, were rippled and bulbous as if formed from a substance which had hardened suddenly in its melting. I had expected irregularities—overhangs, narrows, drops, forks, subsidiary chambers—but there were none. There were patches of moss but otherwise surprisingly little vegetation for so fecund an atmosphere. The temperature dropped swiftly to that of a cold January day in England. We passed the point beyond which we were able to see the entrance to the cave and shortly thereafter we could no longer see the roof above our heads. I guessed that the cave must have been at least five hundred feet high at this point.

The previous year I had listened to a speech at the Royal Geographical Society given by Alois Ulrich who had been exploring the Hölloch in the Swiss municipality of Muotathal which appeared to be at least ten miles in extent. I wondered if we had stumbled upon something commensurate. There were no longer any echoes as such, only a sibilant background to every noise, like a stiff brush dragged across a drum skin. Every so often we stopped and called out, standing in silence afterwards, letting the reverberations die slowly to silence and listening for any answering cries, but none came.

We walked on and the cave grew larger still for we had lost sight of the wall to our left. We adjusted our direction of travel in the hope of regaining the centre of the cave but found ourselves, after several minutes, in a place where we could see neither wall. Around our feet lay two overlapping horseshoes of dancing yellow light from our lit brands. Beyond them was a darkness so complete it felt like a physical substance. We tried to retrace our steps to regain a view of the wall but cannot have done so accurately. Without thinking we spun round, scouring the dark for any clues, and within a few moments we had lost all sense of direction.

Even if we now succeeded in finding a wall the slope of the floor was so shallow that we would not know which wall it was and be therefore ignorant of whether we should follow it to the right or the left to regain the entrance. A hand reached into my chest and fastened itself around my heart. I believe that Bill felt something similar for he confessed that we were in "a bit of a bloody pickle."

We began walking in what we hoped was a widening spiral in search of one of the walls when my brand guttered and went out. We took a spare brand from my pack and tried to light it from Bill's but with no success. The air was too damp and too cold. Some minutes later his own brand went out. We watched the final embers die in the dark. My strength began rapidly to ebb. I told Bill that I needed to sit down for a few moments and did so. He told me that he would carry on searching for a wall. He would bang his machete on the rock every so often and I should do the same, and in this way we would not lose touch with one another.

I heard his individual footsteps distinctly for a while and then they merged into the single, indivisible noise of the cave. However close I held my hands to my eyes I could see nothing. I tried to imagine that it was a moonless night and that, while staying with my brother-in-law, I was out walking on Salisbury Plain but my mental powers were insufficient. Bill banged the rock briskly three times and I returned the call.

After a time I began to see swirls of red and green particles moving upon my retina, the same colours and shapes one sees if one closes one's eyes and presses hard upon the lids. But I could neither dispel them by opening my eyes and looking at real objects nor close my eyes and cover them with darkness. They became heavy and liquid, a great tide of light, not just red and green now but all the colours of the rainbow, gathering and twisting like murmurations of starlings.

I do not know how to describe my state of mind from this point onwards without seeming affected or sensational. I expected my fear to increase but this did not happen. On the contrary I became very calm. My fear of earlier melted away and I felt completely safe. I possessed no body and existed at no point in space, and if one is both nothing and nowhere how can one be attacked? How can one suffer, how can one die? Gradually the coloured phantasmagoria began to resolve itself into images. I was standing on the balcony of a higher sphere, looking down upon my life—my childhood in Chittagong and Patna, the snake that fell onto the breakfast table, the punkawallah with the deformed leg, my ill-matched father and mother, my terrifying Northumbrian grandfathers ("Gog" and "Magog" as my brother styled them), the house in Canterbury, my mother weeping at the rheumatic weather to which she would now be subjected . . . all of it charming and tender and utterly unimportant, a world of toys which would be swept away and leave no trace. The thought filled me with a sense of peace such as I have never felt before. It was perhaps that state of mind sought by certain Hindu fakirs and Buddhist monks.

Then I saw a group of boys from the village bathing naked in the pool where the river slowed and pooled downstream of the mill. My clothes fell away and I was tumbling in a puzzle of white limbs and cold water and silver bubbles. I recognised Solomon, the blacksmith's boy, who kept a knife in his boot. I recognised the ginger boy whom my grandfather had caught trapping rabbits and had beaten with a switch. I recognised my cousin Patrick who died in a house fire at the age of nineteen. I was struggling to keep my head above the surface and frightened suddenly that I might drown. Then Edgar appeared in front of me. I reached out and he put his arms around my chest and I was raised up into the light and the air.

Then he was no longer Edgar. He was Christopher dying, Christopher in those last hours, his sun-browned skin now red and taut and peeling, reeking of sweat and excrement, his eyes wide, as if he could see something dreadful in the distance, nonsense tumbling from his mouth—"Sit down, sit down, sit down . . . The key, for God's sake . . . Horses this morning . . ." I tried to disentangle myself but he was holding on to me too tightly and I knew that he was going to die and take me with him.

Then he was no longer Christopher. He was the creature in Semperson's drawing, part man, part bear, part lizard, rotted meat between the yellow teeth, eyes like orange marbles, lice swimming in its fur.

Then I was alone and back in the utter dark of the cave, frightened and cold, and I longed to return to my nightmare.

§

There was a period of time. It was not like time spent sleeping, after which one is aware of the world having carried on in one's absence, but an absolute vacancy, as if a chapter from the book of myself had been torn out and thrown away. I was naked and wrapped in a canvas sheet. It was night. I could see my clothes hanging in the light of a fire. I was simultaneously hot and cold. Two poles held up another canvas sheet over my head as a rudimentary shelter. I was not well. My life came back to me, as if I were examining a large diagram, homing in on the tiny figure that bore my name. I remembered that we had gone into the cave to look for Edgar and Arthur.

Bill said, "We did not find them," so I must have spoken the question out loud. He was squatting beside me. "Drink this."

I took hold of the warm enamel mug and sipped. He had melted the remains of the mint cake into hot water. "How did we get out?"

"I waited for the bats. Then I knew the way."

I said, "I owe you my life."

He said, "I'm going to lance the bite on your leg."

The lump was the size of a chicken's egg and nearly black.

"I fear it contains something more than putrefaction." He straddled my leg so as to hold it down and keep the cut both small and accurate. He heated the tip of his clasp knife in the flames of the fire. "This will hurt."

On the contrary I felt only a faint nick and warm liquid splash over my leg. Bill cut the sleeve from a spare shirt, washed it and used it to bind the wound. "You should sleep now."

§

I woke to sunshine which was some compensation though it did not drive the cold from my bones. There was no blood seeping through the bandages but my foot was numb and I could not stand. Bill served a breakfast of peanuts and a bitter yellow citrus fruit which I had not seen before and which I found hard to keep down. My mind was cloudy. I asked if Edgar and Arthur were dead.

"We were in the cave for five hours," said Bill. "It is now twenty hours since they entered."

I felt neither sadness at their loss nor any satisfaction at having risked our lives trying to save them, only a dull wretchedness.

Bill left to investigate the graves further. I attempted to read more of the Ovid but my mental powers were not up to the task. Instead I took up this notebook and glanced through some of my entries—a sketch of a terrapin, a description of St. Elmo's Fire, a rudimentary calculation of the volume of water passing over a nameless cataract—recalling the stories evoked by these details. After several hours Bill returned in possession of a new skull and a signet ring bearing the initials "JDC" engraved as three interlocking curlicues. "There are six graves in all," he said. "This was in the last."

He departed on a second errand and reappeared carrying two bladders of water and some palm hearts. He roasted the latter and I ate them with a mug of weak coffee while he boiled and strained the water before pouring it into all our receptacles. He then set about sorting our equipment into that which was now dead weight and that which remained useful. I bridled to see him make himself so free with objects, some of them intimate, which had belonged to Edgar and Arthur but I was too weak to argue.

Bill carried on working throughout the afternoon. He filled two packs with nuts, roots and more palm hearts. I assumed that he was preparing for our forthcoming journey home. Only when he was making supper did he say, "I have provided you with food and clean water for a week though I do not think you will last that long. I will leave you the whisky. I am only sorry that I cannot leave you a gun."

I felt like an idiot for not having predicted this turn of events. I had to think about it only for a few seconds to realise that it would be impossible for me to travel anything but the shortest distance through dense jungle. I said, "You are leaving me," and was embarrassed to hear myself sounding like a child.

He leaned forward and tenderly unbuttoned my shirt to the navel. "Look." My torso was peppered with livid red spots. "My whole life since the age of ten I have served other men for small wages and smaller thanks. The coming few days are worth more to me than to you."

I recalled how I had upbraided him for questioning Edgar's sanity, reminding him that he was merely an employee. I came close to apologising but even here, even now, I felt myself observed and judged by an invisible audience composed of those people whose good opinions I have always sought—my father, my schoolmasters, Christina, my friends—and I did not want to be seen as craven or obsequious. For the briefest of moments I was on the verge of tears, then I gathered myself and wished Bill luck on his journey. He seemed thrown somewhat and I felt stronger as a result.

Darkness fell and the bats came out of the cave. I would see this spectacle only a few more times and be able to tell no one about it. I asked Bill whether he was going to take the signet ring and the skull to the Carlysles. He said that he had not yet decided. There was no financial reward offered and reputation alone rarely put a roof over a man's head. If he reached the river's mouth he might not even sail home. He had skills which, in this country, could make him, if not a wealthy man, then at the very least a man of business. He might simply keep the ring and the skull as mementos.

We sat watching the fire. Every so often the wood spat and crackled and a bright ember was carried up into the dark as if we were cooking stars and adding them to the night sky one by one. I was going to die. I wanted very much to talk about this but I could not broach the subject. I thought of the ayah we had in Chittagong and how she would sit on my bed and ask, "What is the matter with the young master?" and I never needed to say what the matter was because the asking of the question itself was what I needed.

§

The bats woke me at dawn. Bill was already gone. I had a headache and loose bowels. Starting a fire proved too onerous so I ate a handful of nuts, drank a mug of tepid, coppery water and lay wrapped in my canvas sheet watching the sun come up.

I recalled the weekend two years previously during which I had returned to Merton for the Founder's Supper. After an opulent meal I found myself walking in the gardens with Edgar. Pausing at the armillary sundial in the dying light we smoked a pair of cigars looking down over Christ Church Meadow towards the Isis. I don't think, hitherto, that he had ever given me his full attention for more than two or three minutes. I was flattered, and when he told me the story of the Carlysle expedition and his plan to bring back news of the family's missing son I was struck by how pitifully lacking in event my own life had been up to this point.

The memory unsettled me. I drank some more water and added a little whisky to dull the pain in my head. My eye fell on my notebook and I realised that I must try to leave some record of our expedition. If it were never read by another human being it would nevertheless summon a few ghosts and I would be in great need of company over the coming days.

And so I began to write.

Towards the end of the afternoon I relit the fire using the flint and the sealed tin of dried moss which Bill had left me. I roasted another two palm hearts and watched the sun go down. I tried to write more but could not order my thoughts. I had a fever. My left leg was now completely numb and the livid red spots had spread down my left arm. The bats came out to hunt. If I moved quickly my head spun. I drank the last of the whisky and closed my eyes and waited for sleep to take me.

§

I woke thinking that we were still at sea and that we had run into a storm. Lightning ripped the sky from top to bottom and a vast ocean was lit up momentarily in a burst of white light. Then the world was thrown back into darkness and the thunder followed, like barrels rolling off a cart. Lightning struck for a second time and I saw that the ocean was made of trees, that I was not on a boat and that it was not pitching. There was a little canvas roof over my head but I was lying in water. I tried to stand but I could not make my legs work properly. I raised myself onto my hands and knees like a dog. There was another flash of lightning and I saw my notebook wedged into the open mouth of a pack that was filling with water. I pulled the pack under the canvas, extracted the notebook, stuffed it into my shirt and gave myself over wholly to the belief that if I could save the book then I could save myself.

There was lightning, then there was darkness, then there was thunder. I lost the feeling in my hands and knees and feet. I fell asleep, my arms buckled and I was woken by my head and shoulder striking the hard, wet rock. I got back onto my hands and knees. I do not know how many times this happened.

Gradually the gap between the flashes of lightning and the peals of thunder grew longer and both slowly faded. Then they were gone and I was left in complete darkness and pouring rain. I was going to die at some time in the next few days. Only the thought of the notebook gave me any desire to reach the morning alive. My teeth chattered. I saw Christina and her new husband seated on a terrace, their children playing cricket on a long lawn. I saw a flotilla of Spanish ships approaching over the ocean of trees. I was lifted up and carried into the cave by the surviving members of Carlysle's expedition.

§

The bats did not return. Perhaps they could not fly through heavy rain. At dawn a monochrome world became faintly visible. Over the next hour or so the downpour thinned and ceased. The low sky was dirty and grey like a cheap military blanket laid over the world. Drops trembled and fell from every object. The numbness had spread to both my hips. I was still shaking but no longer felt as cold as I had done. Whether this was an improvement in my health or the later stages of hypothermia I had no way of knowing.

The fire was gone. Every piece of wood had become a little boat and sailed away. There remained only a shallow puddle. I took a rough inventory. The moss which I had foolishly left open to the elements had vanished. I could not see the flint. The rain had carried away an entire pack of food. I took the notebook from inside my shirt and opened it. The sodden margins were soaked and in places the paper had begun to disintegrate but I had taken the precaution of writing in pencil so no ink had run and for this I was grateful.

Eventually the sun came out. The temperature rose and steam began to rise from the stretched canvas and the shallower puddles. I drank a little water. I put a handful of nuts into my mouth and chewed them to a paste so that they could pass easily down my constricted throat. I struggled out of my clothes and sat naked on the warming rock. Behind me rose the great opening of the cave. On every other side green jungle ran seamlessly to a misty horizon.

I opened the notebook and waited for the pages to become dry. Then I took up my pencil and began.

§

Now I can write no more. I have been blessed with a final day of brilliant sunshine. For that I am thankful. I hope I have used it well.

The night is coming.

I wish that this were a happier ending.

THE WEIR

He pops the catch and lifts the rusty boot. Quivering with excitement the dogs burst from the back of the car, squirm under the
lowest bar of the fence and bolt across the field in great arcing
bounds. Leo and Fran, big chocolate-and-white pointers. He drops
the chewed and ragged tennis ball into one jacket pocket, the
coiled leather leads into the other, grabs the tatty, gripless tennis
racket and slams the boot. He beeps the lock and climbs the stile.

Grass stretches into the distance. Twenty acres. There are
no sheep this year so half a million buttercups hover just above
the ground. He can smell the May blossom, the same chemicals
in semen and corpses so he read the other day. Wytham Woods
rise beyond the meadow to his left. Up there among the trees is
the Singing Way, pilgrims breaking into song as they passed My
Lady's Seat and looked across the silver flood of Port Meadow to
the inns and spires of the city. One of those spring days that seem
warm and cold at the same time. Enough blue to make a pair
of sailor's trousers. Cirrus clouds overhead. Ice crystals at 16,000
feet. A pied wagtail lands briefly on the path in front of him then
hops back into the air and is carried away.

Leo races towards him and skids to a halt with Fran in pursuit. He barks and half prostrates himself, forelegs flat on the ground, hindquarters in the air. *Throw the ball throw the ball throw the ball.* He lobs it into the air, whacks it hard and both dogs launch themselves backwards, twisting in mid-air so that they land on all fours then run like racehorses in old paintings, the ball still up there, sliding round that big curve.

To his right the river is full from last week's downpour, the surface purling midstream as the water sorts itself out below the weir. A buzzard circles above the scrubby wasteland on the far side. He treads carefully over the twisty poles of the cattle grid and feels, as he always does at this precise point, that he has crossed an invisible boundary which marks the limit of the city's reach.

It's now seven weeks since Maria walked out and he's pleased at how well he's coping. The dogs help, dragging him out on long walks like this. Having the time of their lives, probably. Plus the house is never empty. Knowing they're downstairs when he wakes in the night and finds himself alone. He's learning to cook for himself after twenty-six years: macaroni cheese; shepherd's pie . . . And reading his way through the tower of books which have been glaring at him from the shelf above the TV for God knows how long: John Grisham, Philip Pullman, the one set in Afghanistan the author of which he can never remember . . .

Fran returns with the ball in her mouth. They do a little dance of dodge and feint. She drops it, he picks it up and whacks it away again.

If there are rough patches, that's to be expected. Change gets harder, just as the body becomes less flexible. Today for example. The nagging feeling that his marriage is only the latest thing which has slipped away. The world shifting too fast in ways he doesn't understand, values he'd grown up with become vaguely comic: being a gentleman; respecting authority; privacy; stoicism; reticence. When did holding a door open for a woman become an insult? Teenagers watching pornography on their phones.

He wonders if it all comes down to Timothy, the friction which ended the marriage, this longing for things to be as they were. Or whether, when you have a ready-made answer like that, you use it lazily for every question. The fact that it might be malicious is what makes it hardest to handle, their son wanting them to suffer. Three years without a postcard, an email, a phone call. The anger he felt when Maria said it would be better if he were dead. Her own child. He has dreams of a blurred postmark. Lhasa? Marrakesh? Stepping off the plane into sauna shimmer. Hostels, cafés, a local police chief, feet on the desk under a lazy ceiling fan. The photograph in his pocket getting more dog-eared and less readable by the day, the hope that his son is somewhere nearby, a needle in his arm, maybe, some sign that this was not his choice.

Fran returns yet again with the tennis ball. Leo is busy chasing something. So long as he doesn't bring it back bloody and struggling. He hits the ball into the air. The satisfying boink of the taut strings, the sheer distance of it.

She isn't with someone else, thank God. Unless she's hiding it. Which wouldn't be hard, him being blind to so many things.

There is movement at the edge of his field of vision. Someone is making their way along the gantry of the weir that runs between the farmland and the island. The lock-keeper, presumably, or someone from the Environment Agency. But when they turn he sees a bright red rucksack. It is a woman. She must have lost her way because as far as he knows you can only reach the weir via the unmetalled track that descends from the hard shoulder of the ring road. Black leggings, denim skirt, big tartan shirt, long straight blonde hair. Twenty, maybe twenty-five. She seems unsure of her footing and is supporting herself by holding on to the metal uprights and the rusted valves. It is not a good place to be unsteady on your feet.

Again Fran blocks the path in front of him, tail up, head down, panting, tennis ball between her paws.

"Not now."

She whimpers. *Please please.* He picks it up, wallops it away and starts walking upriver towards the lock. Beneath the woman's feet the whole river is being forced through a single open gate, a fat silver spout curving into the churn of surf. The roar could be a house on fire. She comes to a halt in the very centre of the weir. She is clearly in some kind of trouble. Sudden dizziness, maybe, or that phobia people get on bridges. He can imagine standing there and looking down and being spooked by that torrent. She needs help. He wants to call out to her, reassure her that he will be with her in a few minutes, but there is no way she will be able to hear him at this distance and over that noise. He starts to run. If he remembers correctly there is only a chain to stop pedestrians crossing the lock. Presumably there is some kind of path through the trees. It will take him, what, two or three minutes?

Then he turns and sees her let go of the supports. She stands facing downriver and he realises that she is planning to jump. Understands, too, why she was staggering, because why else would you wear a rucksack if you were planning to do something like that? He feels sick at the thought. "No!" He waves his arms, but she does not turn her head.

She pitches gently forward.

It is both more and less real than anything he has ever seen. Time really does slow down. Her blonde hair rises like a candle flame. She seems completely relaxed, more like someone sleeping than someone falling.

She vanishes into the foam.

Everything is suddenly back to normal, the dandelions, the clouds, the buzzard. For a few seconds he wonders if he really saw it. But Leo is standing on the bank beside him, barking at the water, and he thinks how the woman has a name and a family and is dying right now, somewhere out there, trapped in the stopper, perhaps, being tumbled and battered in that big drum of water. He takes his phone out of his trouser pocket but his hands are trembling too much to dial a number. Then he sees it in the water, the briefest flash of red.

The phone is back in his pocket and his shoes are off. He does not remember doing this. It frightens him because he is not a good swimmer. He removes his jacket.

Red again midstream. Both dogs at the bank now, barking.

He jumps into the shallows. This is a stupid thing to do. Weed and sucking mud. He throws himself forward in a clumsy half-dive and the silty bottom reluctantly lets him go. The water is so cold his chest seizes and he cannot breathe. He gathers his energy and shouts the way he would shout if he were lifting a big weight. His ribs loosen.

It is nothing like the sea, it is nothing like a pool. The water sweeps him sideways. He can no longer touch the bottom with his feet. He realises how big the river is now that he is inside it, how strong, how lost the woman must be and how slim his chances are of finding her. He ducks under the surface but the water is the cloudy green of Victorian bottle glass and he can see for no more than a couple of feet at most. He lifts his head out of the water and sees how swiftly he is being carried downriver. The banks are hidden now behind half-submerged bushes and trapped flotsam, the stream narrowing and picking up speed to squeeze under the bridge. Below the bridge is the weir stream for the next lock. He is suddenly very alone and very frightened, an idiot who has jumped into a swollen river. His sodden clothes are shockingly heavy and it is becoming increasingly hard to keep his head above water.

She looms out of the bubbling green and claws at his face.

Mostly he is angry that she should attack him when he is risking his life to save her. Memories of lifesaving classes at school, Mr. Schiller with his speech impediment, pyjama bottoms knotted at the ankles. He yanks her round so she's facing away from him. Cup a hand under the chin, that was it. Her arms and legs are pedalling hard. Silver bubbles pour from her nose. He can't keep her mouth above the surface. The rucksack. Christ. He'd forgotten. He doesn't have the strength but the idea of giving up now is unbearable. He gulps as much air as he can then ducks under. They sink together, the big red ballast pulling them down. He turns her round and grabs the belt. Which sort of buckle is it? Sudden darkness overhead. The bridge. They're moving fast. He needs a knife. He doesn't have a knife. Yank, squeeze, twist. She is punching him and grabbing his hair but whether she is trying to get to the surface or stop him undoing the rucksack he cannot tell. His lungs are crying out for air. *Don't breathe.* A vicious scrabbling panic. His thoughts are becoming blurred, the brain starting to shut down.

Some fierce animal hunger for life wipes the woman from

his mind. He kicks upwards—*hang on, hang on*—and bursts into sunlight. He heaves down a lungful of air and dirty water, chokes and coughs it out then sucks down another lungful, then a third. She is down there somewhere, dead, dying. He can hear the dogs barking nearby.

She surfaces suddenly beside him, head above the water now. No rucksack. He must have got it off. Her eyes are closed and she's not moving. He grabs her hair this time. No time for niceties. She doesn't respond. Maybe he is dragging a corpse. He swims with one arm and breaststroke legs. Way past the bridge now. Thirty metres until the weir stream peels off and sucks them in. He swims hard in the opposite direction. He grabs the end of a thorny branch. It snaps. He grabs another. It holds. They swing towards the bank and slow down as they move out of the main current. The bottom, he can feel it, thank God. Sludge and roots. He heaves her shoulders upright so she's sitting in the shallow water. A reedy foot of bank between two brambles. The dogs stand side by side watching them. Is she breathing? He can't tell.

One last effort. He gets a firmer purchase under his feet and hoists her onto the grass. So heavy for such a tiny thing. He climbs out over her and drags her away from the edge. Her flopping head smacks the ground as he rolls her onto her front. Recovery position, left knee up, left elbow up.

He collapses onto all fours beside her, breathing hard. He is seeing stars, pinpricks of light swarming across his picture of the world. Absurd quiet all around. Two red admirals. An ant walks over his finger.

Her skin is grey-blue. Her earrings are little chains of turquoise beads with silver spacers, hippyish, the kind he hasn't seen in a long time. An image of her looking into a lacquer box on the bedside table, choosing what to wear on her last day. Would you think about that kind of thing? Her leggings have been ripped and there is a bloody gash down her thigh. His own hand is bleeding. Those thorns? He can't see her chest moving. He takes hold of her wrist to check her pulse and it's like pressing a button. She vomits up a pint of river water and something that looks like breakfast cereal. She coughs violently, brings up more sick then rolls onto her back. Her eyes are still closed, her hair matted and tangled.

He takes his phone out. A single air bubble is trapped under the waterlogged screen like a ball bearing in a child's puzzle. *Damn.* The car is sixty metres away, his shoes and jacket three hundred. He can't leave her alone. The keys are in his pocket, though. "Come on." He squats and slips his hands under her armpits. Fireman's lift. He carries her towards the car. Thistles and sheep shit under his socks. Desperate to have the place to himself most days but today there is no one. Sod's Law. He's freezing. And, unlike her, he's got a decent layer of fat on him. Hope to goodness the dogs haven't gone under a van trying to cross the road. Up the steps and through the kissing gate which clangs shut behind them. Fran and Leo are standing by the car, waiting patiently, eerily human. He shifts her centre of gravity so he can extract the key from his sodden pocket. He beeps the lock and whisks the rug out with one hand before the dogs leap on top of it.

He props her against the car and wraps the rug around her. Mud and hair and dog stink. Her whole body is shivering. He opens the passenger door and lowers her in, banging her head a second time. "Let's get you to a hospital." She makes a noise which might or might not be a word. Seat belt. Don't want to save her from drowning then break her neck in an accident.

He starts the ignition and twists the heater to max. A burst of Garth Brooks till he hits the off button. The air still warm from the journey down, thankfully. Something almost fun about it now, dripping wet, driving in his socks, the glow of post-heroics.

Coming back down the Woodstock Road she says something.

"I didn't catch that."

Slurred words, head lolling. "Not the hospital."

"Well, I'm not going to leave you by the side of the road."

She reaches out and puts her hand on his forearm and it is the first time anyone has touched him with anything approaching tenderness in years. It is this moment which will come back later when he asks himself why he did something so stupid.

"Please."

It's like the shoes. He doesn't turn along the Marston Ferry Road towards the hospital. He is taking her home. The decision has already been taken. Or is he just looking for an excuse?

He parks outside the house and leaves the engine running and there is a moment of balance when the day could roll either way, but when he imagines walking her into A&E and handing her to a nurse and watching her vanish through those automated doors he feels something painful for which he doesn't have a name. He twists the key and takes it out of the ignition. He lets the dogs out, unclips her seat belt, lifts her onto her feet then into his arms.

"I don't want . . ."

"It's not the hospital." He kicks the door shut.

Having juggled her sideways down the hall he lays her on the sofa where she curls up like a dormouse. The shivering has become shaking. He drags the old bar fire from the bottom of the coat cupboard. Central heating on, thermostat to 22. He realises, only now, that he will need to undress her if he is going to get her warm and dry. Maria's voice in his head. *How did this not occur to you?* Fran is in the spare armchair. He can hear Leo eating biscuits from the clangy metal bowl in the kitchen. He goes upstairs. Tracksuit bottoms, sweatshirt, woolly socks, towel.

"I'm getting you into dry clothes." She does not respond. He unlaces her black boots. The smell of burning dust as the elements heat up and turn orange. A flash of Timothy when he was tiny. Buckles and poppers and Velcro. Socks off.

He unbuttons her denim skirt, puts a hand under her hips, lifts her an inch or two off the rug, pulls it out then rolls down her torn black leggings. His hand briefly pressed to her flesh, the weight of her. Scrawny thighs and damp white knickers with pink roses on. A tiny rose of pink ribbon on the waistband. A little curl of pubic hair coming out from under the hem. That long bloody cut on goose-pimpled skin. Memories of being this close to other young bodies. Maria, Jane Taylor, Mona Kerr, Jamila, a woman at a party in Dalston whose name went long ago but whose laugh and whose perfect plump stomach come back to him in dreams every now and then. The thrill of unwrapping someone for the first time.

He starts to take her sodden knickers off but it frightens him, what he might feel, what she might think. He leaves them on and pats her dry as best he can. Blood on the towel. He pushes the bar fire back a little and slips the tracksuit trousers on, one leg at a time. They are ridiculously baggy. He sits her up and slips his socks over her tiny feet.

"Where am I?"

He slides her tartan shirt off and shows her the sweatshirt. "You need to put this on."

She's gone again, fuzzy, uncompliant. *Bloody hell.* He lifts her T-shirt. No bra. The fear that someone is going to materialise at the window or walk through the door. Skinny ribs and small breasts. Such pale skin. He leans forward to pull the T-shirt over her head and down her arms, trying to touch her as little as possible. He sits back and can't stop himself. He looks at her, naked from the waist up, for thirty seconds maybe, unable to take his eyes away. To his surprise he is on the verge of tears. So many lost things. He cloaks her with the towel, gently rubbing her arms and back and shoulders. Like Timothy after a bath. More gently still he presses the towel to her chest and stomach. The soft give of her breasts under his hand. He puts the towel aside and slips the sweatshirt over her head. Right arm, left arm. He lifts her briefly to remove the dog rug and flip the wet cushions over.

Leo comes into the room and stands watching them, unsettled, on guard, never quite relaxed with new people.

He moves behind the sofa so he can dry her hair while holding her head steady against his stomach. Timothy again. Feelings that shouldn't be sharing the same space in his head. He has never felt so old. He puts the towel down. "I'll get you a hot drink." She flops sideways and curls up again. She's shaking less. Or is that wishful thinking?

Only when he tries to put the kettle on does he become aware of how bone-cold he is himself. A slab of ice is stacked against his spine. He feels feverish. It's a relief to have this single, simple sensation consume him. He has to hold on to the banister on the way upstairs. He drops his clothes on the bathroom floor. He should have a hot shower but he can't leave her on her own down there. He dries himself with a new towel from the airing cupboard and pulls on his jeans, a shirt, the big jumper Maria bought for him in Oslo. Walking socks then a scarf from the newel post. That cold slab still sitting at his core.

The kettle rumbles to a climax and clicks off. Instant coffee for speed, with a spoonful of sugar. He sits her up and she helps a little this time. "Hold this." She puts her hands around the mug at least and balances it on her knees.

He says, "You're all right now," which sounds ridiculous as soon as he says it, because it might be a disaster, finding yourself alive after putting yourself through all that. A memory of the water, the sheer mass and speed of it. How close he came.

She leans her head back, eyes closed, and breathes out. She's ugly almost. The blonde hair had fooled him. Big features, wonky nose. "Fuck," she says. "Fucking fuck."

He's never been comfortable with people swearing. "My name's Ian."

She doesn't offer her own.

"Why didn't you want to go to hospital?"

She lifts her head and opens her eyes and looks at the track-suit trousers, the sweatshirt, the socks. "What did you do to me?"

"I put you into dry clothes."

"Did you rape me?"

He is too surprised to think of an answer.

"You took my clothes off." She's panicking. "Where are my clothes?"

A rush of terror. The thoughts that came into his head undressing her. Was she just pretending to be unconscious? "You jumped into the river."

She is suddenly calm again. "Yeh. I do that kind of thing." She laughs a humourless laugh.

His heart is hammering. "But you're alive."

"They stick needles into you." She sounds drunk. He wonders if she took pills before going to the river. Belt and braces. "They cover you in wires, like a monkey in a lab. They find out what you're thinking."

"Your clothes are in the kitchen." The adrenaline is ebbing a little. "I'll dry them for you."

"The small print on that form no one reads?" She drinks the sugary coffee. "They can do anything."

Were they really in the Thames less than half an hour ago?

"I fuck everything up. It's my thing."

The sour self-pity in her voice, daring him to reach out and have his hand slapped away. He's disappointed to realise that he doesn't like her very much. "Sorry I saved you." It's meant to sound wry and funny, but he's shocked by how close it comes to what he's feeling.

"I'm so fucking cold."

He fetches her a scarf left years ago by some forgetful dinner guest. "Why did you do it?"

"Like you'd understand."

"Try me."

"You're just being nice." She does quote marks with her fingers, like she's fifteen. "No one actually cares."

He bites his lip. He's surprised at how angry he is. Then he can't stop himself. "You don't throw a life away." It's Timothy he's thinking about, of course, the nights when he never came home, those God-awful, semi-homeless friends, the smell of them. "Someone cares. Your parents, your brother, your sister, your friends, your neighbours, your doctor, the teachers you had at school, at college, even if it's only the poor bastard who has to pull your body out of the river . . ." He's choking up a little. He's never thought of it this way, that lives are held in common, that we lose a little something of ourselves with every death. Or is it just the desperate hope that some frail strand still connects him to his son, the tiny tug of which might one day bring him home?

"Whoa there." She holds up her hand in a comedy stop gesture but without smiling. "I don't need a sermon."

"I nearly died." He wants very much to have the house to himself again. "I'm not asking you for thanks, but the least you can do is to take this seriously."

She crumples and starts to cry. Are they real tears? He's not sure.

"I should take you to hospital. Someone needs to sort out that cut on your leg."

"I told you. I'm really, really frightened of hospitals." This feels like the truth.

"Because . . . ?"

"I told you. They get inside your mind." She puts her hand against her head as if her thoughts are precious or painful. She is still shivering.

It seems obvious now, the possibility that she's mentally ill. He feels like an idiot for not having thought about it before. She was trying to kill herself. It's not like the signs were hidden. He has no idea what to say. He has never known anyone who is mentally ill.

She says, very quietly, as if she might be overheard, "Everything talks." She sounds younger now. Twelve? Ten? Eight years old?

"I'm sorry. I don't understand."

"Trees, walls, that clock, this wood." She touches the table and for a second she really does look as if she's listening. "Your dogs."

She's so sure of herself that he very nearly asks her what the dogs are saying.

"Stones just repeat themselves," she says, "over and over. *I'm a stone, I'm a stone . . . It's raining, it's raining . . .* Walls gossip all the time. The stuff they've had to listen to over the years. If you go into a graveyard you can hear the dead talking to one another underground."

She's crazy, obviously, but she doesn't sound crazy. She sounds like a sane person who lives in a different world to this one.

She cocks her head slightly, the way Leo and Fran do when they catch an interesting smell. She says, "This house is not happy," which unnerves him more than it should. "I used to think everyone could hear these things. Then I realised that it was only me." She closes her eyes and takes a deep breath. "Some days the only thing I want is silence."

He asks if she has any family. He needs to find someone else who can be responsible, someone who can take her off his hands.

"My brother fucked off to Wales. My dad's got emphysema."

"Your mum?"

"She's got a shitload of her own stuff to deal with."

"You haven't got a boyfriend, a husband . . . ?"

"Yeh, right." Another humourless laugh.

He thinks what hard work she must be, and wonders how many times she's tried something like this.

"I don't want to be here." She's crying again.

He assumes at first that she is referring to his house and he's relieved. Then he realises what she means and he's scared of what she might do. Fran is out of the armchair, both dogs pacing now, the way they do during storms. He says, "I need a hot drink," and leaves the room, to give himself space to think.

He puts the kettle on and leans against the sink. The garden is a mess. A plank is missing from the fence that separates him from the angry Turkish couple next door. Three footballs of unknown provenance are dying slowly in the spring grass which is already too long to mow. He should gravel the whole thing over, get a couple of hardy plants in big tubs, but he hasn't got round to it, the way he hasn't got round to so many things.

"Why are we still married?" Maria had asked.

Companionship? The comfort of sharing your life with someone who knew you better than anyone else in the world?

"I'm afraid of being alone," she'd said. "Isn't that a terrible reason for staying with someone?"

It seemed like a pretty good reason to him.

He's still freezing on the inside. He squats with his back against the radiator. Now he is out of her presence he can see things more clearly. He should have listened to the voice of reason and taken her straight to hospital. He quietly retrieves the cordless from the hall table, closes the kitchen door and dials 999. Ten minutes, the woman says. He feels warmer suddenly. In a quarter of an hour he can put something in the microwave, bring the duvet down, dig out a box set.

He makes the coffee and returns to the living room. She's hugging the green seashell cushion. "You were a long time."

"Sorry."

She looks at him, hard. "Did you ring someone?"

Does he answer too quickly or too slowly?

"Fucking hell. Who did you ring?"

"Look . . ." He puts the coffee down and sits on the arm of Fran's chair.

"You rang for a fucking ambulance, didn't you? You rang for a fucking ambulance. Jesus. All that being-interested bollocks. Fuck you."

He grabs her arm as she pushes past. "Get your fucking hands off me."

She's in the hall.

"Wait. You need shoes."

She fumbles with the lock, the door opens and she runs out. He sees the car before she does. The driver hits the brakes hard, the bonnet goes down and the tail rises. A squeal of hard rubber on gritty tarmac that will leave two black marks for weeks afterwards. She turns towards the car, holding up her hands like Moses parting the Red Sea, and it comes to a halt only inches from her legs, aslant, tyres smoking, like she's a superhero and this is her power. Then she's gone, down Asham Way in his socks.

The driver gets out. "What the fuck are you playing at? What did you do to her?"

The man doesn't seem real enough to warrant a reply. Nothing seems real. He goes back inside where the dogs are waiting for him and reaches the sofa just before his knees go weak with the shock and he is forced to sit down. Both coffees have been knocked over and are soaking into the carpet. The heat from the bar fire stings his lower legs. Leo slides his drooly jaw over the arm of the chair and he lays his hand flat along the dog's warm flank to calm himself.

He stares at the tatty rainbow of VCR cases, the twelve-year-old Banbury half-marathon medal, the framed photo of Timothy

at Wicksteed Park, his rare smile making up for the sun flare
bleaching the right-hand side of the picture. A row of dog-eared
postcards stand along the mantelpiece—the beach at Barmouth,
King Kong on the Empire State Building, the Bruegel painting with the hunters. There is still a gap where Maria's porcelain
chimney sweep used to sit.

He forgets about the ambulance. The male paramedic seems
vaguely pissed off by the wasted journey and not quite convinced
by his story. He shows them the pile of wet clothes on the kitchen
floor. "I saved someone's life."

"Hey, buddy, we're all having a tough day." The man looks
not much older than a student.

The woman gives him a tight little smile which might or
might not be an embarrassed apology on her sour colleague's
behalf. She is plump and ginger, her eyebrows almost white.

The man radios in a description of the woman. "Nope. Nothing as helpful as a name."

Perhaps he's asking too much. They save lives every day. How
often does anyone thank them?

They leave and he returns to the sofa. His body does not feel
cold as such, just restless and wrong and unwell. He picks up the
seashell cushion and hugs it. He can hear the deep, dull sluice
of his blood in his ears and behind it, far away, that faint high
whine, not really a noise at all, the background radiation of the
mind.

*You have to let him find his own way. When he hits the buffers he'll
know where to come.*

Or maybe he'll just break into a hundred pieces.

He sits and listens.

I'm a stone, I'm a stone, I'm a stone.

§

He pictures her heading straight back to the river. He checks the newspapers, wanting reassurance that his failure wasn't catastrophic. He looks forward to being congratulated at the office for his heroics then realises that it will work only if someone else tells the story and he downplays his involvement. *Anyone would have done the same thing.* In any case, the heroics aren't important. Something else happened which he can't articulate, and which he might not risk sharing if he could.

Maria comes round to remove more of her belongings. He doesn't tell her about the incident. She is buoyant, or acts buoyancy with complete conviction. She says, "I'm worried about you," though how—or even whether—this is meant to help he's not sure.

It's true that the house is getting messier and dirtier but he can't be bothered to hoover and sweep and sponge and tidy. Who, in any case, does he need to impress? He senses the beginning of a slippery slope beneath his feet but the tingle of fear is not enough to goad him into action.

It becomes obvious not just that he is depressed but that he has been depressed for a long time, his low mood so constant that it remained invisible, like a lobster in a boiling pot, claws scrabbling at the metal rim.

He wakes in the middle of the night gasping for air. That cloudy green water. Sometimes it is the woman sinking into the darkness below him, sometimes it is Timothy. Sometimes he is crossing the gantry himself with a rucksack full of stones when he trips and falls into the foam while Maria stands on the bank with the dogs and does nothing. Occasionally he lets himself fall willingly and feels a moment of easeful bliss mid-air before he realises what is going to happen to him under the water, and this is the most frightening dream of all.

§

She turns up at the front door on a Saturday afternoon three weeks later. He doesn't realise who she is at first. She's dressed for the office. Cream blouse, charcoal jacket and trousers, hair scraped back.

"I came to get my clothes." It is the surliness he recognises first. "If you've still got them."

He can't conceal his joy. "I'm glad you're OK."

She nods carefully as if she can think of no reason why she shouldn't be OK. Maybe trying to take your own life is not something you want reminding of. She waits outside the door while he fetches the bag.

"You washed them. Wow."

"As opposed to leaving them wet all this time."

"I guess." There is no mention of his own sweatshirt and tracksuit trousers and socks. "Cheers anyway."

"You never told me your name." He doesn't want her to leave, not yet.

She pauses and says, "Kelly," with just enough wariness for him to wonder whether she has pulled it out of thin air.

He had forgotten about the voices. "Do you want a cup of coffee?"

"That's kind of weird."

"Not here. In a café, maybe." As if she really would be at risk coming into the house.

"I've got to get going."

"I have a son." He doesn't talk about Timothy to anyone. "I haven't heard from him for three years. I haven't seen him for seven."

"And . . . ?" Her expression doesn't change.

"I don't know if he's alive or dead."

She clearly has a silent discussion with herself for a few seconds then nods. "Ten minutes, all right? But don't go all strange on me."

She is prickly company on the walk to Starbucks and not much easier over a cup of tea and a Danish pastry. He tells her about Maria leaving. She tells him how she works for the Parking and Permits Office at the council. He tells her about Timothy. She tells him about her father going into the John Radcliffe. Neither of them mentions what happened in the river. Ten minutes becomes half an hour. Reluctantly she gives him her mobile number before she leaves but, to his surprise, it is she who sends him a text the following week saying, "I suppose you want a coffee."

§

"Friends" is the wrong word. She's twenty-four, he's fifty-three. Maybe there isn't a right word. On a couple of occasions they are seen by acquaintances or colleagues who look away as if he is engaged in some kind of moral turpitude. She finds it funny so he decides to find it funny.

She never does thank him for saving her, and slowly he realises that thanks is not what he wants or needs. She tells him about her family, for which her own description, "fucked up," is something of an understatement, her antagonistic relationship with the medical profession, her patchy employment record, the law degree she never finished, the crappy boyfriends she chose because their low opinion of her chimed with her own opinion of herself, the kind boyfriends whose sympathy and patience made them insufferable. She talks about the voices and the changing drug regimes which keep them at bay for a while. She tells him how they torment her but how flat the world seems when she can't hear them.

Twelve years. Once a fortnight or thereabouts. He tells her about the divorce and Maria's remarriage to a man nine years her junior, about a series of internet dates which range from the bizarre to the slightly sordid to the very nearly but not quite right. He tells her about the melanoma on his back which he discovers late and which scares the living daylights out of him for the best part of six months.

She never passes judgement or tries to cheer him up. It irritates him at first but he begins to understand that both of these things are ways of steering someone away from the stuff you don't want to hear. She listens better than anyone he knows. Or maybe it's just that she doesn't interrupt. And maybe that's enough.

She rotates between Danish pastry, almond croissant and millionaire's shortbread. The tea is a constant. Him paying ditto. For a couple of months they have to relocate to the café at the Warneford Hospital when she's going through what she refers to as "a particularly shitty patch." Sometimes she is unforthcoming and ill-tempered. Sometimes they simply sit in one another's company like an old married couple or two cows in a pasture. Companionship, though not in a way he'd pictured it. There are periods when she feels suicidal, though she seems calmer for having discussed her plans in gruesome detail and she always gets back in touch after a week or two.

He still wonders sometimes if Kelly is her real name.

§

Four years after he fishes her from the river Timothy comes home, older and thinner and bearded, with everything he owns squeezed into a single kitbag. His relief rapidly gives way to the disappointed realisation that his son is not greatly different from the young man who went away all those years ago, and he has returned not to heal wounds and build bridges but because there has been a fire at a house he was sitting over the winter for a wealthy couple in Majorca, the details of which are clearly more complicated than his version of the story suggests. He is alternately distant and manipulative and, unexpectedly, it is Maria who suffers most, feeding him and buying him new clothes and letting him stay in their spare room until her new husband delivers the inevitable ultimatum. She loans him a thousand pounds for a deposit on a flat and the first month's rent and three days later he's gone.

"Wow," says Kelly.

"All those years, I imagined this Hollywood homecoming. Him being sorry, us being overjoyed. And now I know it's never going to happen."

"And that feels . . . ?"

"Like being kicked in the stomach every time I think about it."

They sit quietly.

He says, "I'm going to do the garden. I'm sick of looking out onto a piece of wasteland."

He does the garden. He cuts the grass. He lays gravel over black plastic. Tubs, a couple of New Zealand ferns, a bench. He mends the fence and creosotes it. He buys a bird table and puts out seeds and crusts and little chunks of fat. And when he thinks about Timothy it doesn't hurt so much.

§

Leo dies. He is fifteen. Fran takes to her basket and is dead within the month. She, too, is fifteen. Liver cancer, the vet says, though he knows it's heartbreak. They've had good, long lives. And in any case he has arthritis in both hips and walking them had become increasingly difficult.

He says, "I feel lonely."

"Yeh?" She sips her tea.

He says, "I'm getting old."

She says, "I guess you are."

He says, "I'm frightened of dying," though just saying it out loud like that takes some of the sting out of it.

She says, "I'll come to your funeral."

He says, "They'll wonder who you are."

She says, "I'm sure they will."

He pictures her among the trees, twenty yards back from the mourners, his solid little recording angel.

§

He still dreams of the river, the thunder of the weir, the currents unfurling downstream. May blossom and cirrus clouds. He is no longer drowning. No one is drowning. Though they will all go down into the dark eventually. Him, Maria, Kelly, Timothy . . . And the last few minutes will be horrible but that's OK, it really is, because nothing is wasted and the river will keep on flowing and there will be dandelions in spring and the buzzard will still be circling above the wasteland.

ACKNOWLEDGMENTS

With thanks to Clare Alexander, Quinn Bailey, Suzanne Dean, Sos Eltis, Paul Farley, William Fiennes, Kevin Foster, Dan Franklin, Kathy Fry, Sunetra Gupta, Alissa Land, Kevin Leahy, Toby Moorcroft, Debbie Pinfold, Simon Stephens, Bill Thomas, the Jericho Café, and Modern Art Oxford.

"The Island" was published in *Ox-Tales Fire* (Oxfam/Profile Books, 2009). "The Gun" was published in the "Britain" issue of *Granta* magazine in 2012. It was also short-listed for the 2013 Sunday Times EFG Short Story Award and won an O. Henry Prize in 2014. "The Pier Falls" was published in the *New Statesman* in 2014 and was long-listed for the Sunday Times EFG Short Story Award in 2015. "Bunny" was the runner-up for the BBC National Short Story Award in 2015. "The Weir" was published in *The New Yorker* in 2015.